Paula Gosling

DEATH penalties

THE MYSTERIOUS PRESS
New York • Tokyo • Sweden
Published by Warner Books
 A Time Warner Company

MYSTERIOUS PRESS EDITION

First published in Great Britain in 1991 by Scribners, a division of Macdonald & Co. (Publishers) Ltd.

Cover design by Carol Bokuniewicz
Cover illustration by Tim O'Brien

Mysterious Press Books are published by
Warner Books, Inc.
1271 Avenue of the Americas
New York, NY 10020

A Time Warner Company

Printed in the United States of America

Originally published in hardcover by The Mysterious Press.
First Printed in Paperback: September, 1992
10 9 8 7 6 5 4 3 2 1

PRAISE FOR PAULA GOSLING AND *DEATH PENALTIES*

"Gosling herds *Death Penalties* deftly toward an exciting and thoroughly satisfying climax." **—UPI**

"A tense, involving story." ***—Orlando Sentinel***

"Gosling has a ready wit, a cast of cynical coppers you can't help but like, and plots with the exacting precision of an ordinance survey map." ***—Booklist***

"The author has an especially fine touch with her characters." ***—New York Times Book Review***

"Gosling is excellent . . . her works are skillfully and grippingly paced." **—*The Times*, London**

"Breathless suspense and stunning surprises all the way . . . a terrific read." **—Phyllis A. Whitney**

"A chilling, plausible story filled with tension and terror . . . her characters leap from the pages, alive with full-fleshed delineation." ***—Arizona Daily Star***

"With stylish turns of phrase and special insights, Gosling tells an exciting tale that builds to a breathtaking finale in the London tube." ***—Publishers Weekly***

"Her novels are not only cleverly plotted, but brim with power and emotion . . . sure to whet an American's appetite for classic British crime fiction." ***—Rave Reviews***

"Not many mystery writers get better with each book, but Gosling never fails to fascinate." ***—Sacramento Bee***

"Besides constructing a walloping suspense story, Gosling injects a sensitivity in an eerie, metrical prose." ***—Booklist***

This one is for Tess Sacco . . .
and thanks to Ralph Spurrier.

A crime writer couldn't have two better friends.

1

"Dad! You're driving too fast!"

He didn't answer the boy. He *was* driving too fast, but he didn't know what else to do, because the dark-green car that had been following them since they left the house was gaining ground. He couldn't make out the driver's face, for light glared in his rearview mirror, reducing the man in the car behind him to a menacing silhouette. He could just see the pale hands where they gripped the wheel.

Whoever he was, he drove very well, keeping pace, and closing the gap a little every minute or so.

Maybe he was after Max!

They wouldn't. They couldn't be that angry. Could they?

He put his own foot down harder.

It was a long, straight street, unusual in this part of London. Cars lined each side of it without a break, squeezed together right up to the crossing. Large ash trees overhung it, their branches thick with leaves. The warm summer rain that had been falling all day had ceased only moments before, leaving everything dripping and sparkling in new sunlight. The sky was opening, the gunmetal gray splitting like curtains to reveal pure vibrant blue. The sudden, unexpected illumination seemed even greater against the retreating clouds, each crest a cauliflower billow of fire-edged white.

Their brightness blinded him.

That was why he didn't see the old man step out.

When Max shouted, he straight-legged the brake and clutch pedals, twisted the wheel hard, too hard, felt the wheels lock and the tires skid on the wet surface, felt the jolt as they hit the front end of the last parked car, felt the roll begin, saw the street become the sky, with the astonished face of the old man drifting past, like a pink and white balloon, heard the incredible screech of metal scouring the asphalt with a scream not unlike his own, high and thin. The car landed on its side, still moving forward.

Clockwork, running down.

A film, frame by frame.

Suspended in his seat belt, he saw the rush of gutter water surge toward him across the bonnet, followed by the approach of the yellow-painted edge of the curb with its overhanging fringe of grass, each muddy green blade sharp and distinct. Then came the cracked cement of the pavement, with a crumpled chips bag, bright blue and red, lying on it.

The bag caught in the edge of the windscreen.

He stared at it.

Read the words "Ready-salted."

It was all so *clear*.

And then they hit the tree.

2

Detective Sergeant Tim Nightingale stood with his back to the window. Outside, a chilly late-October rain was curtaining across the overgrown rear garden of the house, pushed by a fitful wind. He felt an annoying draft on the back of his neck and moved to one side. The room was cold, and growing steadily colder. That might discomfit a junior investigating officer from the CID, but it didn't matter anymore to its owner.

The old man was dead.

A limp wing of gray hair had fallen forward, obscuring the upper part of his face, and below it the jaw had drooped slightly sideways, giving a sardonic twist to the otherwise blank expression. He lay curled on the floor, making a comma beside the easy chair, his thin body curving around a bouquet of flowers still visible on the worn and faded carpet. His head was tipped forward, his hands caught between his knees as if to warm them. A pipe weighted the drooping pocket of his beige cardigan, and some shreds of carefully hoarded tobacco had escaped from a brown plastic pouch, trickling slowly out to make a tiny pyramid on the floor.

Cartwright, the police surgeon, knelt next to the body. He was a burly man who always seemed on the verge of bursting out of his clothes, and his present position emphasized the unequal struggle between burgeoning flesh and gray gabardine. Beside him the local GP, a neatly dressed Pakistani, was like an exotic exclamation point, dark and thin and tense with impatience. It was past time for morning surgery, and his usual partner was on holiday, so the patients had been left to the ministrations of a rather young and inexperienced substitute. But he hadn't been happy about certifying death—hence Cartwright's presence. The tension between them was obvious.

The rush of traffic in the road beyond the walled garden was like a mechanical estuary, ebbing and flowing with the change of lights at the corner. It had been raining all night, and the passage of tires through the puddles made admonitory whispers that filtered into the room, so that the two medical men unconsciously lowered their voices in deference to what seemed like municipal disapproval.

Despite his apparent calm, Tim Nightingale was eagerly waiting for the verdict concerning the cause of death of one Ivor Peters, first floor on the right, 78 Morstan Gardens, London W11. It was a large bed-sitter, but even so it was crowded by its contents. A full-sized double bed with carved mahogany head and footboards stood in one corner and beside it a matching double wardrobe. The bed was neatly made up with a duvet, the contrast between Victorian and modern made even stronger by the pattern on its cover—a subdued tribute to Mondrian in blocks of brown, black and tan. One corner of the large room had been fitted out as a kitchen. On the sink lay a plate, cutlery, a grillpan and a saucepan, washed and left to dry. A tea towel was neatly folded over the ladder-back chair that stood with its rush seat tucked under a round mahogany table. In one corner was a large rolltop desk, so stacked with papers and notebooks that there seemed little room left for actual use. All the furniture spoke of having been culled from a larger house. The room was very clean, and its curtains and carpet were of excellent quality, but worn and faded—like their owner.

While waiting for the two acolytes of Hippocrates to come to judgment, Nightingale had been trying to deduce the man from the room, looking for clues to Peters's life and death in the objects that surrounded him. It was something he did whenever the opportunity presented itself, trying to train his powers of observation and deduction. He had been in plainclothes for just a few weeks, and so far had done absolutely nothing to deserve the title of "detective," except pass his qualifying exams and find the shortest way to New Scotland Yard from his tiny flat in Putney.

He was tall, with light-brown hair, dark eyes, and a serious mouth not easily given to laughter, although he had a wry, dry sense of humor. Under his wool-lined mac he wore—as casually as possible—a new outfit of gray flannels and tweed jacket. He had tried leaving the jacket under the mattress at night and bashing it against the door of his wardrobe several times before putting it on each morning, but it remained stiff and unyielding, betraying both its recent purchase and his own lack of confidence. He had decided that on his next day off he was going along to the Oxfam shop to find something more lived-in. No suspect was going to be intimidated by such a newly emergent detective, pegged out to dry in new clothes and naïveté. One had to obtain authority where one could these days, and he was convinced it lay in a casual air of having been on the scene for years. Of not caring whether he lived or died one day or had his shoulder cried on the next.

Being a detective was important to him—it was one of the reasons he had joined the police in the first place, and everything he'd done from the moment he'd joined was to reach that end. Now here he was, at the scene of a sudden, unexplained death, ready to be brilliant in the unlikely event that someone asked his opinion.

The difficulty with his secret practice of Holmesian exercises was that he had few opportunities to verify his conclusions, so he kept them simple. The late Mr. Peters had served in a uniformed capacity at one time—from his age probably World War II—for both he and his surroundings were impeccably maintained and each item in it gave the impression of being aligned precisely for inspection. He had been a man of intelligence—the bookshelves were well filled with books that looked as if they had been read and reread, and a chess board with a game in progress sat on a low table in front of the cold electric fire. Peters had been married and had fathered at least two children—photographs on the mantel. He'd been a methodical man—witness the orderly if crowded desk, the very particular arrangement of tins and other items in the kitchen area, and the neatly ticked-off television page of the previous day's *Evening Standard* (he liked thrillers, wildlife programs, and had heavily underlined the entry for a police documentary series). Perhaps he'd been a bird-watcher (the nature programs), or a voyeur—there was a pair of binoculars by a rear window. He wore false teeth (denture powder on the shelf above the basin), which gave him trouble (soft foods dominated his store cupboard and refrigerator), and was a little vain (a tube of hair cream and a bottle of expensive after-shave sat beside the denture powder). He was reflective and quiet by nature—no bright colors in furnishings or wardrobe, not even a red tie kept for Christmas. He'd suffered from insomnia and migraines—both prescription and drugstore medicine bottles were crowded onto the table by the bed.

Nightingale noticed a framed certificate of some kind on the wall above the desk, and moved over to read it. As he did, Cartwright stood up. "Natural causes," he announced. "Myocardial infarction, probably." For a moment the local GP looked as if he still might argue the point. His skin darkened slightly from either annoyance or embarrassment, but Cartwright's official presence looming above him, massive with the weight of experience, carried the day. He pressed his lips together, nodded, sprang to his feet, signed the appropriate form, and started out of the room to return to his waiting surgery.

"Excuse me, Doctor," Nightingale said.

The man turned. "Yes?"

"Was it you who prescribed the sleeping capsules for Mr. Peters?" Nightingale asked.

"Yes—he was my patient."

"Had he been using them for a long time?"

"Oh, no—this trouble was recent. He had witnessed a road accident some months ago, and it rather upset him. He was not eating or sleeping well. I prescribed only mild sedatives, of course, nothing addictive." He did glance at Cartwright, then. "No barbiturates," he said firmly.

"Because of his heart condition?"

There was a flash of something in the doctor's eyes, and he very obviously stopped himself from glancing toward Cartwright again. His chin lifted, but he spoke in an even tone. "He had no previous indication of any heart condition," he said carefully. "Aside from his migraines, from which he had suffered all his life, Mr. Peters was a relatively healthy man for his age. Time was beginning to tell, of course, the little problems of digestion, fatigue, and so on. He had arthritis in the knees and hips, quite painful but not requiring surgery yet, and a troublesome bunion for which we have been awaiting a hospital appointment, but no overt indications of heart illness or circulatory problems."

"I see. Thank you."

"Not at all," the doctor said politely, and left.

Cartwright gazed at Nightingale with some disapproval. "What was that all about then?" he asked.

Nightingale shrugged. "I wondered why he had hesitated to give the certificate, that's all."

"Didn't want the responsibility," Cartwright snapped.

"Mmmmmmm." The fact that the GP had stayed on indicated otherwise, but there was no point in arguing with Cartwright. He was a truculent man who made up his mind and that was the end of the matter. Nightingale indicated the certificate on the wall. "Mr. Peters was one of ours."

Cartwright scowled. "What do you mean?"

"Metropolitan Police—retired as a sergeant in 1965, did the full thirty."

"Hence the crook knees and the bunion, no doubt," Cartwright growled. "Well, he died peacefully enough. Not bashed by a drunken lout or shot by some bank-robbing villain. Just look at the lips and fingertips. Heart failure—which is what it all comes down to, in the end."

"Heart failure," Nightingale echoed. So there would be no need to ask the chief inspector to call in the Scene-of-Crime team, after all, or to set up an Incident Room, or to prepare statements for the press. While he wished violence on no one, certainly not on what appeared to be a blameless old man, there was no denying the disappointment in his voice.

"That's it. Last night, obviously. Rigor is established, but he was in his seventies, rather undernourished, and probably hypothermic, judging by the temperature in this room." Cartwright shivered and glared at the rather splendid electric fire, which they had found switched on but cold. It had apparently gone off sometime during the night, when the money in the meter had run out. "Unless I find something extraordinary in the autopsy, I still say it was just a matter of his heart giving out. It happens." He was gathering his things together, snapping his bag shut.

"He seemed—"

"Dammit, hearts stop when they stop. They don't

always blow whistles and send up flares ahead of time. No history of heart disease doesn't mean a damn thing. It just stopped. All right?" Cartwright was getting cross.

"Then why were *we* called in?" Nightingale asked.

"Mrs. Finch, the landlady, got overexcited," said a bland voice from the door. Detective Chief Inspector Abbott had returned from interviewing the lady in question. "She says the old man had a visitor last night. This morning she noticed he hadn't come downstairs for his milk, so she sent someone up with it. When they found Mr. Peters, she immediately decided his mysterious visitor had murdered him, and dialed nine-nine-nine." He grimaced. "She watches a lot of television."

"Does she know who this visitor was?" Nightingale asked.

"No. The front door is left unlatched until eleven at night, apparently, so the tenants can have visitors as and when they like. Although the rooms are bed-sitters, there's no system for separate bells. There should have been, but her late husband never got around to it. Hence the open-door policy."

"Dicey," Nightingale observed.

"Well, she has arthritis and claims she can't be bothered to get up and down all evening to let people in and out," Chief Inspector Abbott said. He had the knack of mimicry, and for a moment the old lady seemed to be in the room with them, creaky and exasperated by life's unfair demands. Abbott went on. "She heard the door open, heard footsteps going up the stairs, heard them again going down the stairs about twenty minutes later, but she was watching 'Coronation Street' and didn't bother to look out. She heard voices overhead in the old man's room—that's why she realized it was he who had the visitor. She says the voices were loud and she had to turn up the sound on her television, but doesn't think there was an argument. It was just that Peters was rather deaf."

"Man or woman's voice?" Nightingale wondered.

"Man's. She's absolutely certain about that."

"Anybody else in the house hear anything?"

"There are only four bed-sitters in the house, two on each floor. There's a basement flat, but it has a totally separate entrance. A middle-aged couple live there in exchange for doing the cleaning, maintenance, and so on. The woman also shops for the landlady, who can't get out. She's the one who found Peters dead, but claims she and her husband heard nothing unusual during the evening. The other room on this floor is empty at the moment, being redecorated. The two lodgers above on the third were both out. Peters and the old lady were the only two people in the house itself at the time."

"And this didn't worry her?"

"She says it's often like that, and claims she's not bothered, but I think it does frighten her."

"It should. This isn't the most salubrious of neighborhoods."

"No. But they get like that in the city, don't they? Either they put on ten locks, five steel bolts, and a drop-bar, sit shivering in their shoes expecting to be throttled at any moment, and then die because the firemen or the ambulance men can't get to them in time. Or they leave everything wide open because they can't be bothered. She's the last kind, partly because she's naturally bolshie, mostly because she's so disabled by the arthritis."

"And what was Peters like?"

"I gather he was a reasonable old man, 'very brainy,' she said."

"He retired from the Met in '65," Nightingale said, again indicating the framed certificate. "Sergeant."

"Really?" Abbott said, going over to look for himself. "Well, what do you know? I suppose we'd better notify somebody about it then. They usually like to do something in the way of a memorial—flowers, representation at the funeral, that kind of thing." He made a note in his book.

"Did the landlady say anything else about him?"

Abbott shook his head. "She says his daughter was always after him to come and live with her, but he liked keeping his own hours, doing his own thing. He'd lived in the area all his life, and he felt comfortable here, even though it had changed so much. And he was fussy about his food, claimed the daughter's cooking was full of garlic and what he called 'twigs.' Herbs, I guess he meant. So he lived here and cooked for himself and watched his TV and read and met his friends at the local day center and generally was pretty happy, she said. Or had been until a few months ago. She finally admitted Peters had been unwell lately—not eating or looking after himself properly. Seemed to feel she should have done something about it, but hadn't. She said he'd been like that since the accident," Abbott said, gazing down at the old man.

Tim frowned. "The doctor said something about that."

Cartwright stirred. He'd been waiting for an opportunity to interrupt Abbott's flow of words. "Self-neglect," he observed brusquely. "The old story. I see it every day. Delayed shock is more than enough to finish a man his age. Sudden shock even more so. But he certainly wasn't murdered," Cartwright said firmly. He picked up his hat and clapped it on his head. "I'm finished here. You'll have to hang on until they come for the body, I'm afraid. I've got another elderly unattended death waiting in Ealing. God, I hate winter." He left them to it.

"Did the old man have many visitors?" Tim asked Abbott.

"His daughter, two or three times a week, sometimes a friend from the local old people's day center came around to play chess," Abbott said, putting his notebook away. "I expect that's who it was, last night. I took his name, but there's not much point."

"We could go ask him, just to round things off," Nightingale said eagerly.

Abbott shook his head. "You heard him. Natural causes. That's it as far as we're concerned. No crime, no investigation."

Nightingale nodded and looked down at the old man. "We can't just leave him there like that," he said.

Abbott looked too. "Because he was one of us, you mean?"

"I don't know," Tim said uneasily. "It just doesn't seem right."

"It never ceases to amaze me that you young ones still have some kind of cockeyed romantic notion about the Job," Abbott said. "I understand you've done three years uniformed in some of the roughest districts, you've been beaten up twice and stabbed once, you were even assigned to football crowd control for three months to knock the stars out of your eyes, and still you think there's something splendid about being a copper." He looked at Nightingale and Nightingale looked back at him. Abbott wasn't fooling him any more than he was fooling himself. This was a lecture from Abbott's mouth, not his heart.

Tim knew Abbott had been temporarily seconded back to the Met from the West Country, and was not happy about it. Tim, too, had been born to fields and hedgerows, and found the gritty grind of metropolitan life both confining and depressing. They shared that bond—but it was stretched thinly across the chasm of rank.

Tim had heard through the grapevine that Abbott was a good detective and a fair-minded man, but he and the other junior officers had had to take that on trust. Ever since he'd arrived in London, Abbott had been short-tempered and ill at ease. It had been many years since the detective chief inspector had served in the Met—years he had thankfully put behind him. While he'd been endeavoring to reassume the hard manner that armored the city police, it was a cloak that did not settle easily on his shoulders.

"Oh, hell, come on," Abbott said impatiently. Together they picked up the thin, fragile body and carried it to the bed. Rigor had set in, so they couldn't make him look more comfortable, but they laid him gently on his side and drew the duvet over him.

"The daughter will be coming soon," Abbott said, as if to explain why they should have done this simple, decent thing.

"I guess it doesn't take much when you're old and alone," Tim said softly. He looked down at the small mound under the duvet and suddenly felt sad. He knew nothing about this old man, and yet was an official witness to his end. He'd had a family, a career, a life of nearly eighty years, and yet he'd died alone, with no one to hear his final testament. It seemed unfair. He had an irrational desire to wake the old man up, ask him to talk about all the things he had seen and been and done, so they wouldn't be lost forever.

But it was too late for that now. And it was not the kind of attitude encouraged in a detective sergeant of the Metropolitan Police. Sentimentality was allowed off-duty, but there were too many sad stories in London—and everywhere else—for him to spend the limited coinage of his emotions on every one. Save it for a rainy day, he told himself. For a dead child or a lost dog. At least Mr. Ivor Peters had done it his way. Not so terrible, dying in your own home, even if it is on the floor with your pipe unsmoked. Better than in some institution, propped up in a nodding circle.

"I have to get back to the station," Abbott said, glancing at his watch. He turned. "Do you mind hanging on here until they come for him?"

"No," Tim said truthfully. "That's fine."

"Right." Abbott headed for the door, slowed, then turned to look at his new sergeant with some curiosity.

"Why does your willingness to perform this lowly duty worry me?" he asked.

Tim smiled and shrugged. "I have no idea," he said.

Abbott continued to look at him with a raised eyebrow. "It was natural causes," he said pointedly.

"Of course," Nightingale agreed blandly. "Natural causes."

Abbott stared at him a moment longer, then went out, just managing to hide the smile that came unbidden and unwelcome. As if he'd heard it announced, he knew what Nightingale was thinking. He knew how hungry he was to find "his" first good case. But policing was a team effort, and a solitary explorer often stumbled into areas that weren't friendly to intruders. Nightingale's curiosity was something that *could* lead to trouble, and Abbott knew he should have ordered him away from the scene, assigned him quickly to something else, and finished it.

He clattered down the stairs, shaking his head. It probably wouldn't make any difference. And he felt no loyalty to the Met, not anymore. The whole secondment had been a mistake, some Home Office psychologist's bright idea, no doubt, and he resented it deeply. The detective chief inspector who had changed places with him had been on the phone regularly, complaining. They were both out of place and functioning badly as a result. The hell with it—just put in your time and go through the motions, he told himself. Only another four months to go in London, and then you can go back to the Cotswolds, where you belong. You understand the people there, and they understand you. Nightingale's hopes and ambitions aren't really your problem.

Abbott opened the door and went out into the bluster of the day, lifting his face to the stink of exhaust fumes and the wet slap of the rain. God, he thought, for ten pence I'd just turn west and keep walking. The rain is soft there, and the wind smells of cut grass and wood smoke. He teetered for a moment, imagining he could do that, pretending it was a real possibility, a matter of simple choice. Then he turned up his coat collar and climbed into the waiting police car.

As soon as he heard the downstairs door slam shut, Nightingale was across the room. He pulled out the swivel chair and seated himself in front of the cluttered rolltop desk.

He was still there half an hour later when the woman from the basement flat appeared in the doorway, bearing a tray. "Mrs. Finch says would you like a cup of tea while you're waiting?" she asked nervously, trying not to look at the bed and its forever silent occupant.

Tim smiled. "Thank you," he said, clearing a fresh space on the desk. "That would be very welcome."

The hospital room was warm, and the single bed in the center seemed far too large for its occupant. Outside, the scene was one of seasonal conflict. Autumn signaled its supremacy with flags as the breeze-churned branches waved ragged banners of umber, acid yellow, and red. In opposition, the sky was bright blue, fleeced with occasional clouds, attempting an illusion of summer against all the evidence of barometer, thermometer, calendar, and disappearing foliage.

But on this side of the glass, despite the comfort of central heating, Tess Leland felt winter in her bones. She stared down at her son, restless and feverish in the hospital bed, and shivered. Max was moaning with distress, and his breathing was harsh and ragged.

She'd raced for a train as soon as the call had come from the school. It was *not* the kind of place that would panic easily, and the fact that they'd hospitalized him *before* calling her had made the whole thing even more of a nightmare.

The door opened behind her and she turned, startled. "Oh, Richard," she said, and was infuriated to feel relief flood through her. Why should she be glad to see him? Wasn't she capable of handling this alone? Hadn't she handled everything else herself?

Richard Hendricks was pale as he crossed the room and put his arms around her. His normally lively face seemed to have gone slightly flaccid and blank, rather than tighter with worry. "My secretary tracked me down," he said. "How is he?"

Tess took a deep breath. "It's rheumatic fever," she said, trying to keep her voice steady, but achieving only the unpredictable flutes and wavers of an adolescent boy. She cleared her throat and tried again. "He had a cold a few weeks ago, but it seemed just the ordinary—" Her voice seized, suddenly grown too large for her throat. "The doctor says—" She couldn't go on, decided not even to try, and gestured helplessly.

"Come outside for a moment," Richard suggested.

The corridor was long and impersonal, with pale green walls and scuffed mock-marble linoleum. Benches were spaced along it at regular intervals, and nurses with rubber-soled shoes squeaked along carrying trays and bowls and mysteriously shrouded objects. In the distance a trolley rattled, and someone laughed, the sound strangely distorted and somehow out of place. Richard sat down, took Tess's hand in his, and patted it awkwardly. "Take a deep breath and then tell me all about it."

She took the deep breath, and retrieved her hand. "They're giving him antibiotics and other drugs, apparently, which will overcome the initial infection in a few days. There's no reason to think that he won't get through it all right—he's always been a very fit little boy. But . . . but . . . there may be heart damage." She stopped for a moment, kept control, and went on. "If he's very unlucky, he may even have to have operations later on—valve replacements—" She felt the tears coming, tears she had held back before. Damn it! Stop this at once! she ordered. But it was no good. Old habits die hard, even when kicked hard, and knowing someone else was there to share the burden betrayed her into the old familiar reactions.

Her late husband's will had named Richard as co-guardian, so it had been only polite to notify him that Max was ill, but she had never expected him to appear like this.

Any more than she had expected to start crying.

Sit up! she commanded. Behave yourself!

But the troops were rebellious.

Damn. *Damn!*

When she eventually lifted her drooping head, she saw Richard deep in conversation with the doctor. She cleared her throat, and they both turned. "Feeling better?" Richard smiled.

Don't patronize me! she thought. And smiled back. "Fine, thanks," she said.

His tone had implied failure on her part. Well, it hadn't been a faint, or anything like it. Just a moment of quiet reflection, that's all. A little rest, a gathering of loose threads, nothing more. What could have happened of importance in the world during those few minutes? What had she missed? Probably nothing at all.

Richard really did look concerned, and she felt momentarily ashamed of her resentment, but she was cross at him for rushing up here like some self-appointed knight in armor. She wanted to face this alone. It was so much easier to control yourself among strangers. Friends supplied too many excuses to the weak of will.

The consultant had glanced at the clock on the wall as covertly as possible, but it was obvious he had other things to do. "Do you feel well enough to discuss Max's prognosis now?" he asked tentatively.

"Yes," Tess said firmly. "I want to know exactly where we are."

The consultant nodded approvingly, and came over to sit beside her. He had blue eyes, and one wayward gray hair curling out of his left sideburns, like a cat's whisker, giving the impression he was listening in to other worlds, receiving other messages. But his glance was direct and his voice was perfectly, wonderfully calm. "A good convalescence will make all the difference to Max. A matter of damage limitation, I suppose you could say." He carefully explained exactly what rheumatic fever was, how he would be treating Max for it, and what would be needed, once the crisis had passed.

Richard scowled when it came to the details of the boy's convalescence. "That may not be as simple as it sounds. Tess is a widow on her own. She has a career as an interior designer and can't nurse Max during the day. Naturally, Max should have the best possible care, and I'll be glad to take care of it. If you could recommend a suitable nursing home, I'll—"

Tess interrupted, in a voice perhaps more icy than she intended. "That's a very kind offer, Richard, but once Dr. Shaw says Max can leave hospital, he's coming *home*. He's my son, not a parcel to be posted off to strangers."

Richard had flushed at her rebuke. "You try to do too much, Tess," he said impatiently. "I wish you'd let me help you more, take some of the burden from your shoulders."

It was a point of honor with him as much as anything. Richard Hendricks had been her late husband's business partner in what had been a most successful international public-relations firm. But after Roger had been killed in that horrible car crash, it immediately became apparent that most of the company's success had stemmed from his brilliant creative abilities. Richard Hendricks's business expertise alone hadn't been enough to hang on to their clients—in public relations it was ideas that counted. He'd practically wept when he'd had to tell her that the business was going to be wound up, and there would be almost no money from it for her and Max.

"I know you want to help, and I appreciate it," she continued—using almost the same words she had used then. And almost the same mixture of feelings rose in her as she looked at his anxious, familiar face. Dammit, why did he have to look so worried? Why didn't he and everyone else just leave her alone to get *on* with things? Guilt, her constant companion these days, came to sit beside her.

It was Roger's fault, of course.

Blithe spirit, lately flown.

Oh, he'd made a will.

Once. When drunk. On a form from the stationer's.

Everything to my dear wife.

Including all the responsibilities.

She had developed an inexpressible rage toward her late husband in the weeks following his death. As a grieving widow, how could she admit that, as each new problem presented itself, her secret anger grew at his intransigence, his grasshopper views on finance, his refusal to worry about tomorrow, his selfish determination to "live for today," his casual assumption that he could take care of everything, manage anything, and would be around to do it forever.

Because, in the end—he wasn't.

It was true that when he died, the mortgage had automatically been paid off. For that she was undoubtedly indebted to some anonymous stranger at their building society rather than Roger himself. There proved to be two life insurance policies in Roger's desk. One, very small, had been taken out when he was still a student and subsequently left to the vagaries of the standing-order system. It had barely covered the funeral expenses and their outstanding bills.

The other insurance policy had been taken out the day Max was born—to pay his school fees at Roger's old school. A typical Roger gesture. But fees were only the beginning. When Roger had won a place there, his parents had gone without so that he could dress well, take part in sports, go on school trips, and generally keep up appearances with the other boys. She'd been trying to do the same for Max, for he loved the school and would undoubtedly want to go back when he was better.

Tess had lived in England for fourteen years now, but she had been born and brought up in Amity, Iowa, and her conscience was still nagged by stringent, contrary Iowa standards. Because she was an American, everything in her rebelled at the thought of elitist education. Equally, because she was American, something in her was impressed by traditional ways. And, because she was a mother, she conceded the undoubted advantages such an education gave to *her* child as he progressed from snotty-nosed schoolboy to future Prime Minister.

But lately, she'd been losing both the moral and the financial battle.

"As a matter of fact, I'd been wondering whether I was right to send Max back to school so soon after his father's death," Tess said, lifting her chin and keeping her voice firm. "His housemaster has written to me several times about his nightmares. He's been very unsettled this term." She thought of Max's face—flushed and small on the pillow, his mouse-brown hair clinging damply to his forehead. Dammit, Max was her *son*.

"Well, we'll want to keep him here for at least ten days—perhaps a couple of weeks. A matter of assessing damage—if there is any. I'm hopeful there won't be," the doctor concluded. "But this rather long convalescence afterward is vital, I'm afraid. No question of his returning to school for quite a while. I expect he'll require tutoring as well as nursing if he isn't to fall behind." He glanced at Tess and smiled. "But I'm sure you'll manage to work it all out, Mrs. Leland. You look a very capable young woman. I'll look back in on Max later this evening." He nodded and smiled to them both, then hurried off down the corridor.

Richard watched him go, then turned. "There's an answer to all this, Tess."

"Only one?" she asked, and tried a shaky laugh that didn't quite come off.

"Only one that makes sense."

She stared at him wearily. "No, Richard."

"Tess, if you married me, you could give up work, stay at home, make sure Max was properly looked after." He flushed slightly. "And you know I wouldn't pressure you about—anything. But I do care for you, and I'd do all I could to make you happy—"

"We've been over all this so many times," she protested.

"Yes, I know. I was willing to let it ride for a while—"

"Decent of you, old thing."

He grinned, suddenly, engagingly. "Circumstances have changed, Tess. Even you can see that."

"You mean even without my glasses?" She had to smile at him, the successful businessman who could never pass up a chance to make a sale, puppy enthusiasm contained by a firm jaw and handshake. Here is my product, he said, standing tall in his Gieves & Hawkes suit, Turnbull & Asser shirt, and Church brogues. How can you resist?

At first he'd left her alone with her grief, but lately he'd begun calling round, taking her out to concerts and plays, even going up to the school to visit Max. She hadn't known whether his attentions were out of love, kindness, or pity—and she still didn't. But, as appealing as he could be, she knew marrying him was no answer—not as far as she was concerned.

Not now, anyway.

Eleven years of being financially and emotionally dependent, of letting Roger make all the decisions, of playing the game of Letting Daddy Look After Me, had nearly proved her undoing. Because it was what Roger had wanted, because it fitted in with his self-image, she had adopted the rapidly dating guise of a proper Englishwoman. She'd done the charity round, been a lady of leisure, a white-glove drone, played the role of the successful Roger Leland's wife.

Then, without warning, she'd become Roger Leland's widow.

His death made her realize what she had forsworn, and lost—herself. For some days after the accident, she'd felt boneless, foolish, and weak. But, in the twenty minutes between leaving the limousine at the door of the crematorium and reentering it to be driven home, she had made a resolution. She could—and would—take charge of her life again.

It had been hard, so much harder than even she had suspected, but gradually, doggedly, she had sorted, compartmentalized, organized her life and got it running again. Not smoothly, not always easily, but under control.

There had been, unfortunately, no compartment set aside for a seriously ill child. Measles or mumps she could have coped with, but this was more. She had a responsibility to herself, true, but an even bigger one to Max. Wouldn't it make sense to marry Richard? He was attractive and kind, and could provide them with a good life. Physical passion might arrive later, but its absence could well be a plus. Stability—in the upright and wonderfully English form of Richard Hendricks—beckoned her.

"You're very kind, Richard—" she began, but he held up his hand.

"That still sounds too much like a refusal. If so, I don't want to hear it." He smiled his gentlest smile, and she detected definite signs of wavering within. No, she told herself. No.

"Look, Tess, I care for you very much." He cleared his throat and glanced up and down the corridor. "More than I can say standing here." He touched her hand, ran a finger over her wrist and into her palm. "I have to go to Paris tonight, and I'll be away for some time. You concentrate on Max, because he needs you. But whenever you have a moment—think about marrying me. Just . . . consider it. All right?"

"All right," she said. "But no promises." He squeezed her hand and Tess shivered—it was cool in the corridor. She got to her feet abruptly, despite Richard's anxious protest that she should rest awhile longer, and hurried back to Max's room. Something felt wrong suddenly.

Richard followed, and as they stood by the bedside, Max half-opened his eyes and gave a sudden whimper. He was only semiconscious, and he stared at the wall behind Richard with a kind of horror, as if he saw something there, something awful.

"No, I won't. I can't. Dad? Dad—please don't go away, Daddy—please—tell me why—please, come back . . . oh, please . . . I don't want to be bad. . . ." Max's voice, which had risen practically to a shout, faded to a whimper, and then his eyes closed again.

"What was all that?" Richard wanted to know. His face was pale and he looked shocked. It had taken an effort of will not to turn around and look at the wall, so realistic had been Max's fear.

"Probably just the fever," Tess said unsteadily. She, too, had been unnerved by the passion in her young son's voice. "It sounded like the nightmares his housemaster described. Apparently, they're always about the accident. He seems to feel some kind of guilt—I don't know why." She leaned down. "Max," she whispered. "It's all right. Mommy's here, darling. Everything's going to be just *fine*." Max moved restlessly under the layers of white cellular blankets and turned his head away.

She patted his hand, smoothed his cheek.

He knows I'm lying, she thought.

And so do I.

But Adrian, there's no other way," Tess said a few days later. She stood in the middle of the workroom, hands on hips, glaring at her boss. "It's not just that Max needs care, he'll need to keep up with his schooling, too. An au pair would be useless when it came to lessons. I'll simply have to turn Mrs. McMurdo's work over to you and—"

"Not me, love. The bloody woman makes me break out in hives," Adrian Brevitt said, and gave an elaborate shiver. He picked up a block of damask samples and began flipping through them, while keeping a corner of his eye on her. "Anyway, she specified you, remember? This is your big chance to make your name. And mine. I want Brevitt Interiors to rise right to the top. I'm not ready *just* yet to dodder off to my little cottage and rose garden."

Tess had to smile, despite her problems. The image of elegant, fastidious Adrian Brevitt forking manure into the rose beds was ludicrous in the extreme. He could never stray more than a mile from Mayfair without coming over faint.

"Adrian, you know how grateful I am. You were more than kind to take me back when Roger died, but—"

Adrian put the damask down with a thump. "It had nothing to do with kindness and you know it," he huffed. "You needed me, and—after Jason's *treacherous* defection—I needed you. It might have been a coincidence, but it was a very happy one as far as you and I are concerned. Now that I have you back, I do not intend to let anything—not even the sickroom requirements of my beloved and precious godson—take you away from me without a fight. Frankly, my dear, I *do* give a damn. We need the work to survive, and we need you in order to *do* the blasted work. You have a cachet, Tess—you're American. That's instant rapport for a lot of our expatriate and foreign clients."

"And instant turnoff for others," Tess reminded him wryly.

"Well—there aren't many landed gentry left who can afford my prices," Adrian sniffed. "Anyway, of course we can manage your *smaller* assignments while you're staying with Max at the hospital, no trouble there, but *not* Mrs. McMurdo. There must be a way around it, Tess. After all, we do have a little time."

That was true enough, Tess acknowledged reluctantly. Mrs. McMurdo, a wealthy Australian widow, had recently returned to "the old country" to inspect her husband's "heritage." She had found it to be a rambling and nearly derelict Victorian house which sat in the midst of its overgrown garden like a huge toad, a warty and crumbling eyesore in a newly gentrified area of London.

Perversely, Mrs. McMurdo had fallen in love with the place. She decided to "restore it to its former glory" as a tribute to her beloved husband's family, and she swept into the project with vigor.

Of course, nothing but the best would do. She made inquiries and appeared one day in the studio of Brevitt Interiors. After ten minutes of loud and cheerful conversation, she decided that Tess and only Tess was right for the task of restoring The House.

Glad of something which would absorb her and her grief, Tess had set to work. Rather like the man scheduled to hang in the morning, the task of restoring the McMurdo house concentrated her mind wonderfully. She had gone far beyond the remit normally given to decorators and, along with their usual consultant architect, was overseeing the physical reconstruction as well. This was due to be completed in another month, at which time she would be free to bring her magic to bear on the interior. Given a free hand and a generous working budget, it was—or could have been—her big chance. But the situation had changed.

She followed Adrian as he tried to avoid the issue by walking around the studio. "Well, Mrs. Grimble could hardly handle teaching Max, could she? The nursing would be hard enough, what with running up and down the stairs fifty times a day, and her own health is delicate. . . ." Mrs. Grimble had been with Tess since before Max was born. She was eccentric, nosy, and opinionated. Tess put up with her odd ways because by now she was the only one who knew how to find anything in the house.

"You mean her alcoholic level is variable," Adrian sniffed.

"Don't be so damn snooty. She's been very good to me. She put up with Roger and—"

"And Roger put up with her, I imagine. Darling, the woman is a jewel—when she's sober. I quite agree that she's not exactly ideal to either look after or tutor Max. But neither are you. You don't understand the British way of education—"

"Very few do."

He refused to be sidetracked. "You haven't the patience to teach—and you're far more valuable elsewhere. Specifically, *here*." He glanced at her sideways as he leaned over a drawing pad and sketched in, quickly, another window treatment for a luxury houseboat he was redoing.

"I *could* take Max back to Iowa," she said slowly.

Adrian shuddered delicately. "I shall ignore that," he said, tearing off one page and starting another. "There *are* other things coming along, you know, things you don't know about yet. When the McMurdo job is finished it will definitely get publicity for you. And us." He flicked the pen over the paper and stood back slightly to see the effect. "Get enough new commissions on the strength of it—and you will—and you'll be in a position to call your own tune, Tess. I might *even* be stretched to consider a partnership, one day."

Tess stood watching him for a moment. She had known Adrian Brevitt for years, and found him now—as always—to be both exasperating and engaging. He was playing his high cards—something he rarely did—simply in order to keep her. She was flattered—and also tempted to kick him up his beautifully tailored backside. Partnership, indeed. "Richard has asked me to marry him," she blurted out, as if in confirmation of his assessment concerning her intrinsic value.

"You're not accepting, of course." It was a statement, not a question. He put his pen down and turned to face her, arms folded.

"I'm thinking about it," Tess hedged. "I know he's been lonely since his wife died some years ago and—"

"Ridiculous. I won't allow it. He's ten years older than you, and he'd never have time for you or for Max. He's one of those go-getters the media are always on about, thrusting and pushing and shoving and grabbing. Besides, he has absolutely *terrible* taste. I went to dinner there once with you and Roger, remember? The dining-room wallpaper gave me indigestion for *weeks* afterward."

"Perhaps his wife chose it."

"No—he did. He absolutely *bragged* about it. If it

hadn't been for you and Roger, I would have quite happily peed on it just to force him to redecorate."

Tess had to laugh—Adrian really was outrageous when he put his mind to it. The fact that he had a very firm grasp of the practicalities of plumbing as well as the lure of interior couture contributed to his success, of course—but it was the irrepressible and mischievous side of Adrian Brevitt that people remembered, and talked about. He was never cruel and always discreet when it was required, but he never left an inflated ego unpunctured, or a room unnoticed. Privately and recently, Tess had discovered that though he might try to hide it from public view, he was a solid and dependable friend in need.

He was also stubborn.

"What about that ethereal creature who lodges with you?" he asked abruptly. "Couldn't she do bed-baths or geometry?"

"Miranda? She's drifted off to warmer climes with her latest boyfriend. He's 'something' in movies, but I'm not sure what."

She perched on a stool beside the drawing board and hugged her knees. Some years ago, glorying in an unexpected windfall from a grateful client, Roger had had the attic of their large terraced house converted into a studio. He said it would give him a place to work, provide extra guest accommodation, and increase the resale value of the house. The latter possibility was yet to be tested. Due to Roger's penchant for bringing home lame ducks and the walking wounded, they'd suffered a strange procession of visitors in the studio. Miranda had been the last in a long line of non-paying guests. As for working up there—he'd used it only for designing and building conference displays too large for the office and, twice, too large to get down the stairs. Dear, fascinating, exasperating Roger. If only she'd smiled at him when he'd driven off that morning . . .

She sighed for all the might-have-beens. "There's

really only one way out of all this, Adrian, and that's for me to quit my job, sell the house as quickly as possible, buy a small flat, and live off the difference. I'll look after Max myself. I'll learn to be patient. I'll enjoy it."

"Balls," he said uncompromisingly.

She went on doggedly. "Later, when Max is better and goes back to school, perhaps you'll have me back? I hope someone will."

"You're assuming, I see, that I'll still be in business," Adrian said in an irritated tone. "Tess, the McMurdo thing is our first showpiece since Jason left. If you go, dear Dolly may well go, too—probably straight to Jason!" His voice cracked slightly, and he walked away across the room. The very line of his shoulders shrieked perfidy, perfidy!

"Nonsense," Tess said weakly, but she knew it was true, which gave her more to feel guilty about. Adrian spoke from across the room, where he now stood gazing moodily out of the window into the stylish depths of Knightsbridge.

"I'm accustomed to getting my own way, you know," he said. "I shall think of something, Tess, my love—never fear."

And he did.

I think your mother was frightened by a copy of *Tales from the Round Table*," Abbott suggested wryly.

"Maybe. But I want to look into it," Nightingale insisted. "I think there's something there."

"What?"

Nightingale tried to lean back in his chair and found it impossible, the chrome-and-plastic construction being astutely designed to prevent just such attempts at comfort. "I think Ivor Peters was frightened to death," he said.

"Oh?" Abbott raised an eyebrow. "And under exactly what statute do we find this listed as a crime, pray?"

"None. That's not—" Tim began.

"None. Correct. You might try to establish a case for Threatening to Kill—if you had a witness. But you don't have a witness. And you don't have any evidence. And he wasn't killed, he just *dropped dead*," Abbott said, leaning forward and stubbing his forefinger rhythmically on his blotter. "Cartwright did the autopsy and it was heart failure pure and simple. He uses a lot of medical terminology, of course, but the upshot is the poor old man dropped in his tracks approximately seven hours after consuming his evening meal, which—according to his landlady—was taken with clocklike regularity at six every evening, coincidental with the television news. This puts time of death after midnight, and his visitor had come and gone long before then." He leaned back and regarded his junior officer with amusement. "Unless, of course, you're suggesting the existence of some diabolically clever device which produces a delayed BOO! and then self-destructs, leaving no trace?"

Nightingale ignored that and seized on the one thing that seemed pertinent. "You asked the landlady about his dining habits?" he asked in some surprise.

"Cartwright did."

"Ah." Tim seemed gratified.

"I gather Dr. Cartwright likes things tidy. He probably got his secretary to ring the old girl up."

"Oh."

Abbott leaned back and wriggled slightly—his chair had been designed for a smaller man. He regarded his fledgling detective sergeant with benign exasperation. He liked Nightingale, he thought he was bright, and probably marginally mad. It was the university training that did it, of course. Abbott had long since decided, from his own experience, that university education merely fined down craziness from the general to the specific and made it socially functional. Nightingale had taken his degree in history—so there was definitely a touch of the knight in armor there.

However, he reminded himself, Nightingale had been a late starter in the Job. Before he'd joined the police he'd been at Lloyd's, working as a risk assessor, so he was an odds-on odds-against man. Which meant he'd thought this through before risking a superior officer's inevitable sarcasm. Even *he* must have realized how crazy it sounded.

"What bothered you?" he prompted.

"The conjunction of the mysterious visitor and the unpredicted heart failure," Tim began.

"It was probably his chess-playing chum from the day center," Abbott interrupted impatiently. "He came around for a game, Peters told him he wasn't feeling up to it, which was hardly surprising seeing he was brewing up a heart attack, and so the friend left." He saw Nightingale was shaking his head and found himself shaking his own in response. "No?"

"No. I checked. He always played with one of two men, either Ralph Gleason or a character called Chatty Corcoran. He'd played Chatty that afternoon, and told him that he was spending the evening in front of the box."

"Well, then—"

"He also told him why. He said he was frightened to go out at night."

"He and I both. Especially in that neighborhood."

"It had never bothered him before. He told Chatty he thought he'd 'gone too far' about something, and that if he wasn't careful it was going to come back on him."

It was Abbott's turn to say "Ah." He said it despite a growing conviction that he was being sent up, and that Nightingale was either playing an elaborate practical joke on him, which seemed very unlike Nightingale, or was cracking up under the strain of trying to be the new Sherlock Holmes, which was possible and probably an indication that a transfer to Traffic was on Nightingale's cards. He'd be sorry to see him go.

"And did he say what it was?" Abbott asked, with some certainty as to what the response would be, and was proved correct.

"No."

"Inconvenient." Abbott looked at his watch.

"But I know what it was."

Abbott raised an eyebrow. "I don't remember seeing 'clairvoyant' on your personnel file."

Nightingale grinned. "It was under 'Nosy Parker.'"

He shifted forward in his chair. "The reason I got on to it was because of what I read in the notebooks," he said rather desperately. He knew he had no case, but he wanted to spell it out and he wanted Abbott to listen—if only, perhaps, to help convince himself that what he suspected was worth going on with. Although he'd only seen him pushing papers around and staring out the window, he believed the gossip about the tall man from the West Country. Abbott was supposed to have cracked some really complicated cases, and they said he had the right instincts about people and their behavior. Maybe he wasn't happy here, and functioning through clenched teeth, but to hold his attention at all might prove something.

"What notebooks?" Abbott demanded.

"On his desk. I looked through a few while I was waiting for them to take the body away," Tim confessed.

"Oh, dear," Abbott said. "Invasion of privacy. I am shocked."

Nightingale faced him down. "And I took three away with me," he said.

Abbott's expression altered. "And *that* was thieving," he snapped.

Nightingale sighed. "I asked the daughter, when she arrived, and she said it was okay."

"Did you give her an explanation?"

"I said I thought her father had been investigating something criminal, and that I would like to carry on for him."

"And what did she say to that?"

Nightingale shifted in his chair. "She was a little too upset to say much about anything."

"In other words, you took advantage," Abbott said. Now his tone was censorious.

"Only because of what I'd read in the notebooks," Nightingale said defensively. "As far as I could tell, he'd always kept private notes of things he worked on when he was on the force. He kept up a diary of sorts after he retired, too, but it was mostly reflections, observations, that kind of thing. I got the feeling he was always meaning to write his autobiography, but never got around to it."

"And so say all of us," was Abbott's comment. "James Herriot has a lot to answer for."

"Yes. Well, the last three notebooks were altogether different—closer to those he'd done while working. He was investigating something in his spare time."

"My God, a kindred spirit. No wonder you got sucked in," Abbott said, not unsympathetically.

Nightingale looked injured, but went on quickly. "It all started with that accident Peters witnessed. He wrote it up very carefully, regulation-style. He'd been retired for fourteen years, but his instincts were still sound. According to him, the accident was triggered when he inadvertently stepped out in front of a car that was being pursued by another, causing the first car to swerve abruptly, turn over, and hit a tree, killing the driver. He felt responsible, in a way—but he said the *real* culprit was the driver of the chase car."

"Not one of ours in close pursuit?" Abbott said in an alarmed voice. Recent publicity had left everyone sensitive on that subject.

"No—a Ford Escort, dark green."

"Ah." Relieved, Abbott picked up a pencil and began to rotate it between his right and left hands.

"Yes. Peters jumped back, naturally, and tripped over the curb, so at first he heard more than he saw. The second car screeched to a halt—to help, he assumed. But when he stood up he saw that the driver who had been doing the chasing was actually trying to open the boot of the crashed car instead of seeing if he could help the driver. Peters shouted, and the man ducked back into his own car and drove off."

"Drove off?"

"That's right. But Peters got the number, and got an

old friend of his in DVL Swansea to put a name to it."

"Naughty," Abbott said, rotating the pencil a little faster.

"It was a hire car."

"It would be." Abbott sighed and put the pencil down.

"And the person who'd rented it had used a false license naming him as John Rochester, with an address in Leeds, gave his current address as the Mount Royal Hotel, and never brought the car back. They finally found it abandoned in the Park Lane underground car park. By that time he'd checked out of the hotel, paying his bill in cash. There had never been anyone named Rochester living at the address shown on the driving license."

"Life is like that." Abbott nodded. "Look, Tim—"

"But Peters kept on. He felt anybody who'd gone to such lengths to hide his true identity must have had something else to hide, too. He thought maybe this Rochester had planned to use some kind of accident to cover up murder from the beginning. Anyway, he had time on his hands, didn't he? It bothered him. It ate at him. So he used his old contacts in the force to get a look at the accident reports. They had it down as 'reckless driving,' no mention of a pursuit car from any other witness except Peters, who did report it at the scene. The trouble was, nobody else was on the street when it happened, and by the time people did come out to see what the noise was, the other car was gone."

"A lot of people seem to have come and gone in all this," Abbott said, standing up and turning his back to look out of the window. On the roof of the next building, a man in a uniform bearing the name of a television rental firm was checking out a television aerial. "For all I know, that chap over there is planning to electrocute the next person to turn on his television set. If I ran downstairs and across the street and up the stairs again, he'd be gone, too."

"Does he look suspicious? Do you think he's up to something?" Nightingale demanded.

Abbott turned. "Don't be daft," he said.

"But that's just it. You have a lot of experience, you're trained to spot the unusual, you've developed a sense of what's normal and what's suspicious. Peters was the same. And he couldn't get over the feeling that something was *wrong* about the accident—he says it again and again in his notebooks. He made a pain of himself at the scene. He made them open the boot, but it was empty. I've seen the report myself. The officer who did it said Peters was suffering from shock."

"He probably was," Abbott pointed out.

"Yes. But he was an ex-copper," Nightingale stressed. "He knew how to cope with shock—"

"He was also seventy-four years old," Abbott said gently.

"And still sharp enough to play good chess."

Abbott shrugged. "So? Make your point, Tim, *please*. My ulcer is getting restless."

"According to the Forensic report, there were no fingerprints in the abandoned car."

Abbott's expression sharpened briefly. "None at all?"

"None at all."

They stared at one another. "Go on," Abbott said slowly.

Nightingale shrugged. "Nobody seemed to think anything of it. The report went into the files as fraud toward the Avis people—naturally he never paid up—and that's that. They made a stab at tracking him down, but the car was undamaged and he'd only stuck them for a few days' rental, less the usual deposit, since he didn't use a credit card. They gave it a try, and then put it in the back of the drawer."

"You can't chase ghosts forever."

"But Peters went on."

"Tim—"

"He got a look at the reports—he had a lot of friends

around here—and he talked to people at the hotel, especially one of the maids who had been friendly beyond the call of duty with this Rochester—"

"Tim—"

Nightingale sped up his delivery. "And she gave him an address, which led to another, and so on. He went on looking, and eventually tracked him down. Then, for some reason, he stopped the whole thing. In the last notebook he says something about finding out more than he wanted to know, and being too old—that sort of thing. But he'd gone too far. I think this Rochester was alerted somehow. He tracked *Peters* down, came to his place, and either threatened or frightened him so badly that the old man had a heart attack."

"Tim!" Abbott had gotten his attention at last. He spoke evenly and slowly. "Did it ever occur to you that, far from being noble or enterprising, Peters's interest in this man might have been to blackmail him? And that when Rochester refused to pay up, Peters got angry and popped his valves?"

Nightingale shook his head. "No. Never. If you'd read the notebooks, you'd understand. He wasn't like that at all."

"I haven't got time to read the notebooks, or to go on listening to this. Neither do you," Abbott said wearily. "In case you have forgotten, we have something called a Priority Points System for ranking this kind of thing—on which I would estimate this whole mess you've dreamed up would register as about a negative eight. We deal in serious crimes here in the CID. Put it down and forget it. I assume you gave a receipt to the daughter for those notebooks you 'borrowed'?"

"Of course."

"Of course. I don't know why I bothered to ask," Abbott told his desk lamp. He looked at Nightingale, and his eyes were sharp and cold. "What I *will* ask is whether this is some kind of bid for attention. Do you want to impress everybody, make some kind of fancy investigation out of nothing because you figure it will look great on your record?"

"It's nothing to do with my 'career,'" Tim said quietly. "And if I messed up, it would hardly look good on my record, would it? I just think that—well—Peters was one of us. I looked into his record while I was at it, and I've talked to some of the older officers who worked with him. He was straight and he was smart and he was a good copper. If he had a feeling something was wrong, then I think there was something wrong."

"So do I," Abbott said wearily. "In particular, there's something wrong with you wasting so much time and energy on a nothing case that's going nowhere. Give the notebooks back, Tim. Forget it. Let it go. If you think you have so much time to spare from your present assignments, I can give you approximately twelve to fifty other cases that also require attention and energy devoted to them. Old cases, new cases, robberies, homicides. You call it and you're on it."

Tim sighed and looked down at his knees. He folded his hands, inspected his thumbs, measured them one against the other. "What do you want me to work on?" he finally asked.

The capitulation was complete, and—if anything—too fast. Abbott, wrong-footed, looked around his desk for a quick inspiration. "You're on that Primrose Street burglary, aren't you?" Nightingale nodded. "Well, if you get stopped on that, there was a homicide at a disco last night. They've got about two hundred suspects to sift through. Check with DI Holliman if you want to lend a hand—I have no objection."

Nightingale stood up. "All right," he said quietly, and went out of the office.

Abbott watched him close the door, and after a moment, confided in his desk lamp. "He's not going to offer to help on the homicide. And he's not going to give the notebooks back, either," he said in a resigned tone. "He's going to *say* he gave them back, but he's not going to give them back. In two months I've learned just one important thing about Tim Nightingale, and that is that when he seems the nicest he's really planning to do his worst. On that basis, he'll probably go far. Meanwhile, he's going to sit at home and look at those bloody notebooks and think about poor old Peters. He'll read a little Sherlock Holmes or Raymond Chandler before going to sleep, and when he wakes up he's going to start investigating on his own time. That's what *I* would do—which proves that after all these years I haven't learned a thing." The lamp was not much of a conversationalist.

Two months back in the city and I'm talking to electrical fittings, Abbott thought. Tomorrow during breakfast I will undoubtedly make a serious speech to my toaster concerning the front-page news or the state of my shirt collars.

He sighed, and thought about Tim Nightingale's apparently insatiable curiosity about people, his developing instinct for the "wrongness" of things, and the years ahead in which these traits would grow and either drive his superiors crazy, get him killed, or make him a good detective. He considered the abundant energy and the refusal to be daunted that Nightingale displayed, and wondered whether the feeling he had might be envy.

He hoped not.

He'd been having enough trouble dealing with boredom.

"What do you fancy tonight?" he asked the lamp. "Chinese or Indian take-away?"

Probably be one of them weirdos with purple hair and leather trousers, flapping all over the place," sniffed Mrs. Grimble, making another stab at the sink drain with the plunger. Mrs. Grimble and the drains had been waging war on one another ever since she'd first come to work for Tess over ten years earlier. The sink gave a sulky gurgle, surrendered some discolored water, and slowly emptied.

With a triumphant smirk on her face, the old woman smacked the plunger down onto the windowsill and turned to face Tess, who was seated at the big kitchen table, peeling vegetables. She had been late getting home and had hurriedly tied one of Mrs. Grimble's huge aprons over her dark suit. She was wielding the peeler awkwardly, trying to keep the mess from staining her sleeves. Mrs. Grimble picked up a paring knife in one hand and a carrot in the other. Busy hands did not stop her from speaking her mind, however. Very few things did.

"What did you want to say you'd see him for? We

don't want the likes of him living in the house. Waste of time."

"It's the least I can do," Tess said, standing up and going over to tip the potato peelings into the bin. "He's hardly likely to be weird if he teaches at Cambridge. He's a lecturer in history, and recently lost his wife."

"Carelessness or divorce?"

"Neither—he's a widower."

"Hmph. They're all the same, thinking they're so wonderful when they can only put their pants on one leg at a time, like anyone else. What you want is a nice little retired *lady* teacher. Plenty of those around, I'll wager."

Tess ignored this advice and went on determinedly. "Mr. Soame is taking a year's sabbatical to do research for a book on nineteenth-century London and needs a place to live. Anyway, Adrian talked to him—"

"Oh, my Gawd, I might have known Fancy Pants was somewheres behind it!" moaned Mrs. Grimble.

"—and Mr. Soame is very interested in trading rent for tutoring Max. If we can work out complementary schedules, it should be an ideal arrangement," she finished triumphantly.

Mrs. Grimble looked hard at the cooker in case it, too, decided to do something to make her life miserable. "I hope you don't take it wrong that I can't help out more," she muttered. "But what with Walter's stomach and my back . . ." Walter Briggs was Mrs. Grimble's younger brother. He'd moved in with her the day after Mr. Grimble had died, and had remained ever since. According to his sister, Walter was "delicate"—particularly, it seemed, on the day he collected his dole money.

Tess reached out and squeezed Mrs. Grimble's hand. "I couldn't get along without you, but I certainly don't want to risk your health as well as Max's, do I? Who'd look after us all, then?"

The old woman looked at her fondly. "You *need*

looking after, you do," she said. "Too soft, that's your trouble."

The front doorbell rang, startling them both. "That must be Mr. Soame now," Tess said, wiping her hands hurriedly on the apron and then dragging it off over her head, causing her hair to stand up in errant spikes. "Do you think you could be a darling and finish the vegetables before you go?"

"As if I wouldn't," sniffed Mrs. Grimble, reaching for a potato. "I'll be right here if you need me," she said meaningfully, and waved the knife in a vaguely menacing manner.

Tess went down the long dark hall and opened the front door, expecting the worst. For a moment she thought she had gotten it.

On the top step stood an angular man in a wrinkled tweed suit. He had a mac over one arm and a bulging briefcase in his free hand. Someone seemed to have been holding a party in his jacket pockets—and from their shape there was still a lot of clearing up to do in there. His features were somewhat obscured by heavy horn-rimmed glasses.

"Soame," he announced. When she didn't reply, he seemed to shrink slightly. "You *were* expecting me, weren't you? I'm almost certain we settled on Tuesday. . . ." His voice was hesitant, and despite his height he seemed ready to bolt if Tess showed the least sign of disapproval.

"Of course we did." He rewarded her—or himself—with a sudden half-moon smile. For a moment Tess was reminded of the young Alec Guinness, and involuntarily smiled back. "Come in," she told him, and stepped back. He followed her down the dark hall and into the sitting room. "Won't you sit down?" She indicated the battered old sofa that sat like an elderly camel in the bay window. He perched on the edge of it rather warily, putting his briefcase down on the floor beside him and then—after jabbing it first toward the side table and then the coffee table and then the lamp—he put his rather forlorn tweed hat on the cushion beside him. He seemed so ill at ease that Tess began to feel nervous, too.

"Would you like a drink—or something?"

"I don't drink much," he said apologetically. "Wine with meals, occasionally, but nothing . . ." He stopped himself and took a breath. "Coffee would be very nice, though—if you had planned to make some for yourself, that is. There's rather a chilly wind outside and I walked from the tube station, not realizing it was quite so far. . . ." His voice trailed off.

"Of course—it won't take a minute."

Tess fled to the kitchen, where Mrs. Grimble was glowering behind the door, knife in hand. She'd obviously been playing Peeping Tom through the crack. "I'm not leaving, don't you worry," the older woman muttered ominously. "He's big."

"He's also scared stiff, if you ask me," Tess said, plugging in the kettle.

"Hmph," Mrs. Grimble said. "That's just you being soft, as usual. And what's he been doing with that hat, I want to know? Looks like someone sat on it."

"He probably did," Tess said. "Poor lamb."

Mrs. Grimble snorted. "You just remember what can be inside sheep's clothing, young lady. Don't be fooled by all that 'Pardon my toe in your eye and pass the marmalade.' I think he looks loony."

"Nonsense," Tess said, pouring boiling water onto the instant-coffee powder she'd spooned into mugs—three mugs, not forgetting Mrs. Grimble, who had an insatiable thirst.

"Don't tell me nonsense, because *I* read the papers. It's the meek ones that go berserk and chop people up," Mrs. Grimble said briskly, coming across to pick up her coffee, but not relinquishing the paring knife, which she dropped into her apron pocket. "I'll be right here. Listening to his every cunning word."

Tess returned to the sitting room with the coffee, much entertained by Mrs. Grimble's suspicions. She found John Soame still perched on the sofa, absent-mindedly rubbing one knee over and over again as he looked around the room in a bemused fashion. Tess followed his glance, and understood his puzzlement. The rather nice wallpaper was loose in two corners near the ceiling, due to damp, and in several places above the wainscoting it still bore faint traces of Max's infant experiments with crayons. The curtains in the bay window were newish, but clashed terribly with the faded carpet—she'd been shopping for its replacement on the very day Roger had been killed. She hadn't had the heart—or the money—to complete her mission since.

The furniture was a mixture of solid old pieces she'd picked up at various auctions and sales. She'd stripped and renovated them as they came along, always in a hurry, always with a new color scheme in mind, and always intending to redo everything to match—one day. The entire effect was more that of a room created by a nearsighted color-blind junk dealer than a highly trained artist and experienced interior decorator.

"You know the tale of the cobbler's children, don't you?" she said. "The same thing applies here. This is the place I have always *meant* to make wonderful, but never seem to find the time to do it."

Soame shook his head. "Actually, if I were rich, I would commission you to create one just like it for me."

She laughed. "You're not serious, of course."

"I am. You see, when Adrian said you were an interior decorator, I thought it would be so perfect that I'd be afraid to sit down." He leaned forward confidentially. "I tend to spill things."

"So I see," Tess smiled, as a few drops of coffee escaped his mug and disappeared into the carpet.

"Sorry, sorry," he said, jerking it back so quickly that even more spattered out, this time hitting both his knee and the sofa. "Oh, Lord," he muttered, brushing ineffectually at the spots.

If I don't do something to distract him, he's going to fall apart at the seams, she thought. Leaning down, she picked up the black-and-white quilt she was working on and began to stitch.

"That's very attractive," Mr. Soame said.

"It's called a Widow's Quilt," Tess said. "It's a traditional American pattern—always black and white, and always made to fit a single bed. I believe the theory is that by the time you've finished it, the worst of your grief is over."

"And will it be?"

The needle balked. "Damn."

She saw that he looked stricken. "The worst of it is over already," she assured him. "I just jabbed my thumb, that's all. I do it frequently—whatever I sew always has my blood on it, one way or another. I find patchwork very soothing, hand-quilting even more so. But this particular pattern is a bit boring, I must say. I don't know what made me start it."

But she did know. It was a penance for all the wicked thoughts she'd had toward Roger since his death. Not being Catholic, and confession not being available to her, she had found her own punishment—the sewing of this damned quilt.

There were many examples of her handiwork around the house, covering all the beds, hanging on the walls, even curtaining the downstairs cloakroom. But those patchwork pieces were bright and vibrant, done to her own designs. Working this traditional quilt was monotonous and dull, but she was determined to finish it, even if it killed *her*.

"Are the black arrows supposed to represent something?" Soame asked. "Or are they your own creation?"

"Oh, they're traditional, too. They're called the Darts of Death." And they are many, she thought. They cause the wounds that come after—longing, loneliness, frustration, remorse, reproach, resentment, rage, the constant wish to live the time over and repair the wrongs of the past, the bitter knowledge that such a wish will not be granted. A widow's mite. A widow's pillory.

"I see," he said quietly. And, remembering belatedly that he was himself a widower, she thought perhaps he did. He watched her for a minute, then looked around the room again.

"Is there something wrong?" she asked, deciding she could stand it no longer. He was making her nervous, too. Working the quilt wasn't helping, and neither was the coffee.

He gazed at her through the heavy-rimmed lenses and spoke with utter sincerity. "I have faced many things, Mrs. Leland, but none of them compares with the prospect of pleasing a small boy and his mother with my somewhat limited teaching credentials."

"I'd hardly call them limited," Tess protested. "Of course, Adrian told me about your research and why you need to be in London for the next twelve months. Did he also explain my situation to you?"

He nodded vigorously, causing his glasses to slide down his nose. He peered at her over them. "Oh, yes. Adrian said you need a combination tutor and babysitter." He flushed slightly, and rushed on. "As for me, all I require is peace and quiet, a place to sleep, and a large table on which to lay out my reference books. At present I am in a bed-and-breakfast hotel which is on a very busy street. I'm not very happy there. Most of the other inhabitants seem to be foreigners on holiday. All very jolly, of course, but they are constantly asking for directions which I cannot give, or translations which I cannot make. The very few permanent residents all seem to be subject to fits. There is usually someone *shouting*, or crying, or falling down the stairs."

"Oh, dear," Tess said.

"Yes. I've only been there a week, mind. It could have been an unusual seven days for them, I suppose." He didn't sound convinced. "In the place I stayed before that, someone deliberately set fire to the dining room."

"Good heavens."

"Yes." He reflected. "I think it was out of pique, really—the bacon was always burned, so why not everything else?"

"Why not indeed?" Tess said faintly.

He warmed to his refrain. "On another memorable occasion there was a fistfight between two very large and angry women at three in the morning. I got a black eye trying to separate them—they both turned on me, you see. People *will* do that." He sighed. "It is all so exhausting, and hardly conducive to serious study. In addition, London is proving to be very expensive and I'm not exactly wealthy at the moment, what with . . . one thing and another."

He paused, swallowed, and took off his glasses to polish them, oblivious to Tess's efforts to keep a straight face. His eyes, thus revealed, proved to be dark blue and oddly unfocused, like an infant's. She thought she recognized him at last—a fellow sufferer at the hands of willful fate, one to whom things happened without warning, and without explanation.

She'd heard there were natural victims, but until Roger's death she had never considered herself in that category. Yet, for the past few months, she had definitely been got at. She'd been burglarized, for a start. And then there were the little things, like silent phone calls, people staring at her and then turning away, letters that looked as if they'd been opened by someone else first, deliveries of things she hadn't ordered, lost deliveries of things she *had* ordered. All petty, all ridiculous—probably just the vagaries of life in a big city—but unsettling.

From the expression on Soame's face, he too felt gnawed by the rats of misfortune.

He sighed, replaced his glasses, and went on. "But all that's neither here nor there." He cleared his throat. "If you and I can come to some satisfactory mutual arrangement, it would be a great relief to me. Of course, I'd have to meet your son first."

Tess stiffened defensively. "He's a perfectly nice little boy," she said.

Soame nodded. "I was thinking more of whether *he* would approve of *me*, actually."

"Oh, I see." She felt embarrassed at having misunderstood, and decided theirs was probably doomed to be a relationship of continual mutual misapprehensions. She was already resigned to it. "Well, if you can spare the time, we can go up together the day after tomorrow to see him. I'll pay for your ticket, of course. It's not far out of London. I'm staying over, but there are plenty of trains back."

"Very kind," he said quickly. "Very kind."

There was a pause.

"How old is Max, by the way? Adrian probably told me, but I can't remember. . . ."

"He's nine." She felt a stab of concern. "Won't it be boring for you to teach a youngster after teaching university students?"

He leaned sideways to put his empty mug down on the end table and gazed earnestly at her. "Mrs. Leland, it would be sheer delight," he said. "That is, I assume he's the usual kind of nine-year-old boy? No long hair, no beard, not given to beer-drinking contests, pot smoking, arguing theories of genetics, demonstrating rugger tactics at four in the morning, making anarchistic plans for revolution, playing the guitar badly, or bringing aggressive feminist girlfriends to tutorials?"

"Not so far," Tess grinned. "He collects stamps."

John Soame sighed deeply, leaned back, and produced again that engaging half-moon smile. "A proper boy," he said in gratified tones. "I'll take the job." Then he leaned forward, apparently startled by his own enthusiasm. "That is—if you'll have me?"

7

Tim Nightingale leaned back in his chair and opened the notebook. Slowly and carefully, with déjà vu born of what felt like a thousand previous examinations of the same facts in the same file, he read over the information that had been accumulated by Ivor Peters.

It didn't take long.

"Are we going out to lunch or staying in?"

It was Detective Constable Tom Murray standing by his desk, looking harassed. "Because if we're going out, we'd better get a move on or we'll never get a table; and if we aren't, we'd better get a move on or all the decent food in the canteen will have been snapped up."

"That wouldn't take long," Nightingale said, leaning down to put the notebook carefully into the bottom drawer of his desk, which he then locked. Murray raised an eyebrow.

"You still crooning over that?" he asked in surprise.

Nightingale shrugged. "It bothers me."

"Lately they all bother you," his friend said.

"Only the ones that don't make sense," Nightingale said with a wry smile.

They walked out of the office they shared with two other detectives and started down the hall. "But it was days ago," Tom protested, shrugging into his coat. "I thought Abbott told you to shelve it."

"As far as I'm concerned, it's still open," Nightingale said. "Still very much alive."

"Which is more than the old man is."

"Yes." Nightingale pushed the lift button and the indicator lit up, showing it was high above them. The light did not change. They glanced at one another and then turned and started for the stairs. As they clattered down, Nightingale spoke over his shoulder. "By the way, you didn't see me looking at that file. It wasn't there, all right?"

"I don't know what you're talking about."

"The no—— oh, right. Thanks."

"But I reserve the right to think you're nuts."

They emerged from the stairwell and made for the street. A slight drizzle was misting down, and the prospect of the busy, grimy, soggy street did not please.

"God, I hate the city," Nightingale said, turning up the collar of his mac. "The only green thing I've seen lately is the mold on my last piece of bread when I got it out of the wrapper this morning."

"Country boy."

"So?" Nightingale glanced at him. "I'm not ashamed of it. I grew up in beautiful surroundings, and I miss it. We weren't rich, God knows, but we could look up and see hills and trees and sky. If an old man dropped dead there, people would be upset, people would want the thing explained, settled, tied up. Here, we do nothing but make a report, and then we have to shove it to the back of the shelf, because another one comes along. And another. They're all human beings, they all deserve more than that. A little anger, at least."

"Which you seem to be supplying."

"Which I'm tired of supplying," Nightingale grumbled.

They went out into the drizzle and made for the Italian restaurant they both favored. The traffic moved slowly past them, tires peeling stickily from the wet tarmac, windscreen wipers thunking in many rhythms. Windows were steamed because the drivers were complaining and cursing one another, their lips moving silently behind the misted glass. The gritty shuffle of pedestrians was the only sound from the pavement. An occasional umbrella forced them to dodge or duck to one side, otherwise their progress was slow but steady. People didn't want to linger outside any longer than they had to today.

They reached the restaurant, went in, and were instantly enveloped in exotic aromas of pesto, tomato, garlic, cheese, and sharp red wine. Relayed softly through speakers placed with merciful discretion were Neapolitan love songs. There was one table left—the smallest one, of course, in the corner, where their elbows would knock the wall and waiters would constantly pass and mutter, but it would have to do.

"What are you on at the moment?" Nightingale asked when they'd settled themselves as well as they could. "Still that camera-shop break-in?"

"Yes. Personally, I think it was the owner himself, looking for the insurance payoff, but I can't make it out enough to hold up in court."

"Law's old sweet song." Nightingale smiled. It was not a happy smile.

"For the next hour let us forget our work," Tom suggested. "Let us wine and dine and talk of cabbages and kings."

Nightingale eyed him. "It's beginning to get to you, too, isn't it?"

"What is?"

"Everything. The city, the frustration, everything."

Tom shrugged. "Maybe. But if you're going to start in again about transferring to one of the regions, forget it. I am not interested. I will never be interested. I am a city boy. Down today, up tomorrow—swings and roundabouts, that's the way it goes. You'll get used to it."

"You could get used to hills and trees."

"And having to drive twenty miles to the nearest town to get a meal like we're about to have? In fact, having to drive twenty miles to the nearest town to get *everything?* Forget it."

"I can't forget it. I can't forget anything."

Tom leaned forward and put on an Austrian accent. "Dat is your trrrouble, Herr Nightingale, you cannot forget anyting. Lie down on ze couch und tell me about zis compullllsion you haff to valk in se hills vot are rrround like brreasts, and see the trrees vot are tall and strraight like—"

"Like zis bread stick vot I will place in your eye?" Nightingale opened his menu and gave Matt a dangerous look across the top of it. "Let's order this meal. I think your blood sugar is getting low."

"Just trying to cheer things up."

"I don't want to be cheered up. I want to get back to the office. I have an idea."

Tom Murray looked disgusted. "Great. Have your idea. Me—I'll have spaghetti."

Nightingale grinned. "They have something in common, at that."

"What?"

"Loose ends."

The McMurdo family tree had sprung from strong roots, but it had suffered from blight. Now, the only remaining branch was that which had sprouted from a young twig who had emigrated to Australia to make his fortune. Sheep and opal mining, mostly, but a bit of timber, too, had been the basis of his endeavors, and he had prospered. However, Australian weather being what it can be, even that McMurdo branch eventually withered down to just Burdoo McMurdo, a successful manufacturer of plumbing fixtures. It was Burdoo's childless widow who had come to Britain to trace her husband's roots and claim his heritage. Uncle Harry McMurdo, last of the English line, had written to Australia long ago, boasting about how he was leaving Burdoo "a great inheritance—the family treasure." He had conned Burdoo out of some money to "protect" it. Nothing more was heard of or from Uncle Harry until his executors got in touch, and the great inheritance he'd bragged about proved to be a great disappointment.

Dolly McMurdo was what generous friends might

call "a character," and what everyone else called a case of all mouth and no taste. Dolly's saving grace was that she knew she was loud, knew she was gauche, and knew she was laughed at, but didn't give a damn. She was rich enough to soothe any ruffled feelings she might engender through an unkind but truthful observation or a misjudged slap on the back, and rich enough also to buy the good taste she lacked from those who had it—and were willing to sell.

Dolly had swept into the Savoy like a bleached beached whale become woman. Large in girth and gusto, she'd won over the staff with her good humor and large tips, and the other guests by involuntarily becoming a source of delicious disapproval to one and all.

One horrified look at the old McMurdo mansion—now occupied mostly by wasps and black beetles—had convinced Dolly that she had a mission in life, and that was to renovate this fallen symbol of the family's former power and prestige. No matter what it cost.

"My God, would you look at the rotten heap!" she had trumpeted on alighting from her rented chauffeur-driven Rolls. "Burdoo always told me it was a mansion, a dream of old England, and all that dingo dribble." Apparently she had then fixed the heavens with a mean eye, and had spoken to the sky. "Burdoo, you always were a liar—I should have flushed you down one of your own toilets when I had the chance, bless your little dried-up heart." On the chauffeur's later telling of it, she had marched up the path through the nettles, given the front steps an almighty kick, then leaned back and looked up at the scabby paintwork and sagging roofline.

Again, she had addressed a passing cloud. "Burdoo, I guess I'd better make an honest man of you and get this place back in shape before I die. Mind you, another shock like this one may send me along sooner than I think. Enjoy yourself up there while you can, you old wowser." She had then turned to the chauffeur and demanded to be driven to her friend Noelene Arletta Hanks's house in Chelsea. Noelene was always bragging how she knew the finest interior decorators, wasn't she? Well, here was the chance to prove it.

The task set by Mrs. McMurdo was a daunting one, for the structure of the house had suffered through many transformations (bed-sitters, ever decreasing in size and ever increasing in number), encrustations (wallpapers from William Morris through Art Nouveau, Art Deco, wartime austerity, the New Look, the frankly fundamental fifties, the hallucinogenic sixties, a brief flowering of Laura Ashley, and finally, flat buff paint over all when it served, even more briefly, as a hostel for recently released sexual offenders), and visitations (families, single women, soldiers, students, young-marrieds, the above-mentioned ex-prisoners, and, at last—through broken windows—the British weather). But it was a task that Brevitt Interiors—or rather, Tess Leland—had taken to with gusto.

And now it looked as if she would be able to complete what she had taken on after all. After a reassuring phone call to the Ward Sister and a brief chat with Max, she spent the next morning talking with the men working on the house, getting firm commitments as to when she could begin scheduling the various stages of her own work. Then she met Adrian for lunch and told him about her interview with John Soame.

"I think it will be fine," she told him. "We're only a ten-minute tube ride from the British Museum. We should be able to work out our schedules pretty easily, since we both work to our own hours. Max won't be able to do much except read at first, so Mr. Soame intends to use the next few weeks to make a start on his basic research. Then, as Max gets stronger, they'll start proper studies. Max's school is going to give me a syllabus, the appropriate books, and a suggested work schedule."

She reached for another roll and buttered it enthusiastically. Adrian watched her with approval—she had gotten so very thin so very quickly after Roger died, and then again when Max first fell ill. He leaned back as the waiter set down their first course. "You must be sure to take advantage of him," he advised.

Her eyes widened. "I beg your pardon?"

"His expertise," Adrian said. "He knows a great deal about the entire Victorian era—particularly architecture—and you could do worse than ask his opinion if you come up against something in the McMurdo house you know little about. I mentioned it to him and he was very interested. He has a great eye for detail, and he's made some unusual contacts in the antiquarian world."

Tess paused with her soup spoon in mid-air, considering John Soame in this new light. "Well, he may be an expert, but I don't think I've ever met a grown man so lacking in self-confidence," she finally said.

Adrian nodded, spreading pâté on a piece of thin toast. "His wife was one of the most unpleasant women I've ever known—and, my pet, I've known a few. I know one shouldn't speak ill of the dead—"

"That's never stopped you," Tess commented.

He ignored that. "Alicia did a proper demolition job on poor John—something about him seemed to bring out a vicious streak in her."

"You sound as if you knew her very well."

"She was my youngest sister." Adrian smiled sadly at Tess's astonished expression. "Hers was a destructive soul. In the end she left him, went on a trip to India with a 'friend,' and was bitten by a rabid dog—which seemed to me simple justice."

"Adrian!"

He eyed her over his wire-rimmed glasses. "She was as lovely as a flower to look at—but as deadly to the soul as cyanide." He sniffed. "There is no law that says you have to love your own family—especially when it throws out a dud like Alicia. My father suspected the milkman, of course—a narrow-eyed goat of a man who was always leaving extra cream. However, I have recently come across an engraving of his Great-Aunt Beulah, who was the image of Alicia in a bustle. Besides, Mother may have been *tempted* by the dairyman—she was a woman of earthy appetite—but she was far too worried about what the neighbors might have thought to have actually succumbed to his ungulate charms." He waved to the waiter and indicated that they were ready for their next course.

"Well, even if dear old John *is* a bit edgy, I still think he'll be ideal for your situation," Adrian continued after they'd been served.

Tess pressed a large bite of Chicken Dijon onto her fork. "Oh, so do I," she agreed. "He could probably use a bit of comfort and appreciation."

Adrian raised an eyebrow and inspected her more closely while refilling her wineglass. "Oh, dear," he said, smiling mischievously to himself. "What *have* I done?"

"You've made certain Max will be tutored and I will have a man—albeit a nervous one—around the house. You've therefore made certain I'll be free to protect *you* from the Monster McMurdo," Tess said briskly. "And that was just what you set out to do, wasn't it?"

"Why, Tess, you make me sound quite *ruthless*," Adrian said in a hurt tone.

"You *are* quite ruthless, Adrian, when it comes to your own peace and survival. But never mind, we love you anyway." Tess grinned and blew him a kiss across the flower arrangement. "All of your devoted slaves adore you—we always clank our chains when you pass."

Coming home that evening, weary but content, Tess hung her coat in the hall and then kicked off her shoes, moaning with pleasure and relief. She had walked about twenty miles since lunch, choosing plumbing fixtures and getting solid delivery dates out of four different suppliers and looking through a warehouseful of junk for just one little table that she finally found under the stairs, and then discovering that nobody had nineteen rolls of "Daisychain." Two had fifteen rolls each, but of course they had totally different lot numbers. Now she had to convince the client to have "Fieldflowers" instead.

She started up the stairs, then had to come back down again as the phone began to ring. "Hello?"

Silence.

Again.

"Hello!"

Silence.

Tess felt familiar fury boiling up in her. This had been going on for weeks now. The phone rang at random times, but the result was always the same—silence. No giggling, no heavy breathing, no obscene suggestions. Just silence. Not the silence of a broken connection or a dead phone, either. Oh, no.

It was the silence of someone listening.

She had complained, of course. Her phone and her line had been thoroughly checked. No fault. And, as nothing was said of either an obscene or threatening nature, it was not a matter for the police. The phone people were sympathetic, but the only alternatives on offer were an interception service that would only ask what number had been dialed and whom the caller wished to speak to by name, or changing her number, both of which would cost money she could not spare. Going ex-directory was free, but wouldn't be effective until the new phone books came out next year.

Tess reached for the whistle she had bought recently and hung by the phone. "Damn it—who is this? I'm sick and tired of being called at all hours of the day and night."

This time, just as she was bringing the whistle to her lips and taking a breath, just as if she could be *seen*, the silence was broken. A sense of movement from the other end of the line, and a whisper, like a snake shedding its skin.

"We want the money, Mrs. Leland."

The whistle dropped from her fingers and rolled under the bench. She was so dumbfounded she could only say, "What?"

"The money, Mrs. Leland. Give it back."

There was a terrible rasp and slither in the voice, and Tess felt the skin of her back and arms raise up in gooseflesh. A cold draft seemed suddenly to swirl down the hallway.

"I . . . I . . . don't have any idea what you're talking about. What money?"

Now it was worse. Not a whisper, but a chuckle.

"You know. *You* know." Like a cruel child, pointing a finger on the playground, chanting, chanting. "*You* know."

"I don't . . . I don't . . ." Tess felt her throat closing, as if an invisible hand had encircled it.

"It isn't in the house—we looked. And you haven't spent it—we checked. So you've got it hidden somewhere, right? If you don't give it back, *someone* is going to be very, very cross!"

Still a whisper, but now a gleeful, maniac whisper.

And then a click. Dead line.

Tess stood staring at the phone, as if she expected it to strike at her, but it was only a white plastic handset, silent again—connection broken.

Slowly, Tess replaced the handset and stood staring at the phone. It had to be children, or some pubescent teenager trying to exert power in a threatening world. . . .

Boy? Girl? Man? Woman? It had no gender, no age.

But it had known her name.

Suddenly she whirled, ran up the stairway, down the hall and into her bedroom. Slamming the door behind her, she twisted the key in the lock and stood, panting, with her back against it.

All was normal here.

The white curtains, the delicate flowered wallpaper, the brilliant intersecting patterns of the patchwork quilt that covered the king-sized bed, the warm dusky-pink carpet, her slippers and robe, the dried flower arrangement on the bedside table. All untouched, and her own. Safe.

Eventually she calmed down sufficiently to move away from the door. Slowly she unbuttoned her suit jacket and went to the wardrobe for a hanger. A bath, some supper, a book in bed . . . she would not think about the call. She would *not*.

She pulled at the door of the wardrobe—it seemed a little stiff—swung it wide, and began to scream.

Things flew at her, mothlike, fluttering, and cold hard pellets poured over her face and body as she flailed about her, screaming and crying . . . and, over it all . . . laughter.

The wild, unceasing laughter of a demented old man.

With an almost imperceptible jerk, the train began to move out of the station. The train beside them seemed to slide backward—an impression which always disconcerted Tess—and then they were out from under the roof and into the rain. In a moment the windows were covered with running drops and ribbons of moisture that converged and spread, blurring the world beyond.

"If you'll pardon me for saying, you look as if you haven't slept well. Has something happened to Max?" John Soame was asking patiently. He seemed to have been asking it for some time.

Tess shook her head and sipped some of the tea he had brought her. It was scalding, but tasteless. "No, he's doing fine. I was frightened by the wardrobe."

"I beg your pardon?"

She shook her head again, and put down the tea in order to explain about the phone calls, the shower of confetti and fresh red cranberries that had cascaded out of the wardrobe, and the mechanical toy called a laughter-bag that had gone on shrieking long after she had stopped. "I felt like such a fool," she said. "It was just some terrible practical joke."

"But whom do you know who would do such a cruel thing?"

"No one, as far as I know. I mean, I don't have all that many friends of my own—we mostly entertained Roger's clients or contacts in the business if we entertained at all. None of the people I know are given to that kind of 'humor.'"

"But when could someone have gotten in the house?"

"Well, the house was empty all morning. But I called Mrs. Grimble, and asked her about it. She arrives at two o'clock, and stays until five, most days. She did the bedroom first, apparently, and there was nothing in the wardrobe then, because she hung up some dry cleaning that she'd collected for me, and nothing happened. She was there all afternoon, except for about forty minutes when she went out to do my shopping—if I'm pressed for time on a particular day, I usually leave a list and the money on the kitchen table. Whoever it was must have gotten in during those forty minutes."

She was suddenly aware that a middle-aged woman sitting opposite them was listening avidly to their conversation, and lowered her voice. The woman looked away, making a pretense of disinterest, but her ears practically seemed to glow with attention. Well, let her listen, Tess thought. Let everyone listen. A sudden recklessness overcame her—this was too important to worry about eavesdroppers or what the neighbors might think!

"You say you'd been getting phone calls before this?"

"Yes, frequently. But only silent ones. Last night was the first time anyone spoke to me."

"And the first time anyone has gotten into the house."

Tess nodded, her mind still filled with that terrible moment, when she had looked down and seen the carpet dotted with red berries and thought it her own blood. "Just when I realized what it all was, the telephone began to ring again."

"Did you answer it?"

"I was afraid to. Eventually it stopped."

"I see." Soame was lost in thought for a minute, then spoke diffidently.

"When your husband died, did you *inherit* any money, aside from insurance and so on? I'm sorry to pry, but someone seems to think you have some available."

Tempted to have a look at a possible heiress, the woman opposite risked a glance at them and met Tess's eyes. Flushing, she turned away again, pressing her lips together. Tess felt some sympathy—the poor thing couldn't have known when she sat down that she would be forced to share these intimacies. To get up would be to admit she'd been listening. And, of course, to get up would be to miss the rest. What price Hollywood when you could get all this drama for free on the ten thirty-eight?

"I wish we had inherited something," Tess said ruefully. "In a sense we lived from hand to mouth all the years we were married. I don't mean we starved. I mean we lived up to and frequently beyond our means. Everything that came in went right out again—Roger was a real grasshopper—he never seemed to think about the future, because he found here and now so interesting, I guess. When he and Richard Hendricks started up their PR agency, they did it with a bank loan—Roger was always amazingly good at talking to bank managers. Even when the agency started to thrive, every penny they made seemed to go straight back into the business. Roger had no secret accounts or deposit boxes."

"As far as you know," John Soame said.

"I know that Roger couldn't hold on to money at all," Tess protested. "I'd certainly have known if—"

"I don't mean to be rude," he interrupted firmly. "But the fact is, the newspapers are always full of stories about wives who are astounded to discover things about their husbands after they've died or run away."

That was certainly true, Tess thought ruefully.

John Soame spoke again. "Was he a secretive man?"

Tess thought about that. "Not in a sly way, no. But he did like to surprise people—he was very generous, always bringing home unexpected little gifts and things."

"What about this—Richard Hendricks, did you say? Your husband's ex-partner? Would he know about any money?"

Tess shook her head. "I'm sure if Richard had known about any money that Roger had, he'd have given it to me long ago. He's been very good to us."

"Did you ask him about this?"

"I rang him last night, but there was only the answering machine. When I rang the office this morning, his secretary told me he's still out of the country on business. He's gone into partnership with someone else, now—doing market research, I think. He and Roger handled a lot of international accounts, and now that the Common Market is coming, anybody with that kind of experience is in demand. I believe he's doing very well already."

"Have you told him about these calls?"

"No. I just thought it was a crank. Mrs. Grimble knows about it, she's taken a few of the calls. She thinks it's one of the neighbors. Or the greengrocer or the butcher—depending on who she's had her latest argument with. That's more or less what I assumed, too."

John nodded. "Well, if Max approves of me, you'll soon know there's someone in the house all the time. And perhaps the police can convince the telephone people to cooperate."

Tess's eyes widened. "The police?"

He glanced at her. "Of course. You've been threatened, and threatening phone calls must be against some law or other. I'll ring Scotland Yard when I get back to London later this afternoon and find out the position."

The middle-aged woman in the blue hat and coat had stopped pretending not to listen. So had the two men in the seats across the aisle. Tess stared at John Soame in some confusion. Why was he doing this? He saw the question in her eyes and smiled that oddly infectious smile of his.

"Blame it on Clark Kent," he said.

The meeting between Max and John Soame went very well. As soon as they discovered mutual passions for cricket, stamps, Sherlock Holmes, and World War I flying machines, the relationship was solid.

While they talked, Tess went over to the window and looked out. Maybe it would be all right after all. Mr. Soame would teach Max, she could look after Mrs. McMurdo's house, Mrs. Grimble could look after *her* house, and everybody would be happy. A thin shaft of sunlight penetrated the gloomy overcast and touched a vase of brilliant yellow roses that stood in the window of a room in the opposite wing, seeming to set them alight. That's a hopeful sign, isn't it? she thought.

There was a tentative knock on the door, and a young man poked his head through the gap. "Hello? Oh—sorry, Max, didn't know you had visitors."

"It's only my mum," Max said.

"Thank you very much," Tess laughed.

The young man came in a few steps and smiled. He was dressed in jeans and a bright-red pullover and resembled a plump robin. His hair was a fluff of light-brown curls that surrounded his high forehead like a halo, which may have been appropriate, for his shirt had a reversed collar.

"Hello—Mrs. Leland?" He extended a pale hand.

"My name is Simon Carter. I've been visiting your son—I hope you don't mind."

"Not at all," Tess said, shaking his hand, which was surprisingly warm and firm of grip.

"He's a vicar," Max said in pretended disgust.

Simon grinned. "I've only just been ordained," he said. "Doing a bit of hospital visiting until I get a parish assignment. Max is trying to convince me that rugby is a much finer vocation. We are fighting the good fight across a chessboard." He produced a folded board and a box of chessmen that he had been holding behind his back. "Mind you, we haven't finished a game yet, but . . . early days, early days."

"I'm going to beat you before I go home," Max said with pathetic determination. He looked very tired now.

"Perhaps. But not today," Simon said gently. "How about tomorrow, after lunch?"

Max looked as if he was going to protest, then sank back on his pillows with a sigh. "Okay," he said. "Tomorrow."

Carter smiled engagingly at them all, and departed.

Tess walked with John Soame to the lifts. After he'd prodded the button to go down, he smiled at her. "I'm sure we can get to the bottom of this business with the phone calls, you know. The police must deal with this kind of thing quite regularly."

She'd almost forgotten—but he obviously hadn't. "I'll bet they've never dealt with a vicious wardrobe before."

He frowned. "I must admit, that was worrying, if only because it shows someone got into the house." He prodded the lift button again, rather viciously. "You must leave the dirty work to those who are good at it," he told her.

She had to smile. "Meaning you?"

"Don't I look the type?"

"Frankly, no."

He nodded, accepting her sympathetic assessment.

"Ah, well, you see—that's my secret strength," he informed her solemnly, and limped away down the corridor toward the stairs, his awful mac flapping around his long thin legs. The lift arrived then, but it was too late.

The caped crusader was gone.

10

Nightingale had become accustomed to hospitals, but was still a long way from liking to be in one. Their internal workings were akin to those of a small city erected to the glory of some mysterious and undeclared religion. The gleaming instruments and machines glimpsed through half-open doors seemed manufactured for arcane ritual, the various uniforms of doctors, nurses, technicians and workers were worn like vestments to delineate both status and function. The whole edifice was riddled with intersecting corridors leading to unlabeled destinations, and surrounded by a seemingly random and organic encrustation of outbuildings, annexes, and chambers, many of which emitted sudden unexplained bursts of noise or steam. Most of all, there was a peculiar sound that flowed down every hall—a humming pulsation of hidden machinery overlaid by the susurrus of unseen people speaking softly in secret rooms, using words one cannot quite catch, but which seem filled with important meaning.

He might have enjoyed learning about it all, were it not for the pain.

He could feel it as he walked down the corridors. Not just the pain of the patients, but the pain of their families as well. Worst of all, he had a heightened awareness of Death hovering in the corners and on the stairways, watching for His chance. To enter a hospital may be to enter a city, he thought, but it is a city at war—with battalions of nurses, doctors, and technicians on one side, and the dark, invisible shadow of mortality on the other. For Death is a guerrilla fighter, and will dart in through any door, any window, given even the briefest opportunity. He'd seen His work, and knew he would see much more in the years ahead.

A haggard-looking young doctor passed him in the hallway.

Death is our common enemy, Nightingale thought. But you're the soldier, and I'm just one of the dustmen, one of the ones who come to clean up after the battle is lost. You might stop Death—I only trace His footsteps back to His instrument.

And I'm here to do that now.

He found the room number he'd been given. The door was open and he looked in to see a woman sitting in a chair beside the bed in which a small boy was sleeping. She was holding a magazine open on her lap but was not reading it, gazing out instead at the rain clouds scudding low above the trees.

"Mrs. Leland?" He spoke softly, and she turned, startled.

"Yes?"

Nightingale introduced himself and showed her his identification. "I wonder if I might have a few words with you?" he asked. "Perhaps over a cup of tea? I noticed a visitors' cafeteria as I came in."

She stood up and glanced at the boy. "Yes, that would be nice. He's just had his medication and will probably sleep for another hour or so." She smiled at him.

He was startled by her American accent, which was still strong. Despite constant evidence to the contrary, his image of American girls was of long-legged blue-eyed blondes who were incredibly efficient and laughed a lot.

Tess Leland had long legs, yes, but she was a brunette with dark eyes, and she had a fragile beauty that aroused every protective male instinct. Police detectives are no more immune to that than other men. She was pale, and her skin had a translucency born of skipped meals and bruised nerves. As a result, her wide-set eyes seemed even larger, and her mouth more vulnerable. And yet there was strength there, too—in the way she held herself, chin up and shoulders back, in unconscious imitation of a soldier facing danger. The fact that she was dressed in a sweater and skirt that accented her slenderness made her rigidity of purpose and backbone all the more appealing—and sad. Because the thinness was not natural, and the bravery was assumed. This was a frightened and weary woman.

The visitors' cafeteria was newly decorated, and obviously popular, but they found a corner table empty. Nightingale brought over a tray of tea and biscuits. He draped his rain-soaked coat over a chair and watched her fill their cups.

"I must say, you don't seem very surprised by a visit from the police," he said.

She glanced up briefly from her task. "Well, I'm surprised by the speed of it," she admitted. "Mr. Soame must have made quite a scene to produce such quick results."

Nightingale stared at her in some puzzlement. "Mr. Soame?"

She put the chrome teapot down and pushed the sugar bowl toward him. "Yes." It was her turn to frown. "Aren't you here because of Mr. Soame?"

"No—I'm here about your husband's death."

She sat back and stared at him. "But that was months ago."

"Yes, I know."

"Then you're not here because of someone asking you to come?"

"I'm afraid not."

"Oh." She seemed quite taken aback. After a moment's reflection, she focused on him again. "I really don't understand. You said it's about Roger's death?"

"Yes. I'm very sorry to cause you any distress, but I need to ask you some questions about Mr. Leland."

"Why?"

This was the sticky part. Particularly as it was his day off and he had no official sanction to question her or to make any other inquiries. He didn't want to upset her, but usually the truth was best. "Because I have some cause to believe his death was not just an accident."

Damn, he'd seriously shocked her. "Of course it was," she said. "He was going too fast and lost control of the car on a wet street. There was no question at the time, and the insurance company was perfectly satisfied." Her voice rose a little.

"Yes, I know. But there was a witness."

"Was there?" Sudden weariness seemed to sweep away her initial alarm. "Oh, yes, I seem to remember them saying there was someone. . . ." She sighed and rubbed a temple, then sipped her tea.

"He was a retired police officer, and he had the distinct impression that another car was chasing your husband's, and that was why he was speeding."

Her eyes widened. "Someone *chasing* Roger? But that's crazy. Who would do that? Why?"

"That's what I'd like to find out."

"Even so—it would still be an accident, wouldn't it? I mean, Roger was a good driver, but—" She paused. "Like a teenager or something, is that what you mean? Because Roger had challenged him at the lights? He'd do that, sometimes, rev the engine and so on. He liked to win, you see."

Nightingale sipped his tea, then shook his head. "I don't think it was like that, exactly."

"No, of course not—because Max was in the car. Roger would never have played games with Max there."

"Max?"

"My son."

Of course, it had been on the report, a child in the car. Nightingale was horrified. "You mean he's still in hospital because of the accident? I had no idea he was so badly—"

"No, no, Max wasn't hurt at all," Tess said quickly. She could see this was a nice man, that he'd been instantly upset to think of Max being hurt. She didn't know what it was all about, why he should be coming along to talk to her after all this time, but perhaps it was just bureaucracy, the slow grinding of the paper wheels. "They had to cut him out of the car, it's true, but he'd been wearing a seat belt at the time of the crash. It was an adult seat belt, though, and he slid out and ended up under the dash, sort of cocooned. Bruised and shaken up, and shocked, of course—but whole."

"He's ill, then?"

She nodded. "Yes. Rheumatic fever. He's at school near here." She stared at the sugar bowl, then looked up at him anxiously and seemed to be seeking some kind of approval. "I wanted to keep him home, but everyone said he should go back to school, that it would be better for him to be busy and distracted. It seemed so—so *English*, stiff upper lip, all that. I wasn't sure."

"Did *he* want to go?"

"He said he did. In the end I could see that probably it would be better for him to go back to school than stay at home and notice the . . ." She raised and lowered her shoulders. "The emptiness. And I had to go to work, anyway. So—I sent him back."

"Children are resilient."

She nodded. "Yes. But the accident and Roger's death must have upset him far more than he let on—he still has nightmares." She took a deep breath and let it go in a rush around her words, as if she had to get them out quickly. "And I think that he got sick like this because he was trying too hard not to show how much it hurt, so his body—sort of—gave him a way out. Does that make any sense?"

"Shock does strange things to people. We see a lot of it, I'm afraid, and it's not always just a matter of a cup of sweet tea. There's something called delayed shock—that could lower someone's resistance, I expect. I don't know if it could give him something as serious as rheumatic fever, but I guess it could make him more vulnerable to the germ or whatever when it came along." (Or make an old man vulnerable to fear, he added to himself.)

She nodded, apparently satisfied with this, and drank her tea.

Nightingale ate a biscuit, giving her time. When she'd topped up both their cups, he spoke. "Did your husband have any enemies, Mrs. Leland?"

She frowned, but there was a trace of amusement in her eyes. "Good heavens, you really do say that."

"I beg your pardon?"

"Oh, I'm sorry, but it did sound like something from a television series." She scowled and put on a husky voice. "'Did your husband have any enemies?'"

He smiled, but shrugged. "I can't think of any other way to ask it," he admitted. "Does it upset you?"

She shook her head. "No. If you mean talking about Roger, that is. I'm over the worst, now." She sighed. "As to whether he had enemies, I imagine he had quite a few."

"Can you remember their names?" Nightingale reached for his notebook.

But she was shaking her head. "No. I didn't mean I knew of any specific ones—just that it wouldn't surprise me if some people hated Roger, that's all. You see, he was very competitive. More than anything, Roger liked to win. He never meant to hurt people, though—

there was no cruelty in him. He was always surprised when they got angry or sulked. People didn't understand or believe he was just out to win for the sheer joy of it, but it was true. Maybe a psychiatrist would argue the point, but I think he was like that because he was always trying to prove to *himself* that he could win. That was what mattered—not beating other people down, but seeing he could succeed at whatever he took on." She smiled to herself ruefully. "Roger was like a child in many ways—he believed in living for the minute, and enjoying everything—it was all games, really. That's why I asked about the car race—what do they call it—a 'chicken run' or something?"

"I don't think it was anything like that," Nightingale said. He looked down at his empty teacup and moved the spoon back and forth in the saucer.

"But you suspect someone was trying to . . . to . . . what?" She was groping for a sense of what he was after. "Catch him? Hurt him? Frighten him?" She paused, then spoke in a whisper. "Kill him?"

Nightingale shook his head. "Any of those, all of them, none of them. I just don't know. Ivor Peters just said there was something wrong, and I believe him."

"Who is Ivor Peters?"

He explained who Peters was, and what he said had happened at the scene of the accident. He added that Peters had since passed away, but supplied no details.

"Poor old man. What did he say this man looked like?"

He gave her the description from Peters's notebook—it was all he had. "About six feet tall, brown hair, regular features, slim-built, wearing dark-blue trousers and a light-blue windcheater over a white shirt; no tie, no glasses, no distinguishing marks."

She looked at him. "That could be you—if you were wearing the right clothes. . . ." She looked around. "Or quite a few men in this cafeteria. Or Max's consultant, come to think of it."

"I know. Peters only caught a quick look, and his glasses had come off when he fell. But the description was more or less the same from the girl who rented the car, and the hotel maid. Except they added that he was 'attractive.' Of course, Ivor Peters was retired, and the official verdict was 'accidental death,' so he wasn't in a position to arrange a photo-fit session or get a police artist to draw the man." (And neither am I, dammit, he thought.)

"Did anyone say anything about his voice?" Tess asked casually.

He stared at her. "His *voice?* No, I don't think that was mentioned by anyone. Why?"

She told him about the phone call, and the silly game with the booby-trapped wardrobe. "Although it didn't seem silly at the time," she admitted. "It frightened me half to death."

"Anonymous threats are always scary," Nightingale agreed sympathetically. "It's not the threat itself so much as the feeling that it could be anybody—a stranger in the street or, even worse, someone you know and trust. You feel the floor isn't solid anymore."

"Yes—that's it exactly." She was grateful for his understanding—she had been feeling so very foolish about it all, behaving so weakly when it was so important to stay strong for Max.

"And you say there have been other calls?"

"Yes—but they were only silent ones. Nobody ever spoke."

"It does seem odd, especially when you add it to that burglary of yours . . ." he said slowly.

She was astonished. "You know about that? That was months ago!"

"Ah, yes. Computers are wonderful things. They can make you see connections." He smiled. "I gather it was on the day of the funeral."

"Yes. That was the cruelest thing about it—to have your house torn apart when you're at your own husband's cremation—I could hardly bear it. Fortunately, after the service, I had sent Max to stay with a friend for a few days, and we managed to clear it all up before he came back. I just didn't want him to know about it—on top of everything else. He was shocked and upset enough as it was."

"I'm afraid it's not all that unusual," Nightingale admitted. "Houses are often left empty during funerals—and burglars can read the obituary columns just like anyone else."

"I suppose so," she sighed.

"The pattern of the break-in seemed rather unusual to me, though," he said.

"It seemed just awful to me." Tess shivered. "I felt there wasn't a room they hadn't invaded, not a thing they'd left untouched."

"And yet they took very little and destroyed nothing."

"Yes. The insurance man told me I was very lucky that they hadn't broken up the house instead of just dumping out drawers and so on."

"It seems more likely to me that they were searching for something," Nightingale said, leaning back and regarding her from grave gray eyes. She felt she was being explored and assessed. His glance seemed to travel along hidden veins and nerves, following them to her heart and brain, but she did not feel the sense of invasion she'd felt from the burglary. Had she been approved—temporarily—or not? It was impossible to tell. She returned his gaze steadily, but he was not open to a similar evaluation. His personal doors and windows were closed and curtained—she could not discover him that way. Just a tall and attractive young man doing the job he was trained to do. Nothing like Kojak at all. Or the town sheriff back in Amity. How much of his kindness stemmed from his own personality, and how much from his training? Was that smile just Lesson 3 on "How to Put a Person at Ease"? Was Lesson 10

"How to Soften Up Someone with Gentleness, Then Pin Her with a Sharp and Unexpected Question"?

"Do you think they were looking for this money the man on the phone asked you about?" he asked suddenly.

Ah, Lesson 10. She hadn't expected it so soon. Steady, now. "But there *isn't* any money. Roger had an insurance policy that paid off the mortgage, and another to cover Max's school fees, but very little personal insurance—even less once they found out he hadn't been wearing a seat belt."

"Was that usual—his not wearing a seat belt?"

A shadow of some distant annoyance crossed her face. "I'm afraid so. Roger was not one to be confined, unfortunately."

"I see. Go on."

"Well, after I'd settled all the outstanding bills, there was only about two thousand pounds left. Enough to set aside as an emergency fund, but certainly not enough to live on. Not even enough interest from it to cover the rates, in fact. I had to go back to work, if we wanted to stay fed and clothed. There was no other way. The house is big, and a drain to keep up, but I wanted to hold on to it if I could—because I thought eventually I could sell it to provide a start for Max or something."

Nightingale nodded, but his expression had become faintly skeptical. Tess felt oddly let down—nobody seemed to believe her. She only wished there *was* some money.

"So you don't know anything about any sum of money that your husband may have had at the time of his death?"

"No, I don't. I really don't."

"I see." He had opened his notebook, but had found no need to write anything in it. Now he closed it and put it back into his inside jacket pocket, watching her face as he did so. She seemed genuine enough. Was this story about the phone calls true? About the booby-trapped wardrobe? She'd said the housekeeper had taken some of the "silent" calls—had they come when she herself was home, or conveniently away?

It was not uncommon for lonely, grief-stricken women to behave oddly, to do things to draw attention to themselves. There was the further complication of her son's illness, the stress and strain of it all, the need for comfort and support from any direction, through any excuse. Was she like that?

He could believe her, he *wanted* to believe her, because it tended to vindicate Peters's conviction that there was something wrong about Roger Leland's death. And, by inference, his own similar conviction about Ivor Peters's death. And yet . . .

There was no proof. No proof for any of it.

And he only had so much spare time.

He looked again into Tess Leland's eyes. She could be imagining things.

So could he.

And somewhere in the back of his mind, he could hear Abbott's dry, quiet voice. "Two wrongs don't make a case."

11

Max arrived home four days later. He was thin, and his pale cheeks were flushed with excitement at having traveled such a distance in an ambulance.

Tess's heart contracted when she and Mrs. Grimble helped the ambulance men transfer Max to his bed. Although reasonably fit for his age, he had never been a robust child, and now his body seemed all skin and bones. He looked around the room, as if checking that it had not changed while he was away, and his eyes widened at the sight of the big television set and matching video recorder sitting on his desk. "It's a present from your Uncle Richard," Mrs. Grimble informed him.

"He's not my uncle," Max objected.

"No, nor mine, neither," Mrs. Grimble agreed. "But he meant well, and you should write him a note to say thank you."

"Okay, I will," Max said resignedly. He'd propped himself first on one elbow and then the other, in order to get the full circle of inspection, and now he flopped back onto his pillows with a thump. His movements were slow and listless, but he seemed more weary than ill. His joints were still slightly painful, but he didn't complain. Tess started to murmur sympathetically, and he glared at her. Apparently she wasn't supposed to say anything about her "poor baby," *especially* in front of the ambulance men.

Mrs. Grimble glanced across the bed at Tess, her eyes brimming with unshed tears at the sight of Max's thin body. She'd only heard about his illness, not seen it firsthand. Now she realized how sick he'd been—how poorly he still was. "Poor mite," she murmured, as they left the room.

"He'll be fine," Tess said, with more confidence than she felt. "All we have to do is feed him, look after him, and love him."

"All any mother ever wants to do," Mrs. Grimble observed, "'cept these days nobody lets her."

Tess looked at the old woman with deep affection. Mrs. Grimble had brought up two sons, both of whom had turned out almost too well, for they were now abroad making careers for themselves. One day, when they'd settled, one of them might send for her—but Tess selfishly hoped it wouldn't be for a long time.

Of course, Mrs. Grimble might refuse to go to a new and unfamiliar life among the palm trees or mountain ranges, far from the London she'd known all her years. And there was always her "baby" brother Walter to consider. Rarely seen but ever-present Walter, the charmer, the weakling, the pay-day drunk. Although Tess had only met him a few times, and had never really talked to him, she felt she knew Walter Briggs and his unfortunate history only too well. She didn't think the Grimble sons would be sending for *him*, one day.

Tess saw the ambulance men out, thanked them for their care of Max, then waved them good-bye. Closing the door seemed suddenly a monumental task. It signaled the end of one phase and the start of the next.

Max was her responsibility now, not the doctor's or the nurse's, or even the school's.

As she came back down the hall, the phone rang. Tess picked it up, glancing in the mirror as she did so, and brushing back some wisps of hair. "Hello?"

"Hello, Mrs. Leland." It was the same horrible whisper, distorted, weird. "I'm still waiting for the money."

She froze, her hand still caught in her hair. "Who is this?" she demanded more bravely than she felt.

"Watch over that boy of yours," the voice advised. Then there came a slow, vicious chuckle.

Mrs. Grimble, who had come down the stairs behind Tess, spoke up, making her jump. "Give it to me," she said firmly, and took it from Tess's terrified grasp. "Hello?" After a minute she spoke again, more impatiently. "Hello?"

Apparently her authoritative challenge evoked no response. As she held the receiver out in front of her and glared at it, there came the unmistakable click of a phone being hung up at the other end.

Mrs. Grimble slammed the receiver down in disgust. "Fish feathers!" she said furiously. It was her worst expletive. "I'm sick and tired of it!"

"What did he say?"

Mrs. Grimble looked startled. "Say? Said nothing—as usual. Never spoke a word. What did he say to you?"

Tess started to speak, then thought better of it. "Just nonsense," she said.

"Hmph," Mrs. Grimble said. A bright-pink flush of annoyance suffused her cheeks. "Wretched kids." She marched back toward the kitchen, mumbling. Tess stared at the phone, black and silent now.

It had been no child who spoke to her.

That evening, as Tess sat in her favorite rocker, looking through dealers' catalogs, there was a knock at the door and John Soame looked in. He had been moving his things into the flat gradually, dividing his possessions and his days between London and Cambridge. Now he was settled in upstairs, but he had been out all that day.

"Everything all right?" he asked. His hair had been ruffled by the wind, and raindrops spattered his spectacles. He took them off and rubbed them absently on the front of his mac.

Tess smiled. "Yes, thanks. The king is in his counting house and, when last seen, was going over his stamp books and checking over his airplane models to make certain everything was intact. Apparently I have committed the sin of tidying up."

"Something no boy can tolerate." He returned her smile, then glanced at the large book she had balanced on the edge of the table. He came across and peered over her shoulder. "What year did you say the McMurdo house was built?"

"In 1875."

He indicated the reproduction wallpaper collection she was considering. "Those didn't come in until the 1890s."

She sighed and closed the book. "I know—but it is so difficult to be exact. Sometimes you just have to settle for what you can get, and trust that the ambience of the whole will satisfy the customer, who doesn't know dates from figs, anyway."

He made a disapproving sound, but there was a twinkle in his eye. "Bad history—but good decorating, is that it?"

"Something like that. I could, of course, have some paper made specially—I have done, for the three large rooms—at a cost you wouldn't like to know about. But this is just for a small bedroom. Unlimited budget or not, I hate to waste a client's money unnecessarily."

He nodded, then glanced up at the clock on the wall. "Is it all right if I go in to say hello to Max on my way upstairs? I won't tire him, I promise."

"Of course." She watched him start for the door, and

found herself wishing him back. "Ummmmm . . ." She hesitated.

"Yes?"

"There was another phone call this afternoon—just after Max came back," she said.

He frowned and came a few steps into the room. "And?"

"That's all. The same nasty whispering voice. He said he was still waiting for the money. And then he told me to look after my son. Then, just . . . silence. But not very nice silence, somehow."

He came a little farther into the room. "No instructions about where this mythical money was to be given over, anything like that?"

"No."

"No specific threats?"

"No. It was more in the nature of a second reminder," Tess said wryly. She picked at a loose thread on her sleeve. "By the way, I forgot to tell you—a policeman came to see me at the hospital the day after you came up. He wanted to know about Roger's accident."

"Oh?" John Soame came a few steps more into the room.

"He said there had been a witness to the accident—an old man—who thought Roger's car was being chased by another car, and that was what caused him to crash. He saw the man driving the other car, and tried to find him."

Soame stiffened. "Why should he do that?"

"Apparently he was an ex-policeman. Instinct, maybe? Or perhaps just curiosity. The detective wasn't sure, I don't think. Not really."

"I see. And has he found him?"

"I don't know. He's dead now, anyway, so—"

"Who's dead?"

"The old man. The witness."

Soame sighed, shrugged, smiled. "So it came to nothing, then."

"Yes." She looked down at her lap, then up at him

again. "I told the detective about the telephone calls. I don't know whether he believed me or not," Tess said. "He left looking very bemused—and I haven't heard from him since. It was all rather . . . upsetting."

He regarded her through his misted glasses. "I should have said you've had more than enough to upset any six people during the past few months," he said gruffly, and went out.

Tess listened to his footsteps going up the stairs, and felt relieved. Although it might mean resigning from the feminist movement if it got out, she was glad to have John Soame living in the house at last. She could lean on him without being emotionally involved. It might seem an odd arrangement, but it made her happy.

Unfortunately, it didn't please everyone.

12

"I can't believe you've done this!" Richard Hendricks said reproachfully. He'd tracked her down to the house and was now following her from room to room as she took measurements and jotted down her latest ideas on colors and patterns. He was very upset.

"I got home late last night. This morning I called the hospital to find out how Max is, and they tell me he's gone home. Wonderful. So I go around to see him, and discover you've actually *installed* a complete stranger in your home, and turned Max over to him."

"Mr. Soame is highly qualified," Tess said calmly, stepping over a pile of bricks and broken tiles. "He's a Cambridge professor, for goodness' sake. Adrian knows him very well."

"Am I to gather you think *that's* some kind of recommendation?" Richard asked. "Honestly, Tess, you are so naive it sometimes frightens me. Adrian Brevitt might be a fashionable name in interior decoration, but he has some very odd friends along with it."

Tess stopped to look at him. Outside there was a cheerful chuckle of workmen and the sloppy churn of a cement mixer. From above there came the intermittent tap of a hammer and a persistent scraping noise as someone removed years of accumulated wallpaper. Traffic rumbled distantly, and a jet growled its way across the sky to Heathrow. Here, however, in what would eventually become a breakfast room, there was silence. When Tess finally spoke, her voice was cold. "Just what do you mean by 'odd friends,' Richard?"

He looked uncomfortable, obviously not expecting quite this reaction from her. "Oh, just gossip, I suppose. But gossip has to start somewhere—and it's said he's popular at a certain kind of party."

"I had no idea you were so narrow-minded. Adrian makes no secret of being gay."

"I didn't mean *that*. What he does in bed is his own business. I meant he's popular because of what he brings with him."

"I don't understand."

He sighed in exasperation. "*Drugs*, dammit. Marijuana, cocaine, Ecstasy, that sort of thing. Oh, come along, Tess—don't tell me you never suspected it?"

"I never thought about it one way or another," Tess said slowly. "Particularly in connection with Adrian."

"Exactly!" Richard pounced on this evidence of her naïveté. "Any more than you thought about getting involved with this Soame character!"

"I am not 'involved' with him," Tess snapped. "He's a lodger."

"He comes into your part of the house, doesn't he? He sees Max, alone, every day. God knows what might happen. Especially if he's a 'friend' of Adrian's."

Tess felt like slapping his face. "In fact, he is—was—Adrian's brother-in-law. And you have absolutely no right to make such insinuations about a man you've never met. He's a good, kind man—"

"They often *seem* like a good, kind man—" Richard began.

"Oh!" Exasperated, Tess turned away and stalked

into the area that would eventually become a dining room, but which at present was simply another rectangle surrounded by walls of laths hung with loops of unconnected wiring cable. Richard followed her.

"You took Adrian's word, I suppose. Did you bother to check up on Soame? Did you find out if he was really from Cambridge, or if he'd been fired from some little school or other—or even whether he was a teacher at all?"

"No."

"Lord, Tess, you are a fool. He could be anything."

She stopped her pacing and faced him. "Now you are getting totally ridiculous, Richard. What would be his point in taking on a task for which he was totally unqualified? And Adrian would never do anything to hurt Max. The decision is made, and that's an end to it. It's my choice, not yours. My life, not yours. I'm sorry if you don't approve."

"It's not that I don't approve. It's not a matter for approval. The whole arrangement simply horrifies me." He ran his hands through his hair and then stood before her, reproach on his face, pleading in his voice. "And then there is this other thing hanging over you. Why didn't you come to me when these silent phone calls started?"

"Because I thought they were just one of those cranky things that happen in a city," Tess said irritably, knowing he was probably right. She should have told him—if only because he knew so many people in useful positions. "How did you know about them, anyway?"

"Your gorgon of a housekeeper told me this morning. My God, I thought she was bad enough before, but since Roger died she's gotten positively bizarre. I swear she was wearing a tea cosy on her head."

"She's fine. I like her just the way she is."

"And what about that sleazy brother of hers? I suppose you like him, too?"

"I hardly know him."

"Well, he had his boots under your kitchen table this morning, and very expensive boots they were, compared to the rest of his getup, which owed more to Oxfam than Oxford Street. Looked like he felt right at home, drinking your coffee and eating your pie."

"Oh?" Tess was momentarily startled. "Well, I don't mind if Mrs. Grimble has him around now and again," she said casually, not wanting to let him see that it was a surprise to her. Mrs. Grimble had never mentioned Walter's coming to the house when Tess was out. Or feeding him, either. Not that Tess begrudged her the privilege, or Walter the pie, but she was rather sorry to learn of it this way. It would no doubt give Richard even more reason to fret and think her unreliable if he realized it had been done without her permission. "I'm just grateful she gives me as much time as she does. I really depend on her."

"Well, she's no protection against people threatening you, is she? I mean, suppose they don't stop at phone calls? You're a woman alone—"

"But I'm not alone now, Richard. That's the whole point. I've organized it all, and neither I nor Max are ever alone now."

"Temporarily. And questionably." His voice softened. "Why don't you just let *me* take care of you and Max, instead of blithely turning yourselves over to some stranger? I'm earning good money again, and my house is more than large enough for a family. You could stay at home with the boy, be a proper mother, a proper wife. You wouldn't have to come out and work in all . . . this . . . mess!" He gestured around at the half-finished interior.

Tess smiled, and looked around, too. "What you don't seem to understand is that I like working in all this mess, as you call it. What's more, I'm very good at it."

"That's all very well, but—"

She didn't want to seem unkind, or ungrateful, but

his persistence was beginning to make her feel a little claustrophobic. "Look, Richard, I'm grateful for your concern, but it is not needed. Truly."

She went into the kitchen and he followed doggedly, trying another tack. "What does Mrs. Grimble think of this Soame? Does she like him?"

"She wasn't sure, at first," Tess admitted, picking up some quarry tiles that had been stacked on the old stone sink. She held them closer to the window, to get the color fixed in her mind. "But then she doesn't like most people. At first."

"Hah. Don't dismiss that—first impressions are important." He seemed to have forgotten his own opinion of Mrs. Grimble and her questionable freeloading brother. He was off again, pacing and thinking aloud. "You said he was Adrian's ex-brother-in-law. Divorced or widowed?"

"Widowed—if it matters."

"Oh, it matters, all right. Don't you see the pattern? All right, you had a few odd phone calls before; as you said, it happens in the city. But I'll bet they only started to get unpleasant when Soame appeared on the scene."

"Not at all . . ." But her voice was hesitant.

He pounced. "Ah—I *am* right, then. You must have mentioned the silent calls at some point in your first conversation with him. Did you?"

"I don't think so. I don't remember, to be honest." He was talking so fast he was confusing her.

"You must have—and it probably gave him the idea. I bet he wasn't in the house when the threatening calls came, was he?"

"No, but—"

"I knew it. Don't you see? He probably wants to frighten you, to make you dependent on him and get some kind of hold on you. . . ." His expression was almost gleeful.

"*Richard!* What on *earth* is the matter with you?" Tess stared at him. "John Soame is a quiet, simple man.

When you meet him you'll see that all this is just *nonsense*."

They glared at one another across the sink.

When Richard spoke again, his voice was icy. "I have met him, as it happens, and he was neither quiet nor simple. I was greeted first by your loony housekeeper, and then by this Soame, who was prancing around Max's bed with a twisted coat hanger, pretending to be a swordsman."

Tess grinned. "Wish I'd seen that."

"It was not edifying—and the boy was far too excited. He's supposed to be convalescent, isn't he? That kind of thing could easily affect his heart."

"What kind of thing?"

"Laughing, getting excited, talking too much. If you ask me—"

"I didn't."

"—Soame is bad for the boy. I talked to him for ten minutes, and he struck me as very odd indeed."

"He's shy—"

"Shy a few marbles."

Tess glared at him. "Do you think I am a complete cretin?"

"Well, of course not, but—"

"Then why do you insist on questioning everything I do where Max is concerned? He's my son, not yours."

"But I *am* a legal co-guardian," Richard reminded her. "Roger trusted me to look after Max's interests. He must have had a reason for that."

She turned away. "Roger had a false image of me that he'd built up in his own mind. Perhaps it was my fault for letting him think I was the clinging, dependent wife—it seemed so important to him. But it was not a true image, Richard, and I think you know it. I am not a fool, and I would never do anything to endanger my son."

"Not consciously, no. But you're too trusting. You always believe the best of people—"

"And you always believe the worst," she retorted.

"I've had good cause," he snapped. "I came up from poverty, Tess. The real, grinding thing, with a father broken by unemployment and a mother driven into a mental ward by despair. It wasn't an easy climb for me, and I encountered some real bastards on the way. I learned how to recognize them, and I learned how to deal with them. They don't always wear their colors on their sleeves, but the signs are there if you know what to look for."

"Especially if you *want* to find them."

His expression became bleak, and he seemed genuinely wounded by her flare of anger and resentment. "I'm sorry, Tess, I really am. But I intend to make it *my* business to find out more about Soame, since you won't."

She put down the tiles and brushed the reddish dust from her hands. "You may do what you like—I am sure you'll find nothing wrong."

He stood watching her. When he eventually spoke, his voice was soft. "Oh, Tess, I don't want to quarrel about this. I want to marry you—remember? I want to look after you."

Tess was unconvinced. She glared at him above crossed arms. "Well, you're going the wrong way about it. Anyway, since you're usually in Amsterdam or Paris or Nigeria or America or God knows where, doing deals, I don't see how you could find *time* to work a wedding into your schedule."

Richard's face brightened—he had only heard the words, not the tone. "Just give me a date, Tess—any date," he said eagerly.

"Miz Leland?" It was Ernie Flowers, their builder. He'd often done renovations for Adrian's firm and knew something of her requirements. "We found this under the molding in the upstairs hall," he said, holding out a long thin scrap of paper. "I reckon it's the original wallpaper."

Tess took it from him, grateful for the distraction. "Red! I knew it! And not flocked, either. Thanks, Ernie."

"That's okay." Ernie eyed Richard doubtfully. "Anything else you want, just call out. I'm not far away." He wandered out into the hall slowly, whistling under his breath.

"You don't seem to lack for protectors," Richard said in a thin voice.

She looked at him. "Some are more welcome than others," she said evenly.

He went over to the bay window and stared out into the unkempt rear garden. "Did you tell Max about the calls?" he asked after a moment.

Tess stared at him in surprise. "No, of course I didn't. He's still very weak, and I refuse to upset him in any way. That includes not telling him about stupid threatening phone calls or any other problems of any kind. The doctor said he must have rest, and rest he shall have."

He turned on her, his voice harsh. "Then Soame must have turned him against me."

"Why on earth would he do that?" she asked, astonished.

"I don't know," he said bleakly. "But when I saw Max this morning he was very distant, almost cold. Max and I were good friends before your precious 'lodger' came along. Now I can see I am going to be systematically shut out."

"Oh, Richard, that isn't true."

He jammed his hands in his pockets and scowled at her. She'd never seen him untidy or upset before—not even when Roger died. It gave him a new dimension, somehow. Controlled, careful Richard Hendricks apparently had a weakness—and it was for her. All the dinners and the attentions she had thought mere kindness were apparently much more—otherwise, why was he so angry, so hurt? She was annoyed by his anger, and even more annoyed to discover she was excited by it. It made her feel foolishly valuable—with the accent on foolish, she told herself abruptly.

"Richard . . ." she began in a gentle voice.

He interrupted, glancing toward the shadow of Ernie Flowers, who was ostentatiously lingering nearby. "Why don't we finish this over dinner tonight? Is eight o'clock still all right?"

"Oh. Oh, dear." She felt herself flushing and looked down at the floor. Presumably this was some previous arrangement, but she couldn't for the life of her remember making it with him. When she looked up again, his expression was wary, as if he knew from the set of her shoulders exactly what she was going to say. But she had no choice. "I'm sorry, Richard, I hadn't realized that was a firm date. As I hadn't heard from you I'm afraid I've made other plans. You see, John felt we ought to have a working dinner . . ."

Richard Hendricks's face went white. "I see very clearly."

"Well, Max *is* getting better, and his lessons have to be organized—"

"I don't think it's only Max who needs lessons, Tess. I think you have a lot to learn about people, and how foolish it is to take them on face value. Well, I wish you both luck in your education. Perhaps, when you find out more about this Soame—as I firmly intend to do—you'll ring me and admit you were wrong. Until then, I leave you in charge of your life, since that seems to mean so much to you. I hope you—and Max—don't have reason to regret it."

Tess stared after Richard Hendricks's retreating figure with resentment. This outburst was simply wounded vanity, the lion growls of a self-appointed king of the jungle who'd gotten a thorn in his paw through grasping the wrong end of the stick. Of course, she would pay no attention to it, none at all. It was outrageous to suggest that there was anything sinister about John Soame.

Wasn't it?

And Richard Hendricks was a jealous, possessive *idiot*.

Wasn't he?

"Hey, how ya goin'?" asked a soft Australian drawl from above her left ear.

Startled into a sideways leap that nearly ended in a broken ankle, Tess found herself confronted by a lanky, sandy-haired man in very large suede boots. He'd appeared so suddenly and so quietly that he might have been a ghost. He was dressed in a brown suit that matched, almost perfectly, his bright-brown eyes. He was tall, tanned, and handsome—a lad from Ipanema by way of Bondi Beach.

"I'm Archie McMurdo," he told her with a devastating grin. "And I don't think Aunt Dolly is going to be very happy with the kitchen windows you're putting in."

Ten minutes later, Tess was in the phone box on the corner. From its cat-scented confines she could see Archie McMurdo deep in conversation with Ernie Flowers, who looked less than enamored of this new source of irritation.

"But Adrian, why didn't you *tell* me Mrs. McMurdo was leaving London?" Tess demanded, when she'd finally got through to her boss.

"I did," Adrian said absently. "I'm sure I did." He sounded preoccupied.

"No, you didn't. I just called the Savoy and they said she'd gone abroad. Where is she, may I ask? And how long will she be gone?"

Adrian sighed heavily to convey that she was causing him pain and suffering. Again. "Dolly McMurdo has gone to Italy, dear Tess. She'll be back in three months or so. She phoned me last Tuesday, I think it was. Or Wednesday."

"But how am I to get on without her?" Tess demanded.

"A great deal more easily, I should imagine," came the bland reply. "She gave you *carte blanche*, darling girl. Use it."

"And do I have *carte blanche* to deal with darling Archie, as well?" Tess asked dryly.

Adrian's attention was finally caught. "Who?"

"Archie McMurdo, Aunt Dolly's dear nephew. He showed up here at the house a few minutes ago and said he was deputizing for her. He then proceeded to complain about absolutely everything." She bent slightly and peered out of the call box. "In fact, he still is."

"Never heard of him," Adrian said. He was trying to sound breezy, but a fretful undercurrent in his voice betrayed him. "She gave us complete authority, my dear. In writing, if you remember—at my very cautious and obviously necessary request. Are you certain he said he was her *nephew?*"

"Yes. He seemed to know quite a lot about her—and he showed me some letters from her."

"About the house?"

"No—just personal letters. But that's not the point, Adrian," Tess continued in exasperation, spacing out her words as if she were speaking to a recalcitrant six-year-old, which, in a way, she was. "I think you should get in touch with her and clarify the position. If he's speaking for her, fine, we'll have to do our best to keep him happy. But if he's not, I want her to say so, preferably in writing, before he drives all the workmen crazy—to say nothing of me."

"Well, I'll do what I can, ducky." He sounded rather doubtful.

"Thank you. In the meantime, what do you suggest?"

There was a short pause, during which she was certain Adrian was doing something other than considering her problem. Like reading a book or filing his nails. Finally he spoke. "Charm him."

"What?" She wasn't sure she'd heard correctly.

"'Charm him,' I said. Tell him how clever he is, and that you'll think over everything he suggests, and perhaps when it's all done Aunt Dolly will invite him round to see it. Bat your eyelashes, dear. Stick out your boobs. Swivel your hips."

"Unzip his fly and suggest we go upstairs?" Tess asked in honey-and-vinegar tones.

"That was unworthy of you," Adrian clucked.

"Well, so was your suggestion unworthy of you."

Adrian sighed—he was a world-class sigher. "I am absolutely certain you can manage him. Now run along and leave me to wrestle with this ghastly list of new requirements from the sheikh's secretary. Would you believe he wants *solid*-gold bath taps?"

"Yes, Adrian, I believe it," Tess said resignedly. "I also believe you will be shortly called to court in order to bail me out for assaulting Archie McMurdo with a deadly weapon—probably a brick."

She hung up on his "tsk-tsk" and marched back up the street to Number 18 to confront Archie, who now stood alone, having been deserted by an impatient and disgusted Ernie Flowers.

"Your little man seems to think he knows best," Archie said with maddening insouciance.

"I am sure he does," Tess said. "Unless, of course, you have a degree in architecture, structural engineering, or are a qualified surveyor?"

He beamed down at her, but said nothing.

"Well?" she demanded. "Are you any of those things?"

"Nope."

"Have you any practical experience in building or construction work of any kind?"

His smile widened—she was amusing him. "Nope," he said cheerfully. "Do you?"

Tess felt her blood pressure start to rise. "I have a degree in art history and over eight years' practical experience in the field of interior decoration, particularly in the restoration of older properties. What is more, all the structural work on this house has been under the direction of a qualified architect whom we consult for all our renovation requirements."

He was grinning now. "Aunt Dolly said you were a beaut sheila, all right," he said admiringly. "Peppery, too. Never told me you were a Yank, though. Generally, I like Yanks. Sympathetic to 'em, you might say, seeing as we all kicked over the pommy traces in our time. Fact remains, that kitchen needs bigger windows. Putting on the style is all very well, but it kind of spoils the effect to have your client cut off a thumb the first week in residence because she can't see what she's doing, don't you think?"

"I'll speak to the architect about it."

Archie smiled expansively, showing wonderful teeth and two dimples. "There you are, that's all I ask. I just want Aunt Dol to be happy in her new home."

"Very considerate of you." Tess was still nettled.

"Aw, now, don't go snaky on me. Let me buy you some lunch. We should get to know one another, because I intend to be around a lot from now on."

"You do?" Tess asked faintly. She envisaged weeks of fruitless argument with this antipodean alarmist. Handsome he might be, but he hadn't the first idea about Victorian authenticity. Or kitchens. But Adrian had spoken.

"All right," she conceded.

It was a very long lunch.

They found a small Italian restaurant nearby. There Archie McMurdo talked of many things—carefully avoiding the subject of interior decor. He told her of his travels, his property in Australia, his hobbies, his ambitions.

In fact, Archie spent so much time and energy systematically attempting to charm her that Tess hardly had a chance to follow Adrian's suggestion that *she* charm *him*. Concerning smiles and graces, the lunch was a definite contender for the Annual Sweetness and Light Award, providing the judges could keep from throwing up.

He *was* very attractive, of course.

Nice voice, nice hands.

Shame about the clothes.

Still, by the time they'd reached the Strega and cappuccino, she'd decided to let him win the charm contest. Why not? He was neither Max's edgy neuter tutor nor her late husband's suddenly possessive ex-partner. (She still felt cross, remembering Richard's demands.) Here was a handsome stranger who thought she was lovely and kept saying so. It is very soothing to be told one is lovely, especially when one is feeling hot and cross and frustrated. If Richard wanted to be jealous, well then, she'd give him reason. Damn him!

After the meal, she thanked Archie, deftly evaded inquiries about her plans for the coming evening, and fled homeward. There had been a great deal of icy white wine with the spaghetti vongole, and while being charmed was one thing, being seduced was quite another. One man in her new life had been pleasant, two had been interesting—but three could be confusing, if she wasn't careful. She needed time to think.

And lots of black coffee.

Mrs. Grimble was in a hurry to get away, and John Soame had gone to spend the afternoon in the British Museum Reading Room, so there was only Max to tell about the initially annoying (but eventually delightful) Archie McMurdo. Max listened to her description with deep interest.

"Why don't you get Mr. Flowers to brick him up in the basement?" he suggested with all the ghoulish delight of a nine-year-old.

"Don't tempt me," Tess said, and started to laugh despite herself. "I think Ernie would enjoy doing it, though."

"Never mind, Mum. These things are sent to try us," Max said, and sighed wheezily, like Mrs. Grimble. "We have to rise above them," he said, in a fair imitation of the housekeeper's lugubrious tones.

"I guess I have to admit it wasn't all that trying in the end," Tess admitted. "He took me to lunch and told me I was a lovely sheila."

"I see." Max eyed her censoriously. "And did you believe him?"

"Shouldn't I have?"

He thought about this, and folded his arms across his

chest. "You're not too bad-looking for your age," he said in a judicious tone.

"Oh, thanks very much."

"But I don't think you should go around flirting with men you hardly know, Mother."

"You're too young to be so pompous. And anyway, what makes you think I flirted with him?" Tess asked defensively.

"Because you're going red, and because your voice went all weeny and horrible when you told about him saying you were lovely. Yeuchhhhhhh. Disgusting." He made as if to poke his finger down his throat and pantomimed vomiting.

"That's quite enough," Tess said. She considered him for a moment. His color was better, and he seemed restless. "Are you getting bored up here all alone?"

"A bit," he admitted.

"Did you have any visitors today?"

"Mr. Hendricks came around," Max said.

"Can't you call him Uncle Richard?" Tess asked. "He's very fond of you, you know."

"But he's *not* my uncle," Max said firmly. "Any more than that other one is."

"What other one?" Tess asked, alarmed. Who had been here?

Max looked sheepish. "I guess he's Mrs. Grimble's brother."

"Oh. Walter Briggs."

"I don't think I was very polite to him—he woke me up and I didn't know who he was. I think he was a little bit . . . you know . . . pissed."

"Max!"

"Well—he was. He scared me, at first, sort of leaning over me and staring the way he did. I thought he was going to fall right on top of me." He went a bit pink. "And he smelled. So I said, 'Who the hell are you?' and sort of scrumpled up the covers over me. And he laughed."

"Oh, dear."

"He said he just wanted to say hello. He brought me that." He pointed to a jigsaw puzzle at the foot of the bed. "I *did* say 'thank you.'" His tone was defensive.

"Good. Richard said he was here."

Max looked grim. "Does Mr. Hendricks own this house or something?"

"No, of course not. I own it. Why?"

Max shrugged. "You'd think he did, the way he stomped around, shouting and everything. It was pretty embarrassing."

Tess straightened the coverlet. "Is Mrs. Grimble's brother here often?"

"How should I know?" Max asked grumpily. "I was away at school and now I'm stuck up here, aren't I? There could be a herd of elephants drinking lemonade in the sitting room, for all *I* know about it."

"Maybe you should start your proper lessons, if you feel so left out of things," Tess suggested.

Max groaned piteously. "No, no, I'm too weak. Watching old movies on the video is all I can stand. My brain is fuzzy, my mouth is dry, I have dry rot in my wooden leg. In fact, I feel a whole new attack coming on," he said, clutching his forehead dramatically. "Oh, the pain!"

Tess laughed. "You *are* feeling better. I'll tell Mr. Soame when he comes in to set you an essay."

Max slid down under the covers. "Tell him I've gone to Timbuktu" came the muffled suggestion. "Tell him I've turned into a frog." He pushed down the duvet, suddenly, and produced an uncanny imitation of his late father. "Tell him I'm in a *meeting*," he growled.

"I'll tell him you're impossible," Tess said, pulling the duvet back up around her son.

"He already knows *that*," Max said. "He said I have a mind like a grasshopper—jumping around nibbling everything and digesting nothing. He said I was a challenge." This judgment seemed to evoke deep satisfaction.

Tess stood up and walked around the room, straightening things idly. "Do you like Mr. Soame?"

"Sure. Why shouldn't I?"

"Was he in here for long, this morning?"

"I don't know. We watched *The Flame and the Arrow*," Max said. "It was medieval and had a sort of motte and bailey castle in it. Did you know that Burt Lancaster used to be an acrobat in the circus?"

"No, I didn't."

"John said that when I'm stronger—"

"John? You call him John?"

"He said I could. It was his dumb idea, not mine," Max said negligently. "Mostly I call him 'sir' because we have to, at school, and it's hard to break the habit."

Tess leaned against the windowsill and regarded him thoughtfully. His hair was sticking up in spikes and his eyes were like Roger's—long-lashed and slightly tilted at the corners. He'd be quite pretty, she thought, if it weren't for that jaw and those freckles. As it is, even thin and pale, he's all boy. "I think calling him 'sir' is good," she said casually. "It shows you respect him."

"Hmmmmm. Anyway, he said when I'm stronger maybe I could do some fencing. Fencing isn't medieval, though—they used broadswords then and hacked bits off one another until they died. But modern fencing is good, he said. Did you know that one year in the Olympics somebody cut somebody else's ear off? A German or a Russian or somebody. Snick, snick, just like that—it flew off and landed on a judge's lap!"

"Oh, nonsense."

"It did. And then he cut off his nose and then—"

"All right, all right. What do you want for dinner?"

"Fried ears and chips," Max said. "And ice cream!" he shouted after her, as she went down the stairs.

Well, it all sounded pretty normal to her, Tess thought, as she went into the kitchen. And Soame was obviously getting a few facts into Max along with the snickersnees and varlets. What was a varlet, anyway? Villains in historical films were always calling people varlets. Or was it "vartlet"? She must look it up.

Putting on an apron, she began to get out pans and plates.

Richard said he would be looking up things about John Soame. Where would he look? How did you go about—what did they call it?—oh, yes—"positively vetting" someone? She stopped in the middle of the kitchen, a frying pan in one hand and a potato peeler in the other.

Perhaps he would hire a private detective.

Would a private detective find out anything terrible about John Soame? Was there anything terrible to find out about him? Or, if there wasn't, would Richard make something up? From the way he had been behaving that morning, she wouldn't have put it past him. Honestly! Saying that John had been the person making those nasty phone calls! Why, the voice had been nothing like his.

She continued across the kitchen and banged the pan down on the sink. Men were impossible, absolutely impossible. They said one thing but meant another.

One never knew what they were *really* thinking.

14

That night, Max had another nightmare.

Tess had been awakened a few minutes before by a faint noise, and had been lying in the dark trying to figure out whether it had been one of the neighborhood cats doing a fandango on the dustbins, or just another of the creaks and cracks the old house was heir to.

And then Max screamed.

Jumping from bed, she grabbed her dressing gown and fled down the hall to his room. She found Max sitting bolt upright in bed, his eyes open. But she knew he was still asleep, caught somewhere in a subconscious limbo of horror. His face was a blank mask, but his eyes were dark with fear.

She and Mrs. Grimble had moved his bed to the bay window that overlooked the back garden and the bird table he and Roger had built together two years before. The afternoon sun would warm him, they'd thought, and the birds would give him an outside interest. His binoculars hung conveniently from the bedpost, and a bird book sat upon the windowsill, ready for consultation.

But now, in the stillness of the night, moonglow streamed over the patchwork quilt she had made years before, while waiting for him to be born. The squares of bright primary colors she'd chosen looked washed out in the strange, pale light. Only the appliquéd tumbling clowns were visible, their frozen antics somehow eerie and ominous.

And then Max began to speak.

"No . . . please . . . don't make me do that. Please . . . I won't . . . I can't . . . please . . . no . . ."

Tess stood stricken, afraid to waken him too suddenly, but John Soame, coming into the room behind her, didn't hesitate. He stepped around her and spoke quietly and firmly, with the unmistakable voice of authority.

"Max, it's all right. No one is going to make you do anything you don't want to do. It's all right, Max. You can wake up now. You're safe now. Nothing bad is going to happen."

He didn't touch the boy or even go close to the bed, but stayed near Tess, still and watchful, talking steadily and evenly. Gradually the fear was erased from the small, thin face. Max slumped in the bed, his eyes closed.

Tess went to him and took him in her arms, cuddling him as she had done when he was very young, feeling the bird-flutter of his heart against her, his soft breath feathering her throat. She looked up at John Soame, and smiled her thanks.

Standing there in his pajamas, without his spectacles, he looked rumpled and young and suddenly embarrassed. He turned away abruptly and said something about making them all a cup of tea. A few moments later there was a sound of cups and clatter from the kitchen below.

Max gave a long, shuddering sigh and snuggled closer to her. He was awake, now—she could feel his eyelashes brushing her collarbone as he blinked away tears he would rather have denied. He sniffed. "Mum?"

"Yes, darling?"

"I didn't mean to be a baby."

"We all feel like babies when we have bad dreams."

"It was bad. It was all . . ." His voice trailed off.

"It was what? It might help you to talk about it, you know."

He was silent for a moment, thinking this over, then shook his head against her shoulder. "I can't remember. When I woke up . . . just for a minute I remembered . . . but now it's gone."

Tess, feeling the tension in his body as it rested against her, decided not to press the point. She was quite sure he *did* remember, and equally sure he didn't want to tell her about it.

Why?

What was it that he so feared both sleeping *and* waking?

John returned, then, with three steaming mugs on a tray. Deftly, as they drank their cocoa—which he apparently had decided was more soothing than tea—he led the conversation into general channels, keeping it cheerful. They left a more relaxed Max behind when the cocoa was gone, tucked up and smiling, his eyes already closing.

Tess and John walked down the hall toward the stairs. "It must be the accident," Tess said. "It can't be anything else."

John stood outlined against the light from below. He held the tray with the empty mugs awkwardly before him. "I'm not so sure," he said slowly. "Come downstairs for a minute."

Puzzled, she followed him down and into the kitchen. He put the tray down on the table and turned to face her. "When I came down to make the cocoa, I found the back door wide open," he said quietly.

"What?"

"Take a look," he suggested. "The lock has been

forced." She went over and looked at the splintered wood around the lock, and felt the hairs rise on the back of her neck, just like in books—only this was real. Burglars, again.

Burglars?

Or someone else?

"It might be a coincidence that Max had a nightmare at the same time as some intruder was sneaking around the house. Or it might be the very thing that gave him one. Perhaps he heard something, or sensed something . . ."

Tess just kept looking from the door to him and back again. It was too much to take in. Someone in the house? Someone in Max's room?

John went on. His voice was calm on the surface, but she thought she heard anger there, too. "I looked around the house and garden before I wedged the door shut. I didn't find anyone, obviously. As far as I can tell, nothing has been taken—but you'd know that better than I would. The question is—do we call the police now, or in the morning?"

15

The police came promptly—two uniformed constables arrived within ten minutes of the call. They were thorough—they inspected the door and looked around the yard and did a quick tour of the immediate neighborhood. They asked a lot of questions: Who had keys to the house? Were neighbors or friends in the habit of dropping by? Had there been any repairmen in the house recently, or insurance salesmen, or vicars of unknown denominations, or charity callers, or people claiming to represent the local council? Did the dustmen come into the garden or collect from outside the gate? Did she know the faces of the regulars? What about itinerant window washers? TV aerial installers? People claiming to be searching for lost dogs or cats? So many questions, so many possibilities. They were kind. They were sympathetic.

But they were not all that helpful.

"About twenty or thirty break-ins a week now, in this area," the big one said. He seemed almost proud of it.

"You're sure nothing was taken?" the smaller one said.

"I think he was frightened off before he could," Tess said, and explained about Max's nightmare screams.

"Ah, well," the smaller one nodded. "If there was something taken—something of value—I'd say call in the CID to do for fingermarks and all that palaver. But I doubt they'd take it on, seeing as how things are so backed up with real"—he paused—"with bigger crimes. We had a jeweler's shop broken into in the High Street last week, they took maybe ten thousand's worth out of there, neat as you please." He glanced at his partner. "What do you think on this one?"

"I think they would let it pass," the big one said.

"But Mrs. Leland has been threatened," Soame protested.

Interest flared momentarily in their eyes. "Oh?" the big one said. "Have you reported this?"

"Yes," Tess said.

"No," Soame said.

She looked at him. "But I thought you said you went to Scotland Yard," she said.

He looked uncomfortable. "No. I rang up and explained the situation, but I didn't give your name or go in to make a formal complaint. They didn't seem very interested, you see."

"This a person you know making threats?" the smaller policeman asked.

"Well, no," Tess said hesitantly. "It's phone calls, really. Silent ones at first. Then he spoke, but it wasn't what he said—more the tone. He demanded some money—I didn't know what he meant, though. And then there was the confetti and the cranberries." She told them about the wardrobe. Even as she was speaking she understood what Soame had been up against—it sounded so feeble and foolish. "Actually, he hasn't called for a week or two. Maybe he won't, now."

"And maybe he will," the big one said.

"Maybe," the smaller one said. "Maybe."

"Then you do believe me?" Tess asked.

The smaller one smiled. "Of course I believe you, Mrs. Leland. We can ask the Exchange to intercept your calls, or to change your number. Would you like us to do that?"

She was momentarily taken aback. "Well, changing numbers is such a big fuss, notifying everyone and . . . all that."

The big policeman and the smaller policeman exchanged a glance. "It's up to you, Mrs. Leland," the smaller one said.

"I think you should," Soame said. "I know it costs money, but I think you should do something to put your mind at rest. It would be worth the expense, really."

"Change the number and keep a list of the people you tell," the big policeman advised. "That way you can narrow it down if this geezer calls again, see?"

"Y-y-yes," Tess nodded. "All right."

"It would be faster if you did it yourself," the smaller policeman said. "Tell the phone people to call us if they want confirmation or anything like that. Here—this is our names—" He took out a notebook, wrote, tore out the sheet and handed it to her. "Tell them either Constable Sims or Constable Cole—or Sergeant Reeder. We'll leave details with him at the station. All right?"

"Yes, all right. Thank you," Tess said.

They gave her a pamphlet on home security, suggested a few improvements concerning locks and routines, and then they got another call. When they had gone, she sank into her rocker and closed her eyes. "They didn't believe me," she said. "They were just humoring me."

"Nonsense," Soame said. "It's all paperwork for them. If they made some kind of official request for your phone number to be changed or calls to be intercepted, it would probably take days and days to go through. I'm sure they were right; it will be quicker for us to request it."

"Yes, but—"

The telephone rang. From the darkness of the hall its jangle cut through Tess's words like a knife, a cold sharp knife. She glanced at the big old store clock on the wall—2 A.M.

"It's him," she said. She knew it as surely as she'd ever known anything. "I know it's him."

"I'll answer it," Soame said. "I'll put a stop to this."

"No!" Tess sprang to her feet. "He'll just hang up on you. Let me answer it—you listen."

He stood beside her, reassuringly close, as she picked up the receiver. "Hello?" she quavered. She tipped the earpiece away from her slightly so Soame could hear, too.

There was only silence. Soame stirred beside her. "Hello? Who is this? Answer me!"

Silence.

Tears of frustration started into her eyes, and she balled her fist and stamped her foot. "Answer me!"

Soame took the phone from her. "Mrs. Leland has no money of her own or anyone else's. There is no point to this persecution when—" He stopped. His shoulders slumped, and he put the phone back in its cradle. "Gone," he said.

"You shouldn't have interfered," Tess said wildly. "He might have said something if you hadn't interfered. Now it will just go on and on until I go crazy!"

"I know, I'm sorry," Soame said. "It was just the look on your face . . . if you could have seen your expression . . ."

She shivered. "I'm cold," she said wearily. "I'm going back to bed."

"I really didn't mean to . . ." Soame said.

"I know, I know." She managed a smile. "I expect I looked pretty desperate, at that. Blame Clark Kent again, I suppose."

He flushed. "Perhaps I've never really grown out of hoping to be a hero to someone, someday. On the evidence so far, I think I'd better stick to printed history."

She wanted to say something reassuring, but nothing came. "Good night," she said.

Warmth came from the electric blanket, but it was a specious warmth, and did not reach her bones. She took a deep breath, sighed a long sigh, and shivered.

You wanted to be independent, you wanted to prove you could run your own life, she told herself. *Do it.*

After a few minutes of this inner pep talk, she fell into a restless sleep, and awoke the next morning with a headache. Never mind, she thought, swinging her legs over the edge of the bed and reaching for the paracetamol. We have no time for headaches, Mrs. Leland. We have to Get On.

And the first thing we are going to do is call that detective who came to see us in the hospital, aren't we?

Atta girl.

Mrs. Grimble conducted Nightingale and Murray to the kitchen. She scowled at them each in turn, and then went out of the room. Moments later, the roar and clatter of the old vacuum cleaner started up in the dining room. Vigorous sweeping sounds could be heard along with an obbligato of muttering.

Nightingale and his partner dutifully peered at the splintered wood beside the lock, looked at the lock itself, inspected the garden, and then looked at Tess.

"You seem to have been very lucky, Mrs. Leland," Nightingale said, accepting a mug of coffee. "If your boy hadn't shouted out with his nightmare, you might have lost some more valuables." He took a swallow of the coffee. He'd risen too late for a decent breakfast, and had left a fresh, steaming cup of tea and a jam doughnut on his desk. Now, having rushed out without his mac, and proceeding unvictualed, his turn round the garden had left him chilled.

"The local police seemed to think we should be used to this sort of thing, count it into a day's expectations," Tess said. "Do you? I mean, considering everything?"

"By 'everything' I suppose you mean your husband's death, the burglary, those phone calls you mentioned?"

"Yes. You said you were suspicious about Roger's death—"

"Indirectly, yes, I was."

She caught the past tense. "But you aren't anymore?"

"I didn't say that. Not exactly. It's just . . . well . . . it's difficult for me at the moment."

"We have a lot of work on at the moment," Murray put in, trying to be helpful. He wasn't certain why Tim had dragged him along on this—whatever it was—but he felt he should say something. Anything.

"Oh." Tess felt deflated. "I'm sorry, then, to have called you out here. I remember now—you said you were doing it on your own time, didn't you?" She blinked quickly, and stood up. "I hope I haven't made any difficulties for you, calling you at your office and everything—"

"Not at all. You see—"

The kitchen door swung open. John Soame stood there, hair still uncombed, shirt half tucked into his trousers, and wearing mismatched socks. He held a coffee mug in one hand and a slightly burned piece of toast in the other. "Mrs. Grimble told me the police are back," he said. "Have they come up with anything?"

Nightingale turned. The two men stared at one another.

"I know you," Soame said, peering at him.

"Yes, you do," Nightingale agreed.

"Why do I know you?"

"Because I used to ask awkward questions," Nightingale said. "If it helps, I usually sat in the front row, on the right. Your left, of course."

Soame considered him. "You had a beard?"

"For my sins. A beard, a mustache, and a chip on my shoulder."

"But you weren't in my tutor group."

"No. In Jon Chappel's. For *his* sins."

"And now you're a police officer?" It seemed almost too much for Soame to take in. Sometimes, Nightingale thought, it was too much for him to take in, too. All those cloistered years, all those dreaming spires, and now this. His parents, were they still alive, would be startled, too, he supposed. Chappel, when he'd bumped into him a year or so ago, had been stupefied.

"I am."

Tom Murray smiled grimly. "For everyone's sins."

"I see. Well, you've seen the damage?" As Soame gestured toward the rear door, a few crumbs flew out from his toast and a spot of marmalade fell to the floor beside his left shoe. "Of course, you've realized this wasn't a burglary attempt at all, but a further example of what has been going on all along. Somebody is systematically trying to frighten Mrs. Leland into handing over money. It's obvious."

Nightingale raised an eyebrow. "Is it?"

"Come along, you were taught better than that by Chappel, if no one else," John protested. "Examine the evidence, for goodness' sake."

"I have, sir," he said. He kept his face neutral, but winced within. The situation might be clear to Professor Soame, but it was far from clear in police terms. About as clear, in fact, as his own position. Officially, he was not connected with this at all. Officially this had been logged locally as a burglary attempt. Officially, he was at his desk in New Scotland Yard drinking tea and wishing himself back in the country.

Unofficially, of course, he was up to his ears in it.

"What is your place in this, sir?" Murray asked as politely as he could, while eyeing Soame's state of dishabille. "Are you a relative of Mrs. Leland?"

Tess Leland explained, and as she did, Nightingale

covertly examined John Soame. His being here was another coincidence, of course, but surely not one related to the case at hand. If there was a case. Soame must have faced thousands of undergraduates in his time. That he should reencounter one of them as an investigating officer was not all that startling. He just wished he could remember more about Soame than he did. Wasn't there something about him having an unsuitable wife, somewhere?

"I'm sure Mrs. Leland is glad to have you on hand, sir," Tim said politely.

"I'm not so certain of that myself," Soame said. "I seem to have frightened off the phantom caller last night, before he could even speak."

"I see," Tim said. That was interesting.

So many interesting things.

He glanced at the broken doorjamb. Was this just an attempted burglary, thwarted by a child's thin cry of fright in the darkness? The local men were quite correct. This neighborhood, marginal, semiresidential, showed quite lively statistics in the fields of car theft, burglary, assault, and assorted mayhem. And this was just the kind of house a thief on the prowl for the quick chance would fancy—single occupancy, slightly upmarket, potentially filled with the kind of small, portable shinies that could be quickly and easily exchanged for cash across a pub table, no questions asked. After all, it had already happened once.

There might be a pattern, yes. But it also might be that, in their twitchy state, this woman and Soame were *imposing* a pattern on events that were really quite unconnected.

What was worse, *he* might be doing the same thing himself.

Leaping to the wrong conclusion now might mean manpower being expended to no good end, hours wasted, resources drained, all in looking for a little man who wasn't there. And on his recommendation. Very bad for the record. Especially the unwritten record.

His problem was simple—was there a problem?

Murray looked uncomfortable, as well he might. He hadn't the least idea what was going on—Tim had carefully refrained from telling him anything on the way over. He wanted clear first impressions from a disinterested party. From Murray's expression, dragging him in on this would cost Tim a lunch, at least.

He looked around the kitchen. A nice room, with the comfortable cluttered feeling of something that had grown organically over many years of various family requirements rather than something that had been imposed according to an ideal of modern efficiency. What little wallpaper there was showed a simple red-on-white pattern of small flowers.

The many glass-fronted cupboards on the wall were, he thought, contemporary with the building itself. Beside the splintered rear-entrance door was another door, slightly open, through which he could see liberally stacked marble cold shelves—an old-fashioned larder, then, still enthusiastically in use and so far unconverted to the omnipresent "downstairs loo." The sink was stainless steel, the taps modern, but the whole unit had been dropped into the existing structure of battered floor cupboards. Their original tops had been covered over with butcher blocking, which had the effect of raising the actual work surfaces higher than the ordinary. That made sense—both Mrs. Leland and the loony housekeeper he'd met on the way in were taller than average. All the cupboards—high and low—had been painted a pale cream with red accent lines, but it had been done some time ago. Scars showed, dents and bruises, and the chips thus incurred showed many layers of old paint beneath. There was a big pine table in the center of the room, scrubbed clean but heavily scarred, with four chairs placed around it. There were plump red printed cushions tied to each one, but the chairs themselves—although of pine and roughly similar in size—didn't match.

What did all this tell him?

That Mrs. Leland, although a professional interior designer, was one of those rare people who knew the value of *not* rushing in, of staying her hand, of letting be. She'd probably moved in, made the changes in her kitchen that were necessary for efficient and pleasant function, and had then done no more. Perhaps she was not a dedicated cook and milk-bottle washer. A practical woman who kept the more modish aspects of her imagination for her work. Even, possibly, a lazy one. Would such a woman imagine dragons where none existed? Worse, would she manufacture them, either consciously or subconsciously?

He drank more coffee and looked at her over the rim of the mug. Now that the burden of the child's illness had been lifted she looked younger than she had in hospital. A pretty woman, once, who could be again, given time and love and security. Not, he thought, over-emotional, but not invulnerable either. She would stand up to a great deal—but for only a certain time. Watching him quietly, standing up to his inspection and concommittant calculation, she was waiting for his verdict on her, and on her predicament.

If there was simply an attempt here at frightening Mrs. Leland—and she was obviously frightened, for whatever reason—then finding and scaring the hell out of the person responsible might be all that was necessary. With the young, the halfhearted and the amateur, realization that the authorities "knew" of their efforts was often sufficient to stop them from continuing a campaign of intimidation against their chosen victim. If the little man *was* there, a brisk outline of the possible consequences resulting from prosecution might do it.

But who was the little man?

And—most important of all—was he the *same* man who had chased Roger Leland to his death, and—still a conjecture—frightened Ivor Peters into a heart attack when he'd got too close?

In all things criminal, evidence—usable evidence—was the prime factor. If a chargeable offense was committed—then it came down to whether the charge could be proved. Going off half-cocked more often than not provided the defense with all they needed to get a case thrown out before it even came to full trial.

"*Well?* What are you going to do about it?" John demanded, annoyed by Nightingale's long silence.

"John, please." Tess could see that Nightingale was having an internal struggle of some kind, and she felt embarrassed by John's insistence on immediate action. "Perhaps there's nothing Sergeant Nightingale *can* do." She felt a wave of desolation sweep over her—perhaps there was nothing anyone could do, she thought. You are alone. This is not your country, many things are strange to you here. And you are seen as a stranger, too. There is no one. Accept it. Live with it. Get on with it.

Nightingale saw the defeat in her eyes, and wished there were a way to remove it. "While all these things are unpleasant, there is no proof that they're connected in any way. Not necessarily."

"It would be an amazing coincidence if they weren't," Soame muttered.

"Not amazing at all. Coincidences do happen, and frequently. Mrs. Leland says she has no enemies that she knows about. Mrs. Leland says she has been threatened—but the threats have not been followed up. Nothing at all has come of it. No lines of communication have been arranged, no instructions issued, nothing specific has been indicated or requested."

"What about the break-in last night?"

"What about it?" Nightingale countered. "A broken doorjamb isn't enough to convince a judge, much less a jury."

"But there was another call last night, within minutes of the police leaving the house," Soame said. "Someone must have been watching the place, waiting for the right moment. It's a campaign of intimidation, I tell you." His voice rose up, verged on—something. Desperation?

Nightingale shook his head. "One of the great modern compulsions is to answer the telephone. Most people think they have to respond instantly to it. That's what phone freaks count on. This caller may be an adolescent with criminal fantasies. Making threats gives him a sense of power. Or a crank—we get plenty of those—someone seeking sexual thrills from an intake of breath, or the sound of fear in a woman's voice. It isn't *necessarily* a dangerous person, or even a person connected with this attempted break-in. Your caller could just be a neighbor who saw your lights on and decided to take advantage of the moment. Failing evidence to the contrary, that's how we have to look at it. I'm sorry." And he was.

Tess looked at Nightingale and tried to imagine him younger, with a beard, and couldn't. But he was recognizably a police officer. Why? She looked at his partner, sitting quietly at the table, listening and watching. A closed face, that was it. They all had it. Eyes never still in ever-still faces, and carefully, professionally, unimpressed by anything or anyone. Would it help if she flew into hysterics? Screamed, threatened? She thought not. They would change mode instantly, trained to do the right things, say the right things—"Sit down, drink this, calm down, it's all right"—but nothing would change within them as they went through the rituals. Impervious, waterproof, seamless. The very best materials, the very finest workmanship, head to toe. She crossed her arms, settled herself. "Suppose I say something was taken. Suppose we did report a burglary. What then?"

Nightingale shrugged and put his empty coffee mug down on the table. "Then it would go into the files as a reported burglary. The item or items taken would go on a recovery list."

"And?"

"That's it," Murray said. "That's what would happen."

"And, of course, it's a very long list," Tess said resignedly. "Don't you see, John? It's no use. There has to be some actual blood shed before they can do anything."

"No," Nightingale said firmly. "There only has to be a clear connection, a clear and specific threat to someone's safety, or clear criminal activity or intent."

"I'm not making it up, you know," Tess said.

Nightingale felt the sharp edge of her bitterness. It made a thin incision in the carefully maintained envelope of his self-respect. He stood up. "I didn't say you were," he told her evenly. "But neither am I. That's simply the position as far as we're concerned."

The kitchen door banged back and Mrs. Grimble erupted into the room. "I knew it. I told her. I told him. All mouth and trousers, the police," she announced, glaring at the detectives. "Ready enough to accuse when it suits you, I'll wager. Ready enough to push people around, yell at them, lock them up just for being alive." She turned to Tess, who saw with surprise that her eyes were filled with tears. "Local rozzers come round at seven o'clock this morning, for Walter, and it wasn't a friendly call, neither. Wanted to know where he'd been last night, wanted to know what he was doing for money, wanted to know why, what, and wherefore."

Tess was stricken. "I'm sorry, that was my fault."

"Why would it be your fault?" Soame asked.

"They asked me about who'd been in the house. I told them Walter was here yesterday," Tess said. She looked at Mrs. Grimble. "I forgot."

She felt a vague guilt, because Walter Briggs had an old count against him. Years ago, at the age of twenty or so, he'd been convicted of grievous bodily harm against another boy, and had served five years for it. There had been some mention of homosexual advances, counter-charges of intimidation and theft. Mrs. Grimble maintained the conviction was a false one because Walter had been too drunk to know what was happening, but the record—however old and however questionable—remained. What was worse, Walter's life since his release did not bear close scrutiny—mostly because of his repeated backslides into alcoholism. He had learned some questionable skills in prison, and made some less than honest friends. He came and went in Mrs. Grimble's life, his presence kept vaguely alive in Tess's mind by Mrs. Grimble's occasional outbursts of despair on his behalf. Tess had always sympathized with the old woman's frustration.

Roger hadn't been easy, either.

"But he *was* here, wasn't he?" she asked gently.

"Well, yes, he was," Mrs. Grimble admitted. "What of it? Aren't I allowed—"

"Of course you are," Tess said quickly. She put out a hand, but the old lady went right over to Nightingale and glared up into his face. Though she was not small, the flowers on her hat came just to his nose, and he had to lean back to avoid being tickled by them.

"It seems to me you police spend so much time hassling people like Walter, there's none left for doing what you're supposed to, which is protecting the public. Mrs. Leland's a member of the public. What's more, she's a woman alone with a little sick lad to look after and money to earn. But you're just leaving her to it. Never mind people keep breaking in here and calling her up and all the rest of it, oh no. What's so important that you haven't got time for her, hey? What else have you got to do?"

"We *are* investigating a murder . . ." Murray began.

Mrs. Grimble whirled on him. "I'll give you murder," she said in a dangerous voice. Her eyes fell on the coffee mug he'd put down. "And look at the ring that mug's leaving on my kitchen table. Isn't enough vandals try to break in, we have to *invite* them in as well! You ought to be ashamed." She snatched up the mug and took it over to the sink. Soame had to leap out of the way to avoid being splashed as she ran hot water at full pressure and added far too much detergent, squeezing the plastic container as if it were someone's neck.

Nightingale had turned slightly pink across the cheekbones. "We'll tell the local men to maintain their drive-bys. You know their telephone number—and ours. Sorry we can't do more. . . ."

"Certainly couldn't do much less," Mrs. Grimble snorted over her shoulder, and jabbed the dish mop into the mug so hard the wooden handle split from end to end.

16

Back in the car, Murray breathed out. "Whew," he said. "I haven't been screeched at like that since my mother caught me smoking in the garage." He shook his head. "Women's voices," he said. "God, how I sometimes hate women's voices."

"The damnable thing about it is, she had a point." Nightingale sighed.

"I'd like to make a point," Murray said. "My point is this—what the hell was that all about?"

Nightingale smiled. "I wanted an objective observer."

"Well, you got an observer who objects, instead. Come on, give. It has to do with that file you've been crooning over, doesn't it? The one that I'm not supposed to know about."

"It does," Nightingale agreed. And he outlined the trail that had led from one old dead copper to this particular house. "Perhaps Soame is right—Mrs. Leland, and her son as well, may well be in danger."

"But from what?" Murray asked. "And why?"

"If we're to go by the phone calls—and they are the

only specific we have—because of some unnamed amount of money she insists she knows nothing about."

"Do you think she's lying?"

Nightingale thought about it. "I don't honestly know."

He looked back at the house, which was the last one in a group that curved around the remnants of a crescent garden. Once, perhaps, there had been flower beds and benches where there was now simply uncut grass plus a great deal of litter beneath two defeated-looking lime trees. The railing around this tribute to municipal negligence was rusting badly, and the gate which implied admittance to only a favored few was wired shut and obviously admitted nothing.

The windows and door of the Leland house had been painted bright red, but the handle and knocker of the door were still the old, plain steel. No expensive reproduction brasswork, there. No doorside flower urns, no coy china number plate. And the brave red paint was beginning to chip.

The other houses in the terrace were a mixed lot—two had been "done up" in the full and accepted manner, and four or five looked neat and respectable, but many of the others had been allowed to disintegrate to such a degree that the contrast was painful. Several had multiple doorplates and bells, indicating bed-sitters within. A mixed prospect, then. Neither a good neighborhood nor a bad, exactly, but something awaiting the inevitable slide into one or the other.

How long had the Lelands lived here? Judging by the condition of the paintwork trim, about ten years. No doubt there had been a moment, back then, when Kingfisher Terrace had looked about to burst into gentrification, and a local real estate man had gotten several people to buy in on that promise, the Lelands among them.

Even so, it wouldn't have come cheaply. Newly or recently married, perhaps, he looking for an investment, she looking for a home to make, they'd taken the plunge. And they had been happy, no doubt, those ten years ago. Full of hope for the future and one another, the way young people persisted in being no matter what they saw around them.

But the estate agent's hope for the neighborhood had died. Why? Absentee landlords, most likely, who continued to profit from those bed-sitters. Or perhaps owners too poor or too old or too uncaring either to maintain their homes or move from them. The city was moving outward, a tentacle here, another there. Once-genteel neighborhoods that had dragged their petticoats in the mud for years were now rising again, and where broughams had waited, Porsches and BMWs now parked. But not in Kingfisher Terrace.

Although he was hardly an experienced observer of marital patterns, Nightingale thought hope had died in the Leland marriage, too. The evidence was clear. Their first expenditure had been the last. Because after the first flush of ownership they had never bought the brass doorknob, or modernized the kitchen, or planted the garden out. They had converted the top floor to a flat. For added income? For company? To increase resale value? What had gone out of the Leland marriage that was reflected in the Leland house? If he'd had money in the beginning, and his business had been doing well at the end, where was the money now?

He had met Tess Leland, but Roger Leland was beyond his recalling. What had been his true character, the inner persona that his wife had discovered, as all wives do, over their years together? Profligate or miser? Had he hoarded? Had he gambled? Maintained a mistress? Played the market? Did it have a bearing on his death? On what was happening now? And—most important—was it worth pursuing? He kept coming back to that, over and over.

Was this a suitable case for investigation or not?

Murray broke into Nightingale's reflective silence

with a reflection of his own. "Loneliness and grief can make women do strange things, Tim. She could have staged the first burglary, broken open the back door herself anytime before the boy woke up. You have only her word for the words spoken in the phone calls—all the calls picked up by the housekeeper were silent. As was the one Professor Soame heard last night."

"But what would it get her?"

"Company. Sympathy. A reason to fail. Who knows? Maybe somebody else has some money she thinks she should have, and she's trying to smoke it out," Murray suggested. "Or, if we're to believe this phantom caller, it's the other way around—she has some money somebody else thinks *they* should have."

Tim sighed. "Where would she have it?"

"How about a safety-deposit box?" Murray said.

"But she's gone to a lot of trouble to get Soame in to teach the boy so she can keep on working. Why would she do that if she has money?"

"Camouflage. She has it—and means to keep it."

"Where would she have gotten it?"

"From her old man, I suppose. Or maybe there's somebody else we don't know about. Maybe she was playing around before he got killed, maybe she was into something he didn't know about—or found out about. Yeah, how about that? Maybe he got killed because of something *she* was up to."

"And maybe cops could fly," Nightingale said, as he put the car into first and, glancing back, pulled away from the row of houses. "Looks like there's a lot more to do before this is finished. I certainly want to check up on the housekeeper's brother and find out what kind of 'list' he's on, for a start. If that's a dead end, I can see about four different directions to go in if I'm right."

"And if you're wrong, the only direction for you is down."

Nightingale banged the steering wheel. "It stinks,

Tom. Peters sensed it and so do I. Something is going on here, and I want to find out what it is."

"For Peters's sake, so to speak?" Murray asked wryly. "Well, if you're going on with this, you'd better clear it with the inspector."

"Don't nag."

"That's not nagging," Murray said. "That's insurance."

The wine bar was very crowded, and Nightingale had to hold the two glasses high to avoid the heads of his fellow-imbibers. He managed to return to the table without dousing anyone, and sank into his chair with surprising gratitude, seeing as it was too small for him and very unsteady. He'd been on his feet most of the day, doing follow-up interviews on the Primrose Street robbery, and had not enjoyed it.

Being on your feet presumably included access to and use of the mind—his employers paid him on that basis—but his had been elsewhere. He hoped it didn't mean he'd missed something vital—probably the clue and the arrest of a lifetime.

He froze for a moment, did an instant replay of the day's confrontations, then relaxed. To hell with it.

"Well, what do you think?" he asked the red-head sitting opposite him. She was tall and sleek and clever, and they had been conducting an on-off affair for the past few years, emotional weather permitting. He had met her during his time at Lloyd's and knew her to be adroit in bed, hopeless in the kitchen, and a demon at the bridge table. She was personal assistant to one of the medium-powered underwriters, and loved her work more than she loved Tim. He found this a source of great comfort, as he felt the same way about his occupation. Neither saw their relationship going anywhere, but neither—at the moment—saw another relationship coming from anywhere. And so it went on. Her name was Sherry, and her eyes were that color too.

"I think you work hard enough without going on unpaid overtime," Sherry said, sipping her claret and raking the crowd with a comprehensive glance to check if there were any clients among the throng that might merit a smile. Her eyes returned to his, and he saw they were amused. "Don't you?"

"I work hard, sure. So do you. That doesn't mean I can't have an outside interest."

"In an inside subject? You risk becoming a law-and-order obsessive, Tim. Pretty soon you'll be reminding me to renew my car tax and put a better burglar alarm in my flat."

"All praiseworthy things. Consider yourself so advised."

"Oh, get stuffed," Sherry said with a grin.

"Come on, come on. You have an opinion. You *always* have an opinion, and this one is ripe. I can see it trembling on your luscious lips." He picked up the battered bar menu and made a pretense of scanning it. She watched him, then sighed.

"Okay. I think you're probably right—there was something wrong and there probably *is* something wrong. One coincidence—'Isn't life strange.' Two coincidences—'Wait a minute.' Three or more—uh-oh, forget one and two. But as far as I can see, what you can do about it on your own is damn-all. Don't homicide investigations require lots and lots of people? That's what it said in the last mystery book I read."

"*Mary Poppins Meets the Bad Person?* Loved it. Very sound, technically."

"Well, then."

"I can look into it a little."

"How little?"

"Too little."

"Exactly."

He fixed her with a flat expression. "Or I can wait around to see if Mrs. Leland gets beaten up or killed—that might alert DCI Abbott that something is amiss."

Sherry frowned. "Do you think—" Her last words were lost in a roar of manly guffaws from a group of pin-striped young things at the far end of the bar.

"What?" He leaned forward.

"I said, do you really think she's in danger?" As usual, a silence had followed the outburst at the brass rail, and Sherry's question turned heads in their direction.

Tim waited until curiosity died, and then nodded. "But how much and from what or whom, I can't say. That's what makes it so damnable. She could have some money in a building society somewhere under a false name—"

"The book would be in the house—that burglar would have found it."

"She might keep it in a safety-deposit box somewhere."

"But you said she seemed genuinely puzzled by the phone call demanding money."

Nightingale made a wry face. "She did. I must admit, she was very convincing. But then, I've only spoken to her once before, so I have nothing with which to compare her attitude. She might be the greatest actress the world has ever lost, or a pathological liar, or have several personalities—maybe Tess Leland is also Griselda Leland, and only Griselda knows about the money."

"You're tired," Sherry said.

He rubbed his face. "Of course I am. Coppers are congenitally weary—wasn't that in your book?"

"Yes, Chapter Four—'Mary Poppins Goes to Bed Alone Again.'"

"I've never been *that* tired," he protested. "Not yet, anyway."

"You will be, if you insist on following every hunch that pops into your head."

"It's more than a hunch."

"I see." She leaned her elbows on the table and ran

her hands through her hair, dislodging the last of the pins that had held it in place. The glossy, deep auburn hair tumbled down over her ears and she shook it back carelessly. It was a moment he always looked forward to with pleasure—when she shrugged off the office and became a girl again. He wished he could perform a similar shrug of responsibility, but hadn't learned the knack as yet. Maybe his hair was too short.

"Could you do a little detective work for me?" he asked.

Sherry looked at him in some surprise. "What could I do?"

"Well, you could find out about Hendricks and Leland Limited. Or it might be Leland and Hendricks. They were a public-relations company with quite a few international clients, according to Mrs. Leland. What I'd really like to get hold of is their client list, and the names of any financial backers they might have had, and their general financial history. It would give me a slant on at least one side of his life. Contacts, things he might have gotten to know about, secrets he might have had, trouble he might have been in or caused, enemies he might have made—particularly the latter."

"You say the company is now defunct?"

"Yes. I gather Hendricks closed it down a month or two after Leland died—he's started up again with someone else. Leland was the creative side of it, Hendricks the administrator."

"What's he called now? Hendricks and Something Else, presumably?"

"I have no idea. It might be one of those other kind of names—Prometheus Unbounded, or Zippy-Nifty Fixers, for all I know. I'd be glad of anything you could pick up—facts, rumors, gossip—anything at all."

She made a little face—funny but not unattractive—and pretended to glare at him. "You mean now *I* have got to have the outside-interest blues, too?"

"Call it companionship," he smiled.

"I call it damned cheek," she said. "What if I get caught?"

"Doing what? All you have to do is make a few phone calls and tap out a few inquiries on your magic computer."

Her face tightened. "I'm not supposed to—"

"I knew your boss, remember? I know you do half his stuff for him, that you use his access code, act for him when he wants to play golf, even commit funds—"

"Shhhhh." She looked really alarmed.

"I wasn't shouting," he said mildly. "I was using a focused voice and only you could hear it."

"My God—you're really serious about this." Her attitude had undergone a sea change.

"Somebody should be."

She leaned back in her chair and studied the absolutely fascinating edge of the elderly table. Around them swirled the after-closing crowd, now well into their third and fourth glasses and considering the dash to Waterloo or the possibility of a few sausages to aid digestion. A rich aroma of claret, mustard, and bangers filled the room, even overcoming the day's last vestiges of Paco Rabanne and trader's muck sweat. Nightingale could smell Sherry's familiar perfume, too, reactivated by her warmth and the wine. He knew what it cost—he'd bought her some the previous Christmas—and blessed the blender while cursing the packager. Its sudden presence told him she was worried.

"All right, look, it was just an idea. If you don't want to do it, fair enough. I understand," he said carelessly. "Really, let it go."

She raised her eyes to his face. "She has a little boy, you said?"

"Yes. About nine. He was in the car with his father when it crashed." He left out the part about the rheumatic fever, thinking it might seem a little over the top.

"The crash that your old policeman thought was deliberate."

"He thought it was a result of Leland being chased—he never said it was intended. There's no way of knowing whether it was intended. Not with what we have now."

"We?"

"Sorry—not with what I have now." He waited.

She gnawed her lower lip, rather prettily, then seemed to make up her mind. "All right. I'll poke around a little."

"Thank you." He meant it. "More wine, or are you ready to toy with a little filet mignon?"

She chuckled. "Those were the good old days, my love. On your present salary, it's more like a little hamburger."

"Nothing wrong with hamburger, is there?"

"Nope." She stood up. "Especially when you can pick it up in a bag and take it home with you." She momentarily transfixed him with a raised eyebrow as she reaching for her coat. "Coming?"

17

Tess stayed close to Max for the rest of the day.

She lay only half asleep that night.

And nothing happened.

The next day, leaving Mrs. Grimble and John Soame on duty, she went back to work on the McMurdo house, argued with Archie McMurdo, soothed the workmen, shopped at a local supermarket. She came home, cooked dinner, spent the evening with Max, watching television. Slept lightly, waking frequently at the slightest sound.

And nothing happened.

Work again. Research at the Victoria and Albert Museum. Initial interviews with two new clients, each with different requirements, different expectations, and widely differing budgets. Lists and drawings. An argument with a supplier, happily resolved by a switch to an alternative small-bore central heating system. A sales representative from a German fabric manufacturer with a tumble of rich colors and textures that covered her desk and filled her office with a kind of visual singing. Another representative from a Berwick-upon-Tweed pottery, offering imaginative shapes, amusing ideas, and an excellent discount for bulk purchase. Home again, dinner again, praise for the model castle, edgy laughter, edgy sleep.

And nothing happened.

Max had a bit of excitement when his friend from the hospital, the newly reverend Simon Carter, appeared on the doorstep with a chessboard under one arm. He and Tess gave one another a nasty moment when, on her way out, she opened the front door and found him standing there with his other arm upraised.

"Good Lord," he gasped. "I was just about to ring the bell."

"I'm glad to hear it," Tess said breathlessly. "I thought you were about to strike me down."

Carter chuckled and lowered his arm. "Sorry," he said. "I don't usually go around frightening innocent women. Or even sinful women, come to that. Not that I've encountered many." He sounded rather disappointed about it. "I've been assigned to a parish in Peckham, actually. Start my duties next week, but I came down a bit early to get used to London. Frightening place."

"Aren't you from the city?" Tess asked, stepping back to let him in.

"No, no . . . a small-town lad, that's me." Carter beamed. "So, I thought I'd call round and see how the invalid was getting on. I hope you don't mind."

"Not at all. He'll be delighted to see you—he's at the very bored stage."

"Ah, then my timing is good, for once. Perhaps I'm getting the hang of vicaring at last," Carter said engagingly, removing his coat and unwinding a very long scarf from around his throat. There was a pink rash around the edge of his collar, and a small piece of plaster under his chin where he'd apparently nicked himself shaving. He seemed very young, and eager as a puppy to please. "Is he up or down?" he inquired.

"Up. I'll show you," Tess said, temporarily removing

her coat and dropping it over the balustrade as she led him up the stairs.

Mrs. Grimble was waiting for her when she came down. There was a burst of laughter from Max's room.

"Mr. Soame went to the London Liberry half an hour ago. Who's that up there with Max?" she demanded. Tess explained. "Well, just so's I know who's around the place," Mrs. Grimble said. "All these people coming and going . . ."

Tess was putting on her coat. "It was very nice of your brother to bring Max the jigsaw puzzle the other day."

Mrs. Grimble flushed. "I never invite him," she said defensively. "He just comes."

"Oh, that's all right. I don't mind it if you have your brother or a friend around for a coffee. But I do like to know . . . the same as you do . . . who's around."

They exchanged a glance of perfect understanding.

"Do I give this person upstairs a cup of coffee?" Mrs. Grimble wanted to know.

"If you're having one yourself," Tess said with a smile. "I'm sure he'd appreciate it."

"Don't hold with Church, much," Mrs. Grimble conceded. "But I got nothing against it, neither." She headed back toward the kitchen. "Might make some biscuits this morning. Got everything in yesterday."

Tess smiled to herself and went out. She was beginning to think, reluctantly but gratefully, that Detective Sergeant Nightingale may have been right—the phone calls, perhaps even the booby trap in the wardrobe—had been meaningless attempts by some unknown enemy to cause her pain. And the other things were quite unrelated to it or to each other. Her nerves still twanged with the sense of being watched, manipulated, threatened—she grew annoyed with herself for leaping into the air when someone dropped something, or seizing up with panic whenever the phone rang, and began muttering "Pull yourself together" so frequently that she wondered if she should have it set to music.

Things were settling down to a familiar routine.

Why, they even had a vicar visiting.

Life was returning to normal.

It would be all right.

A week after the supposed break-in there was a call from Richard. "Still happy with your lodger?" he asked. "Noticed any of the heirloom silver missing yet?"

"No."

"Any more nasty phone calls?"

"No," she said, and wondered why she was lying.

"So everything is perfect?"

"Yes—everything seems to be just fine, thank you."

He pounced like a cat on a mouse, familiar enough with the sound of her voice to detect doubt. "*Seems* to be?"

"Well—there *was* someone sneaking around the house the other night. But there was nothing tak——"

"What do you mean, sneaking around?" His voice was sharp.

Already sorry she'd mentioned it, she explained about the break-in, and Max's nightmare. "The police think he was scared away before anything could be taken. They're keeping an eye on the house now. But Sergeant Nightingale doesn't seem to think there's any connection between that and the phone calls or anything else."

"Oh, doesn't he? And who is Sergeant Nightingale?"

"He's been looking into Roger's accident."

There was a moment of silence. "What do you mean, looking into Roger's accident? That was months ago."

"I know. He came to talk to me in the hospital about it a few weeks ago. So, when the local police didn't do anything about our prowler, I called him. He's Scotland Yard, you see."

"And he says what?"

She sighed. "The same as the local police—just a crank caller, an interrupted burglary, and a lot of coincidences."

"I see. So much for the Met. Tell me, did you find this broken door or did Soame?"

"Oh, John did—when he went down to make some cocoa for all of us."

"How cozy," Richard said snidely. "And how do you know, dear, kind John didn't do it himself and tell you about it later just to make himself look like a hero? Did he offer to spend the night in your room—just to make sure you were 'safe'?"

"That's a rotten thing to say."

"Not when you take a look at his financial position," Richard said.

"What do you mean?"

"I've had one of my banking friends asking a few pointed questions of some old school chums." He sounded unabashed, smug, ready to impart triumph. "I've just had his report. Want to hear it?"

"I'm not interested," she said, picking up a pencil and beginning to doodle on the margin of an invoice from D. H. Listerman, plc., manufacturers of ceramic ware for the discerning (fancy basins and toilets).

"Oh yes, you are," Richard purred. There was a rustle of paper. "According to my impeccable source, Soame is in a world of financial trouble. And not for the first time, either—apparently his late wife was quite the spender. His bank is making legal noises about his overdraft, which is in the high hundreds. There are some large withdrawals of cash that might be to cover gambling debts. Apparently your new friend likes a flutter now and again."

"He told me that he had financial problems," Tess said. "He's been very open about it."

"And there is a tidy sum paid regularly to a Miss J. Wickham. She could be his mistress. Or a blackmailer."

"Or his dental hygienist. Or an elderly aunt in Brighton."

"Her checks are cashed on a Barclays branch in Cheapside, actually."

"I don't want to hear any more, Richard," Tess said quickly, certain there must be some perfectly rational explanation for all these things. Of course there was.

"I'll bet you don't," he said harshly. "Mr. John Soame is obviously not the paragon you thought he was."

"Neither are you," she snapped.

There was a brief silence. "And what is that supposed to mean?" Each word was frozen into a separate icicle.

"All this suspicion, all this sneaking around—I never knew you were like this," she said.

There was silence on the line, and then Richard spoke repentantly. "I'm sorry, Tess. Blame jet lag, if you like. I came back, saw this report, and just snapped. I only had it done because I'm really worried about you. All this sudden determination to make decisions—any decisions—to do things for yourself, to plunge ahead helter-skelter. It scares me, it really does. Whether you like it or not—and for some reason you suddenly seem not to like it—I care about you, Tess. I care very much. I'm still waiting for an answer to my proposal, you know."

"Well, if you want an answer right now—" Tess began.

"I don't," he interrupted. "Not when you're in this mood." He sighed, and his voice became plaintive. "Max's illness seems to have changed you overnight."

"If anyone has changed, it's you," she said tightly.

He immediately adopted a brisk but cajoling tone, undoubtedly developed for use when facing an awkward client. "Look, talking on the phone like this is silly. How about dinner tonight? Unfortunately I have a plane to catch at ten, so our time will be limited, but—"

"My goodness, which country are you conquering

this week, Richard?" she asked, before she could stop herself.

Silence. Then: "Very funny." He slammed down the phone.

By the end of the day Tess decided she hated men.

All men.

Adrian was in one of his most peevish moods, having heard that his former friend and partner, the renegade Jason, had secured a very desirable contract to do an entirely fresh interior design for the flat of a rich, newly arrived American oil executive who had somehow—the mind boggled—secured rooms in Albany. Adrian had been counting on the commission, having been introduced through a mutual friend to the wife of the executive in question—a malleable lady who, it now proved, was less than reliable in her promises. According to Adrian's contact, a minor Embassy aide, she had been "swept away" by Jason's ideas.

"Well, she'll want to sweep them away when she sees them, that's for certain," Adrian huffed. "My God, Jason in Albany—it doesn't bear thinking about. He has no sense of continuity or respect at all—he'll Art-Deco the woman to *death*, mark my words. It's his latest craze, he does it *everywhere*. With *anyone*. Silver walls and silver balls and little triangular dadoes, that's how *his* garden grows." And then, whirling on an unsuspecting assistant who had just entered bearing a stack of newly covered cushions for the window display, he shrieked, "I said delft blue, not dark blue! Take the hideous things out and burn them immediately!"

The assistant rolled his eyes at Tess and turned without a word, bearing the offending items away. Twenty minutes later Adrian was stalking around demanding that they be returned with equal alacrity; why didn't anyone do what he asked around there? Who was in charge, anyway? *Who made the decisions?* WHO PAID THE BILLS?

At four o'clock, weary, frazzled, and slightly deafened, Tess was sorting things into her briefcase when a shadow fell across her desk. Looking up, she saw Archie McMurdo standing there, watching her. "G'day," he said.

She stopped and glared at him. "Well, what's wrong now?" she demanded, slamming her briefcase shut and preparing to do battle. "Picture rails not level? Floorboards too dark? Windows too small? Come on, out with it."

He looked deeply hurt. "I thought maybe you'd like to have a bit of tucker with me," he said. "But, seeing as you're packing it in early, maybe you'd prefer tea at the Ritz?"

"Why?"

"Does there have to be a reason?" he asked, a plaintive note in his voice. "It's a beautiful afternoon, isn't it? I don't know many people in London, and I have a craving for those little sandwiches and some scones with cream and strawberry jam. Someone told me tea at the Ritz is definitely the bonzer thing to do, so I thought why not do it with someone who's nice to look at? Sure wouldn't want to go there with Aunt Dolly, would I?"

Tess tried to visualize Mrs. McMurdo in the marbled and mirrored fastness of the Ritz, bending over one of the little tea tables with pinkie upraised, her red curls frizzing energetically from under an expensive and totally unsuitable hat, her corncrake voice rasping out over the tinkle of the teaspoons and the piano. The visualization was successful, and she giggled.

Archie beamed down at her, a sunbeam from the window gilding his curly hair and sparking the devil in his eyes. "Exactly," he said. "And frankly, you look pretty jacked. I figure you could use some little sandwiches and a cup of that god-awful perfumy Earl Grey tea they probably serve there. Am I right?"

Tess sighed. He was very right. She looked at him

speculatively. Was this a man with secrets? Did that open countenance and Burt Lancaster smile go all the way through, or was what she saw only on the surface? "Give me a minute," she said, and reached for the phone.

A few minutes later, assured by John Soame that he and Max were deeply, happily—and literally—glued to their model-making, she allowed Archie McMurdo to take her to tea at the Ritz.

It was all that he had promised, but he impressed her more than the pillars and the confections. Gone was the loudmouth complainer, the opinionated boor, the troublesome gadfly. Like some antipodean chameleon, he changed his colors to suit the background, and proved to possess all the polish necessary to negotiate the maze of tiny tables, the spindly legs of the gilded chairs, and the ostentatious flurries of the waiters. He ordered exactly the right things in exactly the right voice, but did no more. He sat beside her in his dark suit and cranberry tie and seemed to glow quietly. The heads that turned belonged only to assessing females, and she met several pairs of covetous eyes with, she hoped, total disdain. He poured her tea and treated her like some rare and valuable visitor from another world. She forgot her wrinkled suit and decidedly tired silk blouse. Gradually the images of peevish Adrian and possessive Richard and impecunious John faded from her mind. She was somebody, after all. Somebody who *deserved* tea at the Ritz.

In short, this particular Archie was both a balm and a revelation.

He caught her watching him and grinned.

"Forgiven?" he asked.

"For what?"

"All the strife I've been causing out at the house," he said. "I know you didn't like it—you're a hard-hearted sheila, and you can cast a mean eye on a man when you want to."

"Can I?" Tess asked.

"Scared hell out of me," he smiled.

"I doubt that very much."

"Well, all that's over now. We're going to get on beaut now, aren't we? We're going to declare a truce."

He looked so earnest, so contrite, that she couldn't resist him. "Oh, all right," she relented. "Let frivolity reign."

"Absolutely. Have another cucumber sandwich." He held up the plate for her selection. As she chose, she chanced to glance up at him and saw him staring fixedly at the people passing down the main corridor below the steps that separated the tearoom from the lobby. When she followed his gaze, she saw an older man had paused, hand on a chair as if seeking support in a crisis, and was staring back at him. His face was pale above the velvet collar of his dark-blue coat, and his mouth slowly thinned as he pressed his lips together.

"Good Lord—do you think he's unwell?" Tess asked.

"Who?" asked Archie casually, replacing the sandwich plate on the crowded top of a small table that sat before them.

"That man you were looking at—he seemed about to faint."

He looked at her in some puzzlement. "Sorry?" he asked.

Tess looked over at the wide carpeted corridor. Many people thronged there, going right to the cocktail bar or left to the dining room. The high-backed blue upholstered chair was still there. The frightened man was not.

"Oh," she said blankly. "He's gone."

"More tea?" asked Archie.

18

Secrets," Tim said abruptly.

Murray spoke without looking up, turning a page and keeping his place with one finger. "Whose secrets?" he asked.

"Anybody's secrets. It's secrets that lead to all the trouble in the world, secret thoughts, secret caches of arms, secret scientific developments, secret political moves, secret agreements to do or not to do. . . ." He had been pacing back and forth between the desks for over an hour.

"Listen, if people didn't have secrets, we'd be out of a job," Murray said. "I'd be stuck in my mother's antique shop, and you'd be . . . what would you be?"

"Much happier," Tim said, coming to a stop and a decision at the same time. "Much, much happier." He went to his desk, picked up the file that had been weighing down his blotter all afternoon, and went out the door.

Murray looked after him, smiled, and went back to reviewing for his promotional exams.

* * *

"Well, Nightingale?" Detective Chief Inspector Abbott looked up from his paperwork.

"Could I have a word, sir?"

Abbott threw his pen aside with every evidence of relief and leaned back in his chair. He seemed in an expansive mood, and Tim was encouraged. "What can I do for you this time?"

"It's about the Leland case, sir." Tim sat down and placed the file on his lap, ready to hand.

Abbott's forehead wrinkled. "Is that something new?"

"I'm afraid not."

Abbott gazed at him for a moment, then closed his eyes and groaned slightly to himself. "It's still this Peters thing, isn't it? You didn't give the notebooks back."

"Oh yes, I did."

"Ah."

"After I'd photocopied the relevant pages."

"Oh."

"And I've been looking into things in my free time."

Abbott started to anger, then shrugged. Free time meant just that. He really couldn't stop Nightingale from going around asking questions while off duty, as long as he didn't abuse his position. "Let me guess," he said cautiously. "You have a hunch."

"More of an itch, really." Tim explained about his interview with Tess Leland and his discovery of her situation—the burglary, the phone calls, the interrupted break-in. "I've said to her that it's all coincidence, but frankly I think there's just too much of it to ignore. Peters stirred something up, and whether it killed him or not, it's still stirring. Roger Leland's death could have been a beginning rather than an ending. Or it could be part of something much, much bigger."

"And so now you want to scratch this Leland itch officially, is that it?"

"I think it should be looked into, yes."

Abbott shook his head in what looked like regret. "We've got too big a caseload to go chasing butterflies, Tim."

"And we always will have. But if it turns out that Ivor Peters was right and I'm right and Roger Leland's death *was* more than an ordinary accident, and his widow and son suffer through our negligence, we'd look very bad. And feel even worse."

"Hmmmm." That possibility was not pleasing to Abbott. He scowled. "But the Leland woman could be a hysteric, looking for attention."

"I've considered that. But Soame believes her, and I respect his judgment. He was there when the latest phone call was made, he saw her reaction."

"Who the hell is Soame?" the detective chief inspector demanded.

Patiently, Tim explained how John Soame had recently entered into the Leland household. "He's a well-known historian. I used to attend his lectures at university. He was very sound."

"'Sound,' was he?" Abbott asked, with only slight sarcasm. It was an awkward moment. Abbott was a good detective chief inspector, but only at the Yard temporarily, and thus lacking the aggressive edge that ambition honed so sharply in men who were out to make themselves known to those on the top floors. He liked Nightingale—most of the men liked Nightingale—but he was hesitant to trust his judgment completely. It was always expensive to trust young detective sergeants completely, and there'd been so much fuss about budgets lately. As far as he could tell, in fact, almost everything up here was about budgets.

"Well, I really can't justify it, you know," he finally said with a sigh.

"It would be a lot more expensive to investigate Mrs. Leland's murder," Tim persisted. "And we are supposed to prevent crime as well as detect it, aren't we?"

"Theoretically."

"Well, this might be doing both. We can't be blamed for trying, can we?"

Abbott regarded Nightingale thoughtfully, thinking of the detective chief inspector who would return to this desk in a few months. The man he was temporarily replacing was an officer of the old school, who'd come up through the ranks, whereas Abbott himself—like Nightingale—had received accelerated promotion because of a university degree. He understood Nightingale's impatience with Yard politics, and the niceties of rank, privilege, and rumor. He didn't think Detective Chief Inspector Spry, when he returned, would be so sympathetic. If he encouraged Nightingale, he might only be making future trouble for Spry and the boy himself. If he *dis*couraged him, however, he could nip in the bud the very qualities that were already lifting Nightingale above the others in the service. Which responsibility should he honor first: loyalty to the service and its concomitant infrastructure; or loyalty to the future, where officers like this one could create better and more sensitive policing? He glanced at the clock again, swiveled his chair to look out of his window, and considered. Finally, he turned back and slapped his hands on the desk. "Just keep it down," he said.

"Sir?"

"Get on with whatever you want to set in motion, but keep the costs down and keep your head down, too. We've only got so much time, only so many hands, we've got to do it all the best we can." He stood up. "Unless and until something bigger or more urgent comes along, that is. Understood?"

Nightingale nodded, stood up, and turned to leave the office. He wanted to get out before Abbott changed his mind or put any limitations on him or said anything else, but he wasn't fast enough.

"Nightingale?"

Tim turned in the doorway. "Sir?"

"What do you intend to do next?"

"I want to run up to Cambridge and talk to a few people."

"Why?"

"I've only heard Soame lecture, sir. I know nothing about his private life. He *is* new on the scene, and he *is* right there in the house and . . ." He paused.

"And?"

"And telephones can be rigged to ring on an electronic command—the technology can be picked up in half a dozen shops along Tottenham Court Road. You can be in the same room and call yourself, so to speak. You can also rig a phone to relay taped messages on command—all kinds of things. Just because he was beside her when she got one of the calls doesn't mean he wasn't behind it."

"I thought you said he was 'sound.'"

"He is—on the nineteenth century. And anyway, that was a long time ago. That doesn't mean he's perfect. Or honest. Things may have happened to change him since I was up there. I don't know what his motivation might be, or if he has any connection with Mrs. Leland, but some answers might be available in Cambridge."

"Not trusting anyone is a bitch, isn't it?" Abbott said.

"Yes, sir."

"But good policing, all the same," Abbott said approvingly. The door began to close. "Tim?"

"Yes, sir?"

"Make it a day trip—I'm not authorizing any overnight expenses so you can have a piss-up with your old school ties."

Tim grinned. "All my old school ties are now rich merchant bankers or pop-group promoters. If I do make contact in Cambridge it will probably be with other coppers. And you *know* we industrious, trustworthy coppers only drink tea, sir."

* * *

Tess and Archie moved on from the Ritz to a small Italian restaurant just off Dean Street, where the food was superb and the wine ambrosial. She had far too much of both, and found herself telling Archie all about the phone calls and the mysterious burglar who wasn't there.

"And they're after this money of yours, is that it?" he asked, offering her a bread stick from the basket.

"Yes. Except that there isn't any money," Tess said. "If I knew what they were talking about, it would make sense, but I don't, so it doesn't." She paused. "Any more than that sentence does. I don't think I should have any more wine."

"On the contrary," he said, filling up her glass. "It's just what you *should* have." He topped up his own glass and then raised it to her. "Here's to nonsense."

"I wish I agreed with you," she said. "It would be funny if it wasn't so frightening."

"It looks to me like maybe it has something to do with your husband," Archie suggested. "Maybe he had some money. Maybe he put it someplace and didn't tell you—how about that?"

"Well, maybe, but that wouldn't have been very like Roger. He *was* secretive about some things, but . . ." She paused.

"But?" he asked encouragingly.

She shrugged and sipped more wine. "If there was any money hidden in the house, I expect the burglars found it weeks ago."

"Not necessarily," Archie said. "Maybe your husband hid it in some really terrific place. What kind of things interested him? What did he do with his time?"

"He didn't have much time of his own, really. He was a workaholic. But when he did take time off, he liked to walk, and drink wine . . . and read. . . ."

"Maybe he hid some money in a book."

"I don't think so," Tess said sadly. "He played squash, sometimes. He was quite good at that."

"Doesn't sound very promising," Archie said.

"No," Tess agreed.

"Hey, cheer up. Have some more wine. You're supposed to be having a good time here, remember?"

When they emerged around ten o'clock, it was raining. They began to walk along the pavement toward Shaftesbury Avenue, where taxis would be patrolling to catch the after-theater crowd. "Just like Melbourne," Archie said, moving her around a puddle.

She glanced sideways at him. "I thought you said you came from Sydney."

"Oh, sure—but I grew up in Melbourne," he said.

As they passed the open mouth of a dark and noisome alley, there was a sudden clatter of bins and a shout. A few yards within, two men were grappling together in a drunken argument.

One knocked the other down and stood over him, shouting obscenities. The reek of alcohol blended with the stench of dirt and decaying garbage as the fallen man struggled up from a heap of split black plastic sacks, shouting in turn, waving his arms. He glanced toward the mouth of the alley and saw them. Abruptly his venom was turned on them rather than his more recent adversary.

"Come on, this is no place for you," Archie said.

As they moved on hurriedly, the man leaned down, picked something up, and hurled it toward them. "Piss off, piss off!" he shouted. "Mind your own goddamn business!"

"Jesus, it's a rat!" Archie exclaimed, as the small black missile fell at their feet and began to twitch.

"No, it isn't, it's a cat," Tess said, stooping down to pick it up. "A kitten," she amended, as the tiny, soaking-wet little body squirmed and mewed in her hands.

"Cripes, it's filthy," Archie said with distaste, pulling her away as the man began to come toward them. "Drop it and come on."

"No—he'll hurt it. He's a vile man," Tess said blurrily, allowing herself to be propelled along the pavement toward the lights of the avenue ahead, but still clutching the squirming, mewling little body. "Throwing this poor defenseless animal at us like that. He could have killed it. Ouch." Needle claws had dug into her hand as the kitten sought freedom.

"Defenseless, hell. It's probably covered with fleas," Archie said. "Oh, for crying out loud, let it go. We can't take a cat into a bar."

"We're not going to a bar," Tess said. She opened her briefcase and carefully inserted the bedraggled kitten, closing it gently over its spiky, muddy, reeking head.

"But it's only a little after ten," Archie said in some consternation.

"Time to go home," Tess said carefully.

"Oh," Archie said, as if a light were dawning. "Oh. Right. Got you. Home it is." He seemed pleased suddenly; she couldn't imagine why. She'd had far too much wine. Her throat was sore from talking so much, and her feet hurt. Maybe his feet hurt, too.

She came to a different conclusion in the taxi.

All traces of the wine, the cocktails, and the candlelight were dissipated from Tess's brain as Archie McMurdo made his expectations plain. "No, Archie . . . please . . ." Tess protested in a low but audible voice, prying away his busy hands and leaning back from his looming face, which cut off the light and made her feel trapped and claustrophobic.

He glared at her for a moment, then pushed her away abruptly. "I thought Yank women were liberated," he said.

"Not all of us," she snapped. "And liberated doesn't mean—"

"Leave it out," Archie said brusquely, and turned to

stare out of the window. His Australian accent, softened during the tea and dinner interludes, had reappeared under the influence of this apparently unexpected and certainly unwelcome wound to his self-esteem.

"It's just that—"

"I know, I know, you're not that kind of sheila," Archie said, turning back to face her and leaning into the corner of the seat. "Forget it. I didn't read you clear, all right? Let's leave it at that."

"I did enjoy this evening with you," she said quietly.

He patted her hand in an avuncular manner. "Well, that's good, girl, that's fine. Glad to have been of service, as they say."

And he spoke no more during the rest of the journey through the gleaming streets. Window displays and traffic lights reflected up off the wet asphalt and made puddles of color on the pavements, but once they'd left the theater district there were few pedestrians about to appreciate the rainbowed duplication. The bright rectangles containing heaped merchandise or mannequins frozen in fashionable poses became fewer and fewer, the gaps between them longer, until only the occasional gleam from restaurants, pubs, and late-night take-aways lent warmth to the gray, slanting shafts of rain and the patent-leather sheen of the road. Other cars, secret and sleek, moved beside them, occasionally punctuated by the red wall of a bus or the half-seen and indecipherable lettering on the side of a passing lorry. In front, the driver was listening to a radio phone-in on the decline of public morals, but in the dark cube of the rear-seat area there was only an intermittent squeak and scrabble from within Tess's briefcase.

Now secure in her corner of the taxi, Tess looked at Archie sideways and tried to free herself from the last seductive strands of alcohol. It wasn't Archie's fault at all, but her own. He'd read the signals correctly—she *was* attracted to him. The trouble was, she was physically attracted not only to Archie, but also to Richard, to

Sergeant Nightingale, to John Soame, to that lovely young curate who came around to play chess with Max, and—it seemed to her—practically every male she passed in the street. Even ever-so-elegant Adrian gave her odd moments of speculation. My God, she thought, I'd better be careful. If the taxi driver turns around I'll probably manage to find something devastating about *him*, too. Was this a result of hormone buildup or a reassertion of her own sensual persona?

Clearly, Mother Nature was not a feminist.

Well, she was not going to give in to Mother Nature any more than she was going to give in to Archie McMurdo's apparent conviction that women were supposed to pay for their dinners, albeit not with VISA. Unfortunately, there were other wishes to be considered, and other obligations. She wrestled with the dichotomy, and then her nerve snapped.

"Perhaps you'd like to come to dinner one evening?"

Archie glanced across at her, somewhat startled by this apparent reversal in her attitude. "Well, sure. Maybe. Why not?" He began to smile again. After a minute he began humming to himself, and reached over to pat her hand, allowing his fingers to linger. "Why not?" he repeated.

I'm doing this for Adrian, she thought.

I really am.

19

Tess's briefcase was never the same again.

She got rid of Archie in the nicest way she could, and carried the case inside at arm's length, for it had developed a leak from one corner.

She ran down the hall with it and plunked it into the sink. John Soame, who had been reading on baby-sitting duty, came out with a worried expression. "Is there anything wrong?" he asked. "You ran in so quickly—"

The briefcase gave a squall.

He looked at it and then at her with an owlish expression. "Your briefcase is haunted," he said. He inspected her gravely. "And you are . . ."

"Perfectly all right," she said, not realizing that her struggles with Archie had left her makeup smudged and her hair rather corkscrewed over one ear. "But if they breathalyze me I may be taken in for being drunk in charge of a pair of shoes. Which hurt." She kicked them off and sighed. "Better," she said. "*Much* better."

The briefcase squalled again. Soame raised an inquiring eyebrow.

"He threw it at me," she explained.

"Did he."

"Yes. He was a mean, drunken old tramp."

"Really. I was under the impression he was a client."

"Oh, not Archie. *Archie* didn't throw it."

"That is a relief." There was a pause. "Then who—"

"The man in the alley."

"Ah."

"Outside the restaurant." She looked at him crossly. For a college professor he seemed rather dim. "He was having a fight with another man and he saw us and he threw the cat at us. Didn't hit us, though," she finished triumphantly.

"It's all in the footwork," Soame nodded. He went over to the sink and inspected the briefcase, which had ceased to leak but had begun to rock. "May I?"

"Watch out," she warned him. "It's very fierce."

He gingerly opened the briefcase to reveal the very small, very bedraggled kitten crouching in one corner. "My God," he said. "He *is* a dangerous beast. You're lucky to be alive."

"It was a close thing." Tess smiled, sinking onto the rocking chair in front of the old Rayburn range. "But I thought maybe Max would like it. He isn't happy." She closed her eyes and leaned her head back. "He should be happy."

"I know," Soame said softly, and then watched her fall asleep in an instant. He put a quilt over her, then went down to the local high-street shop which was run by a hardworking Asian family who knew no night. He returned bearing flea powder, a litter tray and litter, a few tins of cat food, and a tiny bright-red flea collar.

He ran a few inches of warm water into the sink and extracted the kitten from the briefcase for a bath. During the following few minutes Tess awoke. In fact, she was surprised the entire neighborhood didn't awake. After most of the water in the sink had been redistributed over the kitchen floor and the two bath attendants, there was a brief pause for iodine and

Band-aids. There followed an interlude of relative peace concerning flea powder and a saucer of milk, and the evening's entertainment was concluded by the ceremonial fastening of the collar.

The exhausted kitten was settled down in an apple box beside Tess's bedroom radiator, and the equally exhausted bath attendants retired to their respective corners for the night. Tess, now plagued equally by doubts about Archie McMurdo and indigestion from the veal piccata, was convinced she would never sleep—and dropped off instantly.

Had she remained awake she would have been aware of John Soame's pacing back and forth above her head until very, very late.

In the morning the kitten's thin cries awakened Tess. She put on her robe and padded over. "Good morning," she said, and gathered up the box to present to Max, discovering in the process that she had a hangover for which bending over was definitely not a cure.

"What's that?" Max asked wearily, when she entered his room. "More books to read?"

"No. Guess again."

He turned his head away and looked out of the window. "Something educational," he said in vast disgust.

"Absolutely," Tess agreed.

Though he had been healing in body, Max was still unsettled in mind. Oh, he would cheer up after a visit from Simon Clark, who seemed always able to make him laugh. And he would be mentally lively after a lesson with John. But there were still too many moments when she would catch him staring into space with a frown. He had begun asking questions about his father, as if he were a stranger he'd never known. More than once she had caught him crying over the stamp collections or the airplane models he had made with

Roger, or going through the box of snapshots of them all together on holiday and stacking them in various and apparently arbitrary combinations, or rereading a childhood storybook rescued from the bottom of his pine chest. But when she'd tried to comfort him he'd become offhand and cross, telling her not to treat him like a baby. He was just bored, he said. Sick of being sick, he said.

And she guessed he was still having nightmares, for she often found his bed light had been turned on in the night, and shadows would come and go beneath his eyes.

They were there, now.

Without another word, she put the box on the bed beside him, and went down to the kitchen to make breakfast.

She spent the morning at the Victoria and Albert museum, sketching and taking notes, researching the final details for the McMurdo interiors. It was the part of the job she most enjoyed, reconciling the stylistic demands of the past with the practical realities of the present. Fortunately for her—and for Mrs. McMurdo—Victoriana was now very much in fashion, and there were many companies reproducing the lovely curling lines of early William Morris designs in both lighting and plumbing fixtures, basic areas in which anachronistic clashes most often occurred.

Tess had also renewed many contacts in the antiques trade that she had made before her marriage, and had several dealers with whom she had a good relationship and could trust to find her authentic pieces to feature in the large rooms of the McMurdo mansion. Proportion was very important here, she felt—and wherever possible she wanted to use original things rather than reproductions, which were often scaled down slightly to fit into the reduced dimensions of modern homes.

In some cases she'd had no alternative but to find craftsmen willing to reproduce the items she'd chosen, and she spent the afternoon with one of them—a cabinetmaker who would be building the special wine racks for the basement. Tess was determined to carry authenticity even to those dark regions.

She arrived home at three-thirty, told Mrs. Grimble she could leave early, and made tea for Max and the kitten, whose name was apparently Albert. Leaving them mutually absorbed and quite transformed by their new friendship, Tess sank into a scented bath—enjoying the rare luxury of being pleased with herself and her day's work. She was just drying her hair when the phone rang.

She froze for a moment, then squared her shoulders and went downstairs to face the worst.

But it was not the mysterious caller.

It was Adrian, and he was in a foul temper.

"Don't tell me that's really you," he said sarcastically. "How nice to know you're still breathing. May I assume, despite finding you at home at this hour, that you are still working for me and have not resigned to go into business for yourself?"

"You knew my schedule for today—or you would if you'd bothered to ask Maud. I phoned her and told her I would be at the V and A this morning, which I was, and with Mr. Greenslade this afternoon, which I also was, skipping my lunch hour, by the way, so I am taking it now." She dropped into the chair beside the phone and inspected her toes. "What is it, Adrian?"

His tone was measured, small doses filtered between clenched teeth. "I have been having a long heart-to-heart talk with Mr. McMurdo, who kindly called into the studio this afternoon."

"Oh, really?" She was amused, imagining how Archie would have impressed Adrian. "Beautiful, isn't he?"

"I hardly noticed."

She laughed. "Oh, come on—"

"His attractions are not in question here. What is in question is *you*, Tess."

"Me?" She was startled.

"Indeed. He seems to think *you're* not up to the job."

"What?"

"He told me some mad tale about burglars and unpleasant phone calls and you having a lot of money. That was quite a revelation, my sweet." There was nothing sweet about his tone. "I was under the impression that you were as stony as I."

"I am. He had no ri——"

"He says you're too 'burdened' by your private concerns to give the restoration of the house your full attention, and that the work is being skimped or not done at all."

"That's not true!"

"He says he's going to ask his Aunt Dolly to name another decorator. Or, preferably, allow *him* to do so."

Tess had been slowly sitting up as Adrian spoke, and was now fully erect and at full attention, her spine stiffened by dismay. "And what does Aunt Dolly say to that?" she demanded.

"How should I know?"

"But I told you to get in touch with her, to ask—"

"Yes, yes, yes." Adrian was in full flow, ignoring her protests, concerned only with what he saw as betrayal and a considerable loss in income. "But the damage is done, Tess, and *you've* done it. I told you to charm him, I told you to handle him. I have enough to do just keeping Brevitt Studios *afloat* these days. . . ." Self-pity was beginning to creep into his voice.

The scene in the taxi came back to her, in every detail. Apparently Archie really hated taking no for an answer, after all. "Adrian, there's more to this than you think. I think you ought to look into Mr. Archie McMurdo's motivations a little more closely, because—" she began angrily, but he gave her no chance to continue.

"That is not all," he continued, his voice growing heavier with each word. "According to our irreplaceable builder—and I underline the word *irreplaceable*, which does not apply to *everyone* in this organization—the good Ernest Flowers, with whom I've just spoken, Archie continues to turn up at the house and tries to get them to change things."

"What kind of things?"

"Oh, doors, windows, ceilings, floors—just *small* items of that nature. He's apparently underfoot at every turn, getting in everywhere, and generally making a nuisance of himself. I'm afraid Ernest became rather heated on the telephone. He wants to know whether to treat Archie like a client, or throw him off the site. We are at risk, here, Tess—Ernest and his workers are threatening to down tools if the situation isn't clarified."

"Then clarify it, Adrian," she snapped. "I can't believe this is—"

"Oh, really? I find it dismayingly easy to believe," Adrian said. "It is a direct result of a slack hand at the tiller, Tess dear. Of *somebody* not tending to business."

"I have been working hard on the McMurdo house," Tess said hotly. "I have rearranged my life entirely so that I can concentrate on the work—you begged me to do it, remember? And I'm doing it."

"I'm beginning to wonder if I wasn't too hasty about all that. I shall be going over to the house myself tomorrow, to see exactly what you've been doing."

"You *know* what I've been doing. I've shown you all my sketches, from the beginning. It's not fair that you—"

He interrupted. "I haven't time to be fair, Tess. I have only time to survive, and however fond I am of you personally, I am not going to let that cloud my judgment. I'm not going to let even you destroy what I've taken years to build up!" Within his wrath, Tess could detect the sound of imminent tears.

"Adrian, dear, you *know* that I—"

"I don't know anything, Tess, but I will know more tomorrow, that is certain. Good night!"

20

Stunned by the sudden ferocity of Adrian's attack, Tess sat back and stared at the small group of framed Bateman cartoons on the far wall. One was slightly crooked, and she noticed that the heavy embossed wallpaper she had chosen so carefully—so long ago, now—had begun to curl away from the wall in the lower corner near the sitting room. It seemed appropriate to her mood that little things that had formed the solid background of her life were becoming skewed and worn. She thought about straightening the picture. She thought about finding some paste and sticking the paper down. But she remained, immobile, on the bench beside the telephone.

Adrian had sounded almost hysterical.

Although he had a temper and temperament, she had never heard quite that degree of angst in his voice. Could it be she *was* doing a poor job at the McMurdo house? It was true she hadn't gone there in the past few days to see what progress was being made, but that was because she trusted Ernie implicitly.

Had she been wrong? Had she made errors of judgment as to concept, overall design, small details? No—she refused to believe it. She knew her work was good. Better than good.

She sat there for a very long time, until the hall grew dark, and beyond. Wind suddenly shook the windows in the sitting room, and there was a mutter of thunder. A little while later, she could hear rain falling, and above it, the sound of Max's television set. Still she sat there, staring without seeing. She was so absorbed in her reflections that the doorbell, going off without warning above her, made her jump in alarm. Perhaps Mr. Soame had forgotten his key. Wearily she got up, pulled her old, comfortable dressing gown around her, tied the belt in a knot, and went to the door.

Suddenly overtaken by caution, she stopped before opening it and called, "Who is it?"

The clamor of the bell, which had continued, abruptly stopped, and an equally loud voice replaced it. "G'day! Is that my sweet little sheila? I've come to bring you joy and merriment, as promised."

Anger swept and shook her. Taking a deep breath, she opened the door. Archie McMurdo stood on the doorstep, grinning, his hair wet and his mac dripping rain. He was carrying a bottle of champagne under one arm, and had a bunch of roses in his hand. As he stood there he wavered a little from side to side—clearly he had fortified himself for the anticipated rigors of the evening ahead.

Tess glared at him, firmly gripping the front of her robe as an alternative to his throat. "How dare you go behind my back to my boss and tell him I was *incompetent!*"

His face fell comically. "Why, the old galah promised he'd let me talk to you first. Damn his eyes!" Archie's voice carried clearly above the hiss of the rain, and Tess glanced nervously at the neighboring bay windows. Archie leaned forward, and a gust of beery breath hit her full in the face. "I ought to have a chance to explain, don't you think?"

"I'm not interested." She began to close the door.

"Here, wait on, sweetheart," Archie bellowed, jamming a foot in the opening. "You and me have got to come good over this. That old wowser only gave you his side of it, I'll bet. I've got a few points to make, too."

"I don't care to hear them."

"Then I'll just stand here and shout them through the door."

She assessed him. He was grinning again, and she decided he would do just what he said, if only for the sheer hell of it. He seemed the sort who enjoyed such little scenes of macho courtship. "Five minutes," she said in a steely voice. He followed her in, his eyes bright, smilingly certain that he could overcome all obstacles in his way, including her anger and the knot in the belt of her dressing gown.

"That's better. Not used to all this rain in Adelaide," he said, shaking himself like a dog.

"I thought you said you came from Sydney," she said, standing with hands on hips while he put down the champagne and roses, after offering them to her without success.

"Adelaide first, then Sydney," he said earnestly.

"But—"

"You look real beaut," he went on, oblivious to her expression. "And you smell good, too." He came closer. "Just stepped out of the bath, I'll bet, and nothing on but that little roby thing. . . ."

"Was it in Melbourne, Adelaide, or Sydney that you learned to be such a . . . such a . . . *creep?*" she demanded, sidestepping his advance. It had been a mistake to let him in, to worry about what the neighbors might think, and she already regretted it. Why, for all she knew, that boyish grin could be the very expression he wore when pulling the wings off flies.

"Now don't go all snaky on me, sweetheart," he pleaded, as she dodged him.

"I have every right to 'go snaky' on you," she snapped. "You've been a bit of a snake yourself, if you ask me. You promised not to interfere at the house, yet I find out you're still hanging around out there annoying Ernie and the other men. Now you've gone behind my back to Adrian and told him I shouldn't be working on the house—"

"You shouldn't."

"—and threatening to write to your aunt suggesting that she hire another interior decorator! How dare you!"

He stopped his clumsy but apparently good-natured pursuit and scowled. "Not a matter of dare, sweetheart. Matter of fact. You've got too much on your mind these days. Your kid. The money. People threatening you. All that. Takes a girl's attention from her work. Changes her priorities." He beamed suddenly. "So, I think you should forget the house and all the rest of it and concentrate on me. Much nicer for both of us when we've got time to enjoy it."

She stared at him. "Do you mean to tell me that you did that just so we could be together?"

"Sure. Aren't you flattered? Just shows how much I think of you, sweetheart."

Drawing herself up, Tess went from stare to glare. "On the contrary," she said coldly. "It shows how little you think of me and how much you think of yourself."

Anger flared to his eyes. "Now, wait a minute—"

"No, *you* wait a minute," she said. "I am a mother and a working woman who is hanging on by the skin of her teeth to her home, her child, her career, and her sanity. Contrary to general opinion, I do not need a man to complete my life. Get out!"

"The hell I will. Not until you and me get a few things straight." He lunged at her, still apparently under the impression that a few deep-tongued kisses would transform her from independent career woman to supplicant, and convert hostility into panting hunger.

She struck him, hard, across the face.

It had a strange effect on him. He went red, then white, and then a terrible expression came into his eyes. She saw, too late, that he was far more gone in drink than she had thought. And that slap had been one mistake too many.

She backed away, knocking over a small pine chair which in turn collided with the small hall table near the front door. A vase teetered and went down onto the scuffed parquet floor with a splintering crash.

Archie McMurdo laughed. It was a vicious laugh—he was enjoying himself now. "Uh-oh, there goes the furniture!" he said gleefully, and returned to his relentless pursuit, moving as suddenly and unpredictably as a spider, scuttling first one way and then another. Dodging around her own hallway, Tess would have felt foolish if she hadn't been so frightened. "Time to squirm for your supper, sweetheart," he grinned, reaching for her. "Time to give old Archie what he deserves."

"I'd rather do that myself," said a voice from above them, and Tess looked up to see John Soame standing on the stairway, arms crossed and staring down. His face was very pale.

Archie, startled into immobility, stared at him. "Who the hell are you?" he demanded. He turned to Tess. "Nobody said anything about a boyfriend. Who's he?"

He was still waiting for her answer as Soame descended the last few steps, took hold of him from behind, and started propelling him toward the front door. Caught unawares, Archie seemed to forget for a moment that he was taller and stronger by far than the other man.

Then he remembered.

"Let go of me, you little bastard," he howled, and twisted out of Soame's grasp, then went for him wildly. Tess put her hands to her mouth, horrified, as the two men began to grapple in the hall. Seeing violence on television or witnessing it in a Soho alley was one thing—having it in your own home was quite another. The grunting, the sudden bitter smell of violence, the wordless struggling was eerie, shocking, and made infinitely more terrible by taking place within familiar walls.

"Oh, John, be careful, oh, darling, *please* stop, please be careful—oh, no—don't—" She could hear herself babbling, as she moved around them, plucking ineffectually at their straining shoulders, mesmerized by the enraged grimaces on their reddening faces as they pushed and shoved one another backward and forward, like animals jockeying for superior position and leverage, or like boys in a playground. It was silly, and it was absolutely awful.

"Open the door," John grunted through clenched teeth.

Tess edged past them and did as she was told. Cold air and rain swept in. She wanted to close her eyes and ears to the sight and sound of the two men, but she couldn't.

A moment later, she was glad she hadn't, for she might have missed the sight of an astonished Archie McMurdo being suddenly thrust through the open front door and thrown down the front steps onto the wet pavement below. It was so quickly done, so adroit and unexpected, that she could only stare at the man who had done it. John Soame stood panting but unmarked in the open doorway, staring down, quite oblivious to her presence in his moment of triumph.

Archie, however, was not. He got up, staggered slightly, brushed at himself and stared up at her defiantly. "Did you enjoy that, sweetheart? Don't laugh too long, because we haven't finished with you yet. We still have business together. And next time I'll make sure you're alone."

John slammed the door shut and then leaned his

head against it, panting slightly, his shirt taut across his thin shoulders, his tie dangling over one shoulder, his hair ruffled up in the back like a boy's.

"Damn," he said under his breath. "Damn, damn, damn."

21

John Soame turned and stared at Tess. "Are you all right?"

She was suddenly aware of her scrubbed face, her old bathrobe, her straggly hair—and her acute embarrassment at having been the cause of a scene.

"I—I'm fine, really," she stammered, feeling the flush rising up her throat and flooding her naked face, like a unfurling banner of shame. "I'm sorry about—it's so—"

"I'm sorry if he was a friend—" He glanced at the abandoned roses and champagne, and managed to imbue the word "friend" with a great complexity of meaning.

"No . . . not at all. He's my client's nephew—the man I had dinner with last night? He's been causing a lot of trouble at the house, and Adrian thought my being friendly might change his attitude."

He offered a wry smile. "Apparently it did just that."

"Yes." She pulled her dressing gown closer around her throat. "But I really gave him no reason to suppose—"

"I'm sure you didn't," he said, rather too quickly. And rather too coldly for comfort.

"In fact, I made things worse. He went to Adrian today and told him he thinks I can't handle the job, said he wants another decorator. And Adrian *listened to him!*" she said miserably. "He's angry with me . . . I don't understand anything anymore."

He came to her then, and put an arm around her shoulders. "Don't worry—Adrian is always flying off the handle about something. You know he has faith in you—he wouldn't have been so determined to keep you if he didn't."

She looked up at him. "Even to the point of inflicting me and my troubles on his poor unsuspecting brother-in-law."

He, in his turn, flushed slightly. "Poor, yes, but hardly unsuspecting. Nobody who has taught adolescents is unsuspecting—quite the reverse, I assure you. And as for—"

"John? What's wrong? What on earth was all the shouting about?"

It was a woman's voice—a young woman's voice, light and soft as gossamer. Startled, Tess sprang away from Soame's encircling arm and looked up. There, outlined in the entrance to the attic flat, was a lovely girl: slender, blond, and barefoot. She was wearing a man's silk dressing gown, presumably Soame's. Suddenly Tess realized that when he had first appeared on the stairs he, too, had been dressed rather more casually than usual. That his tie had been loosened and the first few buttons of his shirt had been undone *before* his encounter with Archie. Her heart, which had been thudding and fluttering a moment before, closed up and went as hard as a fist.

"It's all right, Julia," Soame said. "Just a drunken intruder who needed to be shown the door." He glanced uneasily at Tess—his turn now to be embarrassed. He started to say more, but Tess didn't want to hear it. The situation was all too obvious.

"I'm sorry—I hope I haven't spoiled your evening," she said stiffly. "Thanks again for the rescue." She wrapped her faded robe around her, feeling very foolish, very tired, and very, very old. She fled to Max's room—before she made it all worse.

Max looked up as she came in and closed the door behind her. His freckles stood out against the pale skin, and his hair was standing up in spikes, needing a wash. His pajamas were all wrinkled, and he had a smear of jam on his chin, a teatime leftover. "Hi," he said.

It was enough.

She sat down on the side of the bed and, taking him into her arms, she wept into his spiky hair. "Oh, Max, I'm sorry."

"What for? Gosh, Mum, you're strangling me," he said, squirming in her arms until he was free. He stared at her, startled by her tears. "Hey," he said. "Stop that." He patted her arm and smoothed the top of her head awkwardly.

She wiped her eyes on her sleeve. "Oh, rats," she said crossly, blinking rapidly to recenter her contact lens. She sniffed hugely, and sighed. "It's just that—sometimes I'm so—so—*dumb* about things. People, and . . . things. You know."

"Oh, that." He was half disappointed to find the crisis so small.

"What do you mean, 'Oh, that'?"

"Well . . ." He shrugged. "You are a bit of a klutz, Mum."

"Am I?" she asked, in some astonishment.

"Never mind," he said, patting her hand with an unconscious air of benign superiority. "Girls are *always* hopeless."

"Oh, really?" She gazed at him speculatively, and blew her nose. If that was the attitude his father and that damned school had been inculcating into him, perhaps it would be a good idea if he *did* go to the local comprehensive, at that. From what she'd seen of the little ladies of the neighborhood, he'd soon have that patronizing attitude knocked out of him, and a good thing, too.

"This has been a momentary aberration," she said, giving her nose a final wipe. "Normal services are now resumed."

She began plumping his pillows and straightening his blankets. There was a resentful squeak and Albert appeared from beneath the coverlet, his cozy nest disturbed by her sudden burst of housekeeping. "I think you should have a bath and a hair wash before you go to sleep," she said firmly. "And you need fresh pajamas, too—you've had these on for days."

"I've just got them nicely broken in!" he protested.

She plucked at a hole in the right sleeve. "Broken out, you mean. This top is a diary of disasters—I can see glue, ketchup, gravy, ink, and poster paint, all down the front. Come on, stop moaning. No, leave Albert here. He might fall in and drown."

Grumbling over the unfairness of it all, Max deposited Albert in a huge cardboard box of balled-up newspapers.

"Simon made that today to keep Albert from knocking the pieces off the chessboard," Max said. "It kept him quiet—sort of." As if to prove the efficacy of the young vicar's unusual gambit, the kitten immediately began a mad scrabble, picking out a ball and chasing it around the box, then changing direction when another took its eye. Max grinned. "That's his crazy box."

Tess looked down at the kitten as it excitedly continued its manic circular pursuit. "I know just how he feels," she said.

During a humiliating night of waking and sleeping, Tess confronted herself and was not impressed. What an idiot she'd been—what a fool! Why hadn't she seen it before?

All her troubles had to do with the McMurdo house. They must do.

She thought back to Mrs. McMurdo and their first trip to the house all those weeks ago. Hadn't Dolly said something about "Harry's little treasure"? At the time she'd thought the woman was being sarcastic about the house itself, but could there have been more to it than that? Suppose there had been some family story about the old man having a secret hoard of money, which Dolly only took half-seriously, but which Archie had taken to heart?

Suppose he'd followed his aunt to London and—when she made no fabulous discovery—decided to do a little exploring of his own? Ernie had said, just before they started the restoration work, that he thought "kids" had been in the house at night, disturbing things. What if it hadn't been kids—but Archie, searching for something?

And then she'd arrived on the scene, and gotten in his way.

What would he have done then?

Decided to get her *out* of his way, of course. He could easily have pumped Dolly about Tess—heard all about Roger's death and then Max's illness—and decided to use the situation.

Because he thought she'd found what he'd been searching for.

"We want the money, Mrs. Leland. . . . Give it back." That's what the caller had said. It seemed so obvious now.

The burglary, the phone calls, the threats—that had to have been Archie. When they hadn't worked, he'd decided to try criticizing the restoration work. But no luck. So he'd turned to charm. That hadn't worked, either. So he'd gone to Adrian and tried to get her fired. That would have gotten the work suspended, and while he pretended to be choosing another decorator, he'd really be searching for the money, unobserved and unimpeded.

But where was it?

The house had been almost literally torn to pieces while they installed new wiring and plumbing and put in the central heating system. The attic had been completely exposed when they'd put on a new roof. All the window frames had been removed and replaced, the chimneys swept and repaired, even many of the walls had been stripped right down and replastered. What was *left*, for goodness' sake? She frowned in the darkness, and then her eyes flew open and she stared into the shadows. Of course.

The cellar.

22

While the vista of Cambridge under sunlight is uplifting and noble, Nightingale felt that in mid-morning rain the town revealed its true nature—quiet, enclosed, introspective. Steamy windows in teashops and cafés bespoke earnest conversations within, lights glimmering in the various libraries told of shoulders hunched over books and hurriedly scribbled essays, while brief flares of blue light, random metallic ticks and deadly silences emanating from within the Cavendish laboratories told of heaven knew what next.

He walked slowly across Trinity's Great Court, practically alone in the vast expanse. He passed one or two hurrying scholars and a muttering academic, all head-down into the rain. In the distance two gowned figures marched in almost military tandem beneath a large blue umbrella. The stormy sky pressed down, with torn rags of smaller and darker clouds moving quickly beneath a pale-gray canopy.

The line between town and gown was a sharp one, as always. In contrast to Trinity's peace, the street beyond was as clotted with cars as any London thoroughfare, and a horde of Saturday-morning shoppers jostled over the pavements. Around and between the road and foot traffic wove the bicycles, their riders for the most part encased in plastic ponchos, rain speckling their spectacles and dripping down from hatbrims or noses. In their baskets or trapped over rear wheels under elasticated ropes, rode awkward bundles of books, haphazardly encased in layers of plastic carrier bags. Under the banners of Gateway, Safeway, Sainsburys, Marks and Spencer, and Gupta's Groceries were transports of Herodotus, Thucydides, Darwin, Donne, and Drucker, safe from the rain, but still—and always—vulnerable to undergraduate attack.

The cheekbones of the cyclists were flushed with exertion, but they looked pale and waxy with cold and damp around the jawline. They seemed, for the most part, unbearably young, and he envied them—knowing that his envy stamped him forever old and severed at last his tenuous connection to that age which parents think wonderful but students know to be exhausting, confusing, and full of strain.

He'd been happy here.

He was not happy to be back.

Not, at least, on this mission. Always behind him he could hear the Yard accountants' footsteps, drawing near. He should have had a week to suss out John Soame—to talk casually to academics, students, his bank manager, his landlady if he had one, and so on. The bits and pieces that reveal a man are rarely found in a hurry—one day would never be enough.

It gave him only one real option.

Bardy Philpott.

Bardy had been head porter at Brendan College, Tim's alma mater. Brendan was one of the "newer" additions to the University, being less than two centuries old. Brendan bore its nouveau stigma gracefully. The blatant red bricks chosen by its founder had long since been hidden behind trembling ivy. The paneled rooms and hallways had gradually acquired the desirable patina of age by the simple expedient of successive masters allowing smoking everywhere until well after World War II.

Nightingale made a stop on his way to Little Badger Lane, to acquire a small offering of Bardy's favorite tobacco and malt whiskey. The old man was retired now, and living in a very bijou residence acquired for him by his son, who had "done well" after leaving Trinity with honors and going on to become a Queen's Counsel much given to annoying the Met by gleefully picking holes in their evidence.

Nightingale was astonished to discover that Bardy actually remembered him by name and corridor. When he considered the numbers of young men who had filtered through Brendan before, during, and since his own stay there, it seemed an impossible feat, and he said so.

"'Memory is the warder of the brain,'" intoned Bardy, proving he, at least, had not changed during the intervening years. His speech was still larded with quotes and misquotes from Shakespeare. He was always to be discovered reading the Bard in the Porter's Lodge—hence his nickname—apparently thinking that such a scholarly pursuit was one befitting his position in the college. Bets had been taken as to what other book might be hidden behind the rubbed blue cover of his massive *Complete Collected*, but despite furtive forays into the P'Lodge taken as dares, no rogue copies of Raymond Chandler or *Playboy* had ever been discovered.

Bardy Philpott was unusual in other ways, too. Unlike most porters he was tall, and cadaverous in appearance, his long and melancholy visage convincing callow undergraduates that he lacked a sense of humor. Certainly he was strict in his application of the rules, but those who took the trouble to know him better soon discovered a wry, dry slant of mind lurked behind his lowering brow. And, while he was firm, he was not entirely unyielding, and had often turned a blind page of his Shakespeare while a late returnee skulked past the P'Lodge.

He accepted Nightingale's offering of tobacco and whiskey with grave appreciation, and led him past his retired bowler—which hung in honorable estate on a separate peg in the hall—through to his snug sitting room. He loomed oddly against the chintz and exposed beams, and when Tim commented on the room's attractions, Bardy snorted.

"Daughter-in-law did it all. Never asked me. When she finished, there wasn't a chair in the place I could sit in." He sank into the one jarring item in the room—a huge and ugly club chair covered with cracked brown leatherette which Tim remembered had taken up a great deal of the space in Bardy's lodge. "Bursar let me take this when I retired," he said, tapping his large bony fingers on the worn arms. "Probably would have had to talk to visitors while lying on the floor, otherwise." He grinned, exposing large, even teeth. "Does my heart good to see her wince at it every time she drops by. Which fortunately isn't often."

They spent a few minutes establishing vital trivia, filling in the cracks between the years. Although it was still early, Bardy had provided them both with a stiff drink, and now raised his glass and an eyebrow. "I never would have placed you with the constabulary. You must have changed a lot."

"I hope so," Tim said. "Looking back, I'd say I was pretty much a self-righteous prig in those days."

"Would have thought that was a prime qualification for policing," Bardy said slyly, but there was no rancor in it. The old man leaned back and searched his memory for something suitable. "'In every honest hand a whip to lash the rascals naked through the world,'" he said finally. He opened his eyes and looked at Tim with lively interest. "I'm assuming the honesty, mind."

"Depends on your definition, doesn't it?" Tim smiled. "So far I don't think I've been too bad."

"And tomorrow?"

Tim shrugged.

Bardy nodded. "I suppose that's honest, too," he conceded. He took another sip of his drink. "What particular rascal are you after today?"

"John Soame," Tim said.

"Has he killed someone?" Bardy asked in some surprise.

"No. Why? Would you have expected him to?" Nightingale asked, rather startled by this leap to the worst possible conclusion. Was he more right to suspect Soame than he'd thought?

"Most people expected him to murder his wife," Bardy said, obviously worried that he'd said the wrong thing. "But as bad as she was, he never raised a hand to her that we heard of—and we would have heard."

Exactly. Tim's decision to come here had been based on just that. "Was she so terrible?"

"Yes," Bardy said flatly. "I would have murdered her, if she'd been my wife. 'A most pernicious woman.'"

"You're speaking in the past tense, I notice."

"She died out east somewhere, in the end. Let him off the hook. Funny thing was, he was upset by it." Bardy paused to consider this aberration. "Maybe he felt guilty because he wished it would happen, but never could bring himself to do it. Maybe it was regret. Or annoyance, even. No satisfaction in having her drop dead where he couldn't see it." He began to fill his pipe. "If not for that, then what?"

Tim explained a little of the Leland case, naming no names, and that he was short of time. "As he's new on the scene, I want to find out as much about him as I can," he said.

"Fact or fiction?"

"As much of either as possible."

Bardy smiled. "'If a lie may do thee grace, I'll gild it

with the happiest terms I have.' I take it you know about the two girls."

"Two girls?"

"Yes. The reason he's not here now is because the Master suggested a sabbatical. It was thought better to get him away until the gossip died down. He wasn't really due for one for a few years, yet. They were embarrassed, of course—but they didn't want to lose him."

Slowly the story came out. Two girls—close friends, it later turned out—had alleged that John Soame had subjected them to sexual harrassment in order to ensure good grades. He'd denied it strenuously, and had—in the end—been exonerated. But the damage had been considerable, both to him and to the college. "They should never have let women into Brendan," Bardy concluded. "These two were not good scholars, and he'd been tough on one of them—to the point where she put her friend up to siding with her, figuring it would excuse her poor performance in her first-year exams."

"What happened to her?"

Bardy sucked the flame down from four matches before he spoke. "Father is a magistrate," he said.

"So nothing happened to her," Tim concluded wearily.

"Just starting her final year." He sucked again, blew smoke, seemed satisfied and leaned back. "Not many friends, though. Just the one, now. Just the one."

"And they sent Soame away."

"He was pretty shaken by it. Went a little odd, which is hardly surprising, what with the life his wife had led him for years, and then her dying, and then these girls. And money troubles, too, I hear. Started to drink a bit. Got into a fight with a senior tutor from Trinity—bit of a sarcastic bastard, as it happens. Still, no excuse for public fisticuffs, is it?"

"I don't know," Tim said. "It might be."

Bardy regarded him with some amusement. "You accept excuses, do you? Even in the Met?"

"I hope so," Tim said.

"'Nothing emboldens sin so much as mercy.'"

"'Some rise by sin, and some by virtue fall,'" Tim countered.

Bardy grinned—an unnerving sight—and nodded. "Anyway, the Master decided to grant him his sabbatical so he could pull himself together. But if the Met are interested in him . . ." He waited.

"As far as I know, he hasn't done anything criminal," Tim said. He didn't specify further. "You say he went 'a little odd.' What do you mean by that?"

Bardy shrugged. "Thought people were ganging up on him, conspiring against him. Not just the girls—although it was them that set it off, I suppose—but the other tutors, the Dean, even the Master. I believe it's called paranoia, is that right? Suspicious of everyone."

"Was he 'odd' to the point of imagining things?"

Bardy shifted uncomfortably in his big chair. "I don't like to speak ill of the man, Tim. I liked him, and felt sorry for him. We all did—it wasn't his fault."

"To the point of imagining things?" Tim persisted.

Bardy sighed. "Some."

Tim leaned forward. "To the point of doing something about it?" he asked.

There was a long pause.

Finally Bardy Philpott spoke. "He gave us a few rough nights," he said slowly.

"Had to admit him to Addenbrookes for a couple of days," Detective Sergeant Flynn told Tim that afternoon in the lounge of the Eagle. "They sedated him, made him sleep it off, so to speak. And to give him his due, he stayed quiet after that. Must have put him on tranquilizers, I suppose. We didn't want to bring charges. We like to be discreet about goings-on in the colleges. God knows, there are enough batty ones wandering around to fill a loony bin and overflow into the Cam—we can't arrest them all or there'd be no one to lecture, would there? But barricading himself in his rooms and shouting that he'd kill anyone who came inside—we had to do something about that."

"Did he have a weapon?"

Flynn smiled. "He had a carving set—you know—big knife and fork. Kind of thing you give as a wedding present. Knife was as dull as a bread stick, but the fork could have done a bit of damage. Never used it—never intended to use it, in my opinion. Two minutes after we broke the door in he collapsed and started to cry. Poor bastard. He'd just had too much put on him, that's all. More of a danger to himself than anyone else. My chief inspector thought the same, and decided to let it go. We have to be flexible here, you know. We get heavy with them, they'll get heavy back. Too many of them, too few of us. Not worth it."

"Can you tell me anything else about Soame?"

Flynn shrugged and picked up the other half of his ham sandwich. "My sister-in-law Edna is a bedder at Brendan. She often brought back stories about his wife running around with other men and that, and a rotten tongue on her, to boot. One of the kind that likes to stir things up for the hell of it, know what I mean? Enough to turn God himself into a woman-hater, apparently. A few years of that must have affected Soame somewhere inside—but Edna says he was 'always lovely.' She thought the world of him—all the women on the staff did, according to her. Not what I'd call a Cary Grant to look at, but something about him appealed to them." The last bite of sandwich disappeared. "Mind you, if they'd seen him swinging that carving knife, they might have thought otherwise."

23

When Tess arrived at the McMurdo house, it was locked and apparently empty. She'd expected to find Adrian here, after his pronouncements on the telephone, but he was nowhere in sight. As it was Saturday, there were no workmen around, either.

The prospect of prowling the house alone was not an attractive one, but she'd gone to some trouble to get over here, and was determined to get to the bottom of all this.

The answer had to be here, somewhere.

She opened the front door and entered the unlit entrance hall, which felt cold and gritty. If there *was* something hidden in this old house, something valuable and still undiscovered, it would be pretty amazing. Workmen were here every day, and the place was locked at night. Of course, it could be broken into like any empty house, but she had a feeling—also formulated during the previous long night—that something more was needed.

The oak staircase rose ahead of her, and broad arches opened into rooms on either side. Normally the place was filled with the sound of hammers pounding, boards creaking, the slop of plaster, and the whistling and chat of workmen. Now all was still and quiet—and yet there was a feeling that someone was here. Somewhere.

"Adrian?" she called in a tentative voice. It had started to rain again on the way over, and the house had a dank and gloomy atmosphere. As she went through the empty downstairs rooms, thunder grumbled disapprovingly overhead. She shivered in her damp coat.

They had been decorating the dining room at last. It had been the least damaged of all the rooms, and one of particularly graceful proportions. She had chosen a rich but darkish paper with a pattern of peacock feathers against a green background, and the minute she entered she saw that it had been a mistake. Even with only one wall completed she could tell she had misjudged the mood of the room, had hoped for too much light from the deep bay windows that overlooked the rear garden. Luncheon as well as evening meals would be taken in the dining room. In an evening glow of candlelight the peacock paper might seem mysterious and exotic, but at midday it would probably depress both appetites and conversation.

My goodness, she thought to herself. I hope Adrian didn't see this. Maybe Archie was right, maybe she was losing her grip. She took out a pencil and wrote in large letters beside the last strip: ERNIE—DON'T CONTINUE—WANT TO CHANGE PAPER.

Still thinking she might encounter an Adrian too sulky to answer her call, she went upstairs. Things were not so far advanced here, and in many places the plaster was still too wet to be painted or papered. Wires stuck out of the walls, awaiting the arrival of the special light fittings she'd ordered copied from a pattern she'd come across in an old catalog in the Victoria and Albert. Such a luxury, having an absolutely unlimited budget. Mrs. McMurdo might be annoying, and her absence might be awkward, but if she had interfered the way her damned nephew insisted on doing, the job would never be done.

After an unsuccessful tour of the upper floor, Tess went up to the attic, still with the expectation of meeting someone. Whether it was the rain or just the sounds of the old house adjusting to its new arrangements, she kept thinking she was not alone. But here, too, there was only empty space. She hadn't been up here since her first survey of the house with the architect. She remembered her disappointment when the long dusty area had revealed only cobwebs and spiders, instead of a treasure trove of trunks and old furniture.

They had discussed the possibility of converting the attic to another living floor, but the house was so large there was really no need. Since there were very few cupboards in the bedrooms below, the attic would really be needed for its original use—storage. If Mrs. McMurdo did employ servants, probably only one or two would live in. There was already provision for a small flat off the new kitchen, and there were three good-sized rooms over the garage that could be converted into an easily accessible flat, should the need arise for further employee accommodation.

She walked the length of the attic, which derived only limited illumination from the original dormer windows. This was supposed to have been augmented by the discreet installation of several windows on the rear roof slope, but the overcast sky and the sluicing pattern of raindrops on the slanting glass reduced this benefit considerably. Still, there was sufficient light to see that there was nothing here to interest her—or anyone else. The floor had been up because Ernie and his men had replaced some boards when they rewired the ceiling circuit on the floor below, and the entire roof had been removed and replaced, so any secret rooms or hidey-holes would have been exposed long ago.

If there were any secrets left in the McMurdo mansion, then her midnight thoughts had to be correct—they were in the cellar. And she couldn't avoid going down there any longer.

Uncle Harry had once written to his Australian relatives begging for money to "protect our precious family heritage." McMurdo had sent a few thousand Australian dollars and asked for details, but had heard no more until the solicitor's letter arrived, announcing Uncle Harry's sudden demise. Mrs. McMurdo had thought it a great joke, and told Tess with some glee how her husband had been fooled. "The old wowser probably blew it all on beer," she'd said. "That's probably what killed him in the end."

Or had Uncle Harry been telling the truth?

Had he wanted the money to "protect" something valuable, and then died before he could tell his nephew about it?

Gold? Jewels? Paintings?

And what kind of protection? The more Tess thought about it, the more she was drawn to the idea that Uncle Harry had had some kind of safe installed in the cellar. Installed and concealed.

At some point in the house's checkered history, the cellar had been converted from kitchen and storage to a small flat. She seemed to remember Mrs. McMurdo muttering something about Uncle Harry living "like a mole"—so presumably, when the place had been converted to bed-sitters, he must have spent his last days down there in gritty solitude.

There was an outside entrance, at the side of the house, where tradesmen would have called on the cook who ruled the huge basement kitchen in the old days. The inside staircase that Tess descended also led directly into this old kitchen, now devoid of everything except dirt. The windows that overlooked the small front areaway were thick with muddy grime, and very little light came through. Tess had come prepared with a torch, and was glad of it.

Behind the kitchen, a long passage led back into darkness. The first door Tess opened revealed a very primitive toilet. Other small, windowless rooms opening off the passage had probably been used for the storage of vegetables and preserved comestibles, and possibly for servant accommodation. The scullery maid would have slept down here, certainly, the air of her unventilated room half poisoned with the fumes left on her clothes by the various polishes she was expected to use daily on grates, cutlery, and brasswork. Toward the rear of the passage was a larger room. It had a small fireplace that used the same chimney which served the large library fireplace above. Although this back room was dark, it had a pair of wide, shallow windows that looked out on a steeply rising slope now overgrown with weeds. Next to this room, and sharing the chimney on the other side, was a smaller room, also with windows, although these were tiny and almost blanked out by overgrowth. These two potentially pleasant "garden" rooms would have undoubtedly comprised the cook's accommodation—parlour and bedroom. If the original McMurdos had employed a couple, it would have been for both butler and cook—a common and useful domestic combination.

At the very end of the long passage was a wooden door, and Tess knew that behind it lay the wine cellar, hollowed out beneath the garden, and so far untouched by the workmen. When she turned the handle and opened the door, it came toward her accompanied by a cool, earthy breath of dark air.

Like a grave.

"Oh, for goodness' sake, stop trying to scare yourself," Tess said aloud, and the echo of her voice made everything immediately worse. It seemed to stir rustles and whispers in the room behind her, causing her to glance back over her shoulder in some trepidation. But no one was there. Back at the beginning of the passage, beyond the old kitchen, the sound of a car driving by on the street impersonally confirmed her solitude, its occupant humming past in total ignorance of her existence, the warm purr of its engine coming, passing, gone, leaving an even greater silence behind.

Of course she should have waited until Monday, when Ernie and the men would be around to assist her. The floor within the cellar was uneven, she could sprain an ankle, lie there for days, there might be rats, there definitely were spiders—

But she had wanted to meet Adrian, counter any disapproval or disappointment he might feel about her work. In order to be here to do just that, she'd had to call Mrs. Grimble to come over and look after Max, because John had previously arranged to meet someone at the British Museum this morning. So for better or worse, she was on her own.

"Good God, woman, get on with it," she muttered, and entered the vast but strangely oppressive space beyond the wooden door.

Almost immediately she came up against the end of the first empty rack, crumbling and grimy. Beyond it stood another, and another, rank and file, some ten in all, their cobwebbed honeycombs now empty where once hundreds of green, brown, and crystal bottles had glittered and waited in the cool dark for a summons from above. After all, Victorian gentlemen prided themselves on their cellars, and according to Mrs. McMurdo, the builder and first owner of the mansion had been a noted collector of fine vintages.

All gone now.

Just the empty racks, sentinels of an earlier grandeur, guarding an empty treasury. For wine was valuable—and old wine, fine wine, even more so. But of course! That was it! "Harry's little treasure"!

Poor old Harry, writing blearily to his relatives in Australia about the family "heritage," could simply have meant the hoard of wine kept here. The last of the English McMurdos probably drank his way to oblivion on some of the rarest wines in the world. Many might have turned to vinegar during their long incarceration, but perhaps he'd been beyond noticing. Or perhaps he'd been cannier than that—perhaps he'd found out the value of some of them and had sold them off to an eager dealer. That certainly made sense. And, if that was true, it meant that Harry's little treasure was no more—for not a bottle remained. She played her torch over each rack to verify what she knew already to be true. Not one produced a reflected wink of glass.

Tess frowned. If the wine had indeed been the treasure, she need look no further. But if it was not, there was not much further she *could* look, for the wine cellar was the last room in the house.

True, she had stood in the doorway—as she did now—to do her sketching, and had not explored the room further, leaving that to the architect. But he, too, had seemed reluctant to remain in the oddly claustrophobic room, and so their examination had been rather superficial, a matter of quickly estimated measurements, no more.

"Last hope," Tess muttered, and reluctantly entered.

She walked between the first two racks to the rear wall, and then did a quick perimeter of the room, counting her steps out of habit.

The left wall was five steps shorter than it should have been. And on the floor below it, there was a scraped mark just visible under the accumulated dust of years.

So she'd been right! A false wall had been subtly built in on a slant in front of the original wall, creating a wedge-shaped space between them. But how to get into it? She played her torch across the stonework, and saw that it was not stone at all, but some kind of modern artificial surface that had been rubbed over with dirt to aid concealment. She caught a brief, reflective flash in a line of "mortar," and leaned closer. A ring was embedded there, made of steel or brass. It had been painted over in an attempt to blend in with the mortar, but the paint had flaked away. She rubbed at it, then inserted two fingers and tried twisting it. No. She pulled—and was rewarded with a scraping sound. She pulled again, harder.

With a groan of unoiled and unused hinges, the wall swung toward her. It was surprisingly light for its dimensions, which in a way confirmed its modern construction. When there was space enough, Tess stepped through and used her torch.

More racks. Not for wine, but for books.

Shelf upon shelf of books! Her heart gave a thump. First editions? Rare illuminated manuscripts? Now that she thought back, wasn't there something about the original McMurdo who built this house having been some kind of collector? Where had she seen it, that oblique reference?

She went forward, and propping her torch to give her light, she took a book at random and opened it. Turned a few pages. Returned it to the shelf and took one from another shelf. And another.

After a while, she began to laugh.

And laugh, and laugh.

There was a step behind her.

Behind her.

She turned, went to the opening between the real and the false wall, and saw the dark silhouette of a man outlined in the entrance of the wine cellar. But she was not afraid.

"Here's your 'treasure,' Archie," she giggled, holding out a large, copiously illustrated volume. "Uncle Harry's family heritage. No wonder he wanted to keep it hidden. About two hundred dirty books. As fine a collection of Victorian pornography as I've seen. I don't know what they're worth, but you're certainly welcome to them."

"Bitch."

She couldn't have heard correctly. "What?"

"Stubborn, stupid, silly bitch!" The voice was like a rasp against her, the hatred in it was salt in the wound. The figure took a step forward, out of the faint twilight of the corridor into the blackness of the wine cellar. She could hear his shuffling steps, and tried to put the torch beam onto him, to find his face, but before she could, there was a grunt, and then a most extraordinary sound.

Like huge dominoes falling.

And she knew, although she could not see them, that the wine racks had been pushed and were falling toward her in the dark. She cowered back against the crumbling whitewash of the stone wall behind her.

There was a splintering, crunching, thudding sound as the wine racks began to hit the side wall and one another, still falling toward her. Some instinct made her look up into the darkness over her head and she saw, for an instant, in the light of her rolling torch, the loom and rush of a great dark shape. She held up her arms for protection, but they were not enough against the weight of the rack. Broken, rotten wood cascaded around her as the massive bulk of the rack crashed against the frail barrier of the false wall, but kept falling, taking the new wood down with the old.

She screamed, but her voice could not be heard over the splintering crash of the successive wine racks as they broke over her, one after another.

Afterward, there was only silence.

And then footsteps, walking away.

24

Tess opened her eyes and saw only roses and honeysuckle—a bright flowery print on the folds of waving curtains. Turning her head, and clenching her teeth against a wave of pain and nausea, she encountered a barrier of chrome bars through which the calm gray eyes of a nurse were watching her carefully.

"Hello," the nurse said with a smile. "Decided to rejoin the living, have you?"

"Wha——what happened . . . ?" Tess's throat was raw and her lips were dry. The nurse stood up and lowered the bars to cradle her head while she sipped some water. Then she moved the protective sides back into position.

"You just rest and I'll fetch the doctor," the nurse said. "You've been in an accident, but you're safe in hospital now, and you're going to be just fine."

She went out, and there was a brief and confusing pause, during which Tess was certain her head had fallen off. Then the curtains moved aside and John Soame stood there, white-faced. "Thank God," he said. "I thought you were never going to wake up."

"What happened?"

He came over to stand awkwardly beside the high table onto which she was both blanketed and fenced. "We're not exactly certain," he said. "We expected you back well before tea. We waited and waited, but when you hadn't appeared by four, and hadn't called, I left Max with Mrs. Grimble and went over to the house. I finally found you under about five hundredweight of fallen wine racks." He took a deep breath. "You were so damned lucky, Tess. The racks fell against some kind of false wall, propped themselves over you like a house of cards, supporting each other and leaving you trapped but pretty well untouched underneath. I called the fire department. I could see you under there in the light from my torch but I couldn't shift the damn things. An ambulance man crawled in to make sure you were alive. . . ."

"Sorry I missed all the excitement," Tess said in a dry voice.

"More like it all missed you," John pointed out. "How did you manage to pull it all over on yourself like that?"

"I didn't," Tess said. It was coming back now, the shadowy figure in the wine cellar, the crash, the sound of footsteps going away, and then the blackness closing in. "Archie did it for me." She told him about the dark figure in the doorway. "I don't understand why he didn't bother to look at what I'd found, because I'm certain that's what it's all been about." She explained the theory that had taken her to the house in the first place. "Instead he seemed incredibly angry for some reason. He knocked over the racks out of sheer bad temper. That's what it seemed like, anyway."

"Well, he's obviously mad. He might have killed you."

"Well, in a way he did us a favor—the racks had to be demolished anyway," Tess said. "Did you see the books?"

He smiled wryly. "I was more interested in making sure you were alive, but I couldn't resist a quick glance at one or two, since I assumed they were why you were there."

"And?"

"An interesting collection. Possibly quite valuable."

"What does Adrian say about it?"

An odd look crossed John's face. "Nobody seems to know where Adrian is," he said. "Once they were certain you were alive, I called him, but there was no answer at his house. I tracked down his secretary at home. She was under the impression Adrian had also intended to go to the McMurdo house this morning, but there was no sign of him when I arrived."

"Or when I arrived," Tess said. "One of the reasons I went over there was to talk with him. I thought if I could find what Archie was after, it would prove to him that my work wasn't the problem at all. He was so cross and almost frantic about the possibility of losing Mrs. McMurdo as a client."

"Well, he's been having real financial difficulties since his partner left."

"But we've got lots of commissions," Tess said in some puzzlement. "We're very busy."

"Are you? Or is it just Adrian flapping around the place saying there isn't enough time to do anything, that he must get on, must get on?"

"Oh." She had forgotten how well John knew his ex-brother-in-law. His picture of Adrian was a familiar one. Perhaps too familiar. "He hasn't fired anyone—he even took me on when he didn't need me."

"Oh, he needed you, all right. It's been a long time since Adrian did a full commission himself, and he wanted someone 'special' to give him the cachet he'd lost when Jason left."

"I'm no replacement for Jason," Tess said.

"Ah, but you're American, and attractive, and—according to Adrian—very clever. But his problem is more immediate than that. As I understand it, the perfidious Jason took quite a chunk out of the company's bank account when he left, saying it was a return on his original investment. It might have been, I suppose. He was the onc who handled the books—Adrian doesn't know anything about keeping accounts. I gather some creditors have been baying at the door. Adrian is getting desperate."

Tess was very confused—and it was getting worse. She felt very odd talking to him while lying down like a baby in a cot, and her head was thudding painfully. He kept fading away, like a bad television picture. "But he never said anything about all this to me."

John nodded. "It's a Brevitt trait, I'm afraid, keeping your actions—and your intentions—a secret. They're not exactly the most stable of families, either."

His tone was both sad and bitter, and she remembered his wife had been a Brevitt. Suddenly another and very horrible thought occurred to her. What if the figure in the doorway hadn't been Archie at all?

What if it had been Adrian?

The curtain was swished back, and a white-coated doctor appeared with the announcement that there was no skull fracture, but because she had been unconscious for so long, they were going to keep her in overnight for observation.

"No," Tess said. "I want to go home."

The doctor, a young man with a topknot of very curly blond hair that made him resemble a benign sheep, told her that would be very dangerous under the circumstances. "Should there be a lesion, there might be subdural bleeding, a buildup in pressure—"

"I think you should do as he says," John advised.

"I'm sure you do, and I'm sure he's right," Tess said, struggling to sit up. "But I'm still going home." She got down from the examination table and struggled to get her feet into her shoes. Why was it so difficult? They were just shoes. Damn. DAMN!

For another thought had come plunging unbidden into her aching brain. What if the figure in the doorway had been neither Archie, nor Adrian, but the owner of the voice on the phone? The one who had said, "Watch over that boy of yours"?

John Soame's hand was under her elbow as he put his key in the lock of the front door. "I'm sure everything is just fine," he told her soothingly.

"But she didn't answer the phone," Tess wailed.

"Perhaps they were watching television and she didn't hear it—" John began, then stopped. They had walked down the hall and into chaos.

"My God," Soame gasped, and held Tess up as she sagged against him, her eyes wide with disbelief.

"Oh no, oh no!" she moaned.

The house had been torn apart. Pictures had been taken from the walls and smashed, furniture was slashed and stripped, rugs were up as well as floorboards. There didn't seem to be a single thing left whole or untouched anywhere.

"Max!" Tess screamed.

There was an answering wail from upstairs. John Soame's long legs took him up the stairs three at a time, and he was in front of Max's door in seconds. The door was locked. "Max! Mrs. Grimble!"

"Saints alive, it's the perfessor. We're all right!" He could hear Mrs. Grimble within, and there was a scrabbling as the door was unlocked. He was nearly knocked flying as she erupted like Vesuvius into the hall. "Where is he?" she screamed.

Tess had managed the stairs, and her heart nearly stopped at the old woman's words. Then she saw Max's face peering around the doorjamb, and she sank down onto the top step, suddenly legless with relief.

"What happened?" Soame was demanding.

Mrs. Grimble glared at him, as if it had all been his fault. "About ten minutes after you left, he come. We were playing Snap, and I heard the front door open. I called down, but there was no answer. Something warned me. Something told me!"

"*I* told you," Max said, clinging to Tess. It was difficult to see who was comforting whom.

"I heard noises, footsteps coming up the stairs. I didn't like it, so I slammed the door and locked it," Mrs. Grimble announced melodramatically. Two red spots of color shone high on her thin cheeks, and the flowers on her hat seemed to tremble with indignation and excitement. "He come to the door, he rattled the knob, he said he wanted to talk to Max. Said he wanted to take him to his mother, because she was badly hurt and was asking for him. Well, if that had been true, he would have been a policeman, wouldn't he? With a woman constable, because of the boy. Even *I* know that. So we didn't say a word, Max and me. We just sat there, and he just stood outside the door there for a while. It was as if we could hear him thinking. I suppose he could have knocked the door down, but he didn't. He went away. A few minutes later, the crashing and the banging started up."

"Did you recognize the voice?" Soame asked.

"No," said Max over his shoulder.

"What's he done?" Mrs. Grimble demanded, starting toward the stairs. Now assured of personal safety, she could afford to enjoy the dramatic aspects of the situation. Her name might even get into the paper. Weeks of being the center of attention at the launderette beckoned her on. She paused by Tess.

"We might have been killed in our beds!" she announced rather inaccurately, and edged past her, grumbling.

"You'd best get back into bed," John said to Max.

"I don't want to get back into bed. I want to look after Mum. What happened to her? Who was here? Who—"

"Hooligans. Hooligans!" Mrs. Grimble was shrieking from down below. "Oh, my God! Oh, my God!" She could be heard going from room to room, freshly shocked by every new discovery.

Max looked at John and then at his mother. His face was drawn and he looked like a fretful little old man. He went over to look over the balustrade, then turned back. "What's going on, anyway?" he asked suspiciously. He looked at his mother. "You look scared," he said. "Who hurt you? Was it the same person who was here? Why did he mess up the house?"

Soame answered for Tess, who was leaning against the balustrade and looked in no condition to answer questions. "Your mother is fine. There was an accident at the house she's been restoring, and she got knocked out, but the doctors have X-rayed her all over, and she's not badly hurt. I don't know what happened here, but I'm going to find out. Okay?"

He and the boy locked glances. "Okay." It was clear that it wasn't okay, but Max didn't quite know how to argue about it. Where to start? His face was pale, and his eyes were shadowed as he looked at his mother. "Mum?" He spoke softly.

"It's all right, Max." Tess straightened up, blinked her eyes clear. "It's my opinion that we have been visited by a poltergeist."

"Oh, sure," Max said, totally unconvinced.

"And it's also my opinion that we should have a cup of tea before we do anything else." She managed to stand up—probably the hardest physical thing she'd ever done. "You go back to bed, and we'll bring it up. All right?"

He nodded, and slowly, reluctantly, he did as she asked. But he knew, they all knew, that it wasn't all right at all.

When Soame returned from the kitchen, where Mrs. Grimble was wailing as she worked, Tess was still sitting in the rocking chair where he had left her, her face paper-white under the slow-running tears. He patted her shoulder, but there was no response as she stared blankly at the overturned and gutted sofa.

It hadn't been much of a house, she thought, but it had been home, full of the small and silly things that had no intrinsic value but were precious to her. Every piece of furniture had a history. Junk-shop prowls with Roger, or early-morning visits to country markets on the rare weekends when they stole away together, afternoons of searching for the right materials, evenings of reupholstering, with Roger handing her the nails while he kept one eye on a televised soccer match. And the pictures, also bought in junk shops or markets, occasionally even on a visit to a friend's gallery when times were good, discussed over a paper cup of tea from a stall or a glass of white wine at a preview, choices narrowed, prizes carried off and hung in various places until the right spot was found. The hugs when they knew they'd been right, the giggles when they admitted they'd been had—all part of it. All important. All still Roger when Roger was gone. Grief overwhelmed her as it had not upon his death, because all that they had had together, all the marriage had been in the beginning and through the years, was tied up in these broken bits of wood and cloth and paper. Roger had still been here, somehow, his presence triggered and maintained by those memories, and now all that had been torn apart.

Now he was *really* gone.

And there was just Max. Thank God, there was still Max.

Seeing she was in a dark world of her own, Soame went into the hall, dragged the telephone out from under the overturned bench, and called the local police. They told him to sit down and touch nothing. It seemed only minutes before they arrived, bringing a sense of order to the scene, their sensible voices and confident manner briskly blowing away the miasma of violence and violation that hung in the rooms. It was a damn shame, they agreed, in tones that indicated they knew lip service to convention was not going to help, but was very necessary. They'd seen it before and they'd see it again, and they knew how to deal with it, so not to worry. "Anything taken? How about a list? No hurry. Who's your insurance agent? You look absolutely shattered, Mrs. Leland, would you like us to call your GP?" They were sympathetic and efficient. While two of them surveyed the damage, a woman police constable comforted Tess with practical suggestions for salvage and a hot mug of tea conjured somehow from the shattered kitchen and the equally shattered Mrs. Grimble, who was now blaming herself for the entire thing.

When she had finished her tea, Tess looked so absolutely devastated that Soame sent her to bed and agreed with the police that calling her GP would be sensible, under the circumstances. The doctor could look in on Max, too, who was now getting a little too flushed and bright-eyed as he waited for an explanation and some kind of comfort. A forensic team arrived from the local police station and began photographing the scene and attempting to find fingerprints. They had to take Tess's prints (she hardly noticed), Max's (who was thrilled and was given a copy of his own to keep), Mrs. Grimble's, and John Soame's—all for elimination.

John then made another phone call. An hour later, Detective Sergeant Tim Nightingale and Detective Chief Inspector Abbott were standing in the doorway, looking around as the forensic team finished their work. Soame glared at Nightingale with a mixture of anger and appeal.

"*Now* will you believe that Mrs. Leland and the boy are in danger?" he asked grimly. "*Now* will you take this seriously?"

25

Tim Nightingale glanced at him. "I always have taken it seriously," he said calmly. "But there wasn't much for me to go on, was there?"

"Is this enough?" John demanded, waving an arm around at the heaps of rubble that had once furnished the Leland home. "It was planned, the whole thing was planned."

Abbott raised an eyebrow. "What makes you say that?"

"It's obvious, isn't it? She was attacked by Archie McMurdo. He knew I would have to go out to look for her, or to identify her body, or whatever, and when I did—he got in and tried to get at the boy, who he probably thought would have been left alone. When he couldn't get at the boy, he did this."

Abbott looked confused. Sergeant Nightingale had returned from Cambridge and brought with him some interesting information—interesting enough to jolt Abbott from indifference to intrigue. He now understood why Tim had become caught up in the case—the people and the situation were ambiguous and somehow did not mesh comfortably. There was a feel of jagged edges, a picture out of focus, and pieces missing. They had been discussing Soame when the call came through concerning the Leland house. And now a new element was being introduced. He glanced at Nightingale and saw that he, too, seemed puzzled. "And just who is Archie McMurdo?" Abbott asked slowly.

"Oh, Archie is—" Soame paused. "I thought you knew about Archie," he said to Nightingale.

"He's news to me."

With a visible effort at self-control, Soame explained about their visitor of the previous evening, the trouble he'd been causing Tess at the house, and the threats he'd made after he'd been thrown out.

"You threw him out bodily?" Abbott asked. He gazed at John Soame with new interest.

"I had no alternative, the man was drunk and objectionable. I felt Mrs. Leland was in some danger from him."

"Fair enough." Abbott sent Nightingale a glance, and Tim went into the hall, where he had a low-voiced conversation with one of the other policemen. When he returned, Soame was standing with his fists clenched by his sides, and Chief Inspector Abbott was gazing into space reflectively. "So you think the scenario is as follows—just let me talk this out, if you will," Abbott was saying.

"Go on," Soame said tightly. He apparently had mixed feelings about the appearance of a superior officer on the scene. While he welcomed the presence of rank as an indicator of the importance of the situation, he resented the authority so represented. It had been easier dealing with Nightingale.

Abbott was reciting for his own benefit as much as anyone else's. There had been too many cases crossing his desk, too many investigations in progress, and he needed to know exactly where they were on this one. "A few months ago, Roger Leland was killed by a hit-and-run driver. His son was in the car with him, but was uninjured. Since that time he has suffered with nightmares, and on top of that he caught rheumatic fever and is now convalescing here at home. In order that Mrs. Leland may continue her work, you have been hired to tutor the boy in exchange for accommodation. Right so far?"

"Yes."

"In the past few weeks Mrs. Leland has received several 'silent' phone calls—"

"Some of them were threatening. They threatened her, and her son, and demanded money."

"Unfortunately, you have no proof of that, other than Mrs. Leland's word. Anyone else who has picked up the telephone has heard only silence."

Soame looked stunned. "Are you saying she's *lying?*"

"Mrs. Leland felt confident enough to go to a large empty house on her own," Abbott pointed out.

"In broad daylight. And she expected Adrian to be there."

"Adrian being?"

"Her employer, my ex-brother-in-law, Adrian Brevitt." Soame was obviously not happy with Abbott's attitude. "And you're forgetting the intruder we had the other night."

"Oh, yes—the intruder, who forced open a door but didn't come in."

"He might have—"

Abbott ignored him and continued his résumé. "Now, in addition to all that, you tell us that for the past few weeks, a man named Archie McMurdo has been harassing Mrs. Leland at her work—a mansion she is restoring for his aunt, Mrs. Dolly McMurdo. He annoys her and the workmen, so naturally she goes out to dinner with him."

"You make it sound irrational," John muttered. "I think she was trying to put the relationship on a friendlier basis—for Adrian's sake." Obviously agitated now, Soame began moving around the room, trying to put a few things back in place. Abbott stayed where he was and continued. Nightingale, fascinated by the older officer's technique, watched and listened. There *was* a case here. He'd been right. And now Abbott was taking it, and him, seriously.

"She was cooperating for her *boss's* sake, then, rather than her own," Abbott said, slightly annoyed at Soame's pedantic interruption. "But then this Archie McMurdo shows up here at the house—"

"Drunk."

"Drunk, and makes an unwelcome pass at Mrs. Leland, which you interrupt. You throw him out. He makes threats and accusations, which unsettle Mr. Brevitt and, through him, Mrs. Leland. So she suddenly decides to go to the house today."

"Yes."

"When Mrs. Leland doesn't return, you decide to go to the house to find her."

"Yes." Soame was continuing to pick up objects, as if searching for something.

"You leave the boy in the charge of the housekeeper."

"Yes."

"And not ten minutes after you leave, someone arrives here and tries to get to the boy."

Soame whirled. "Exactly my point! As if he'd just been waiting for his chance!"

Abbott looked at him and nodded. "Yes. But when the housekeeper locks the door and refuses to come out or to answer him, he doesn't shout, or argue, or attempt to break it down, but goes meekly away and vents his anger on the house itself." Nightingale glanced at Soame, gauging his responses to Abbott's questions. "Does that sound like he really wanted to kidnap the boy?" Abbott asked, with what sounded like sincere interest.

"How would *I* know what he really wants?" Soame

demanded. "How can you? How do we know he's even sane?"

Nightingale shifted his position, leaning against his other shoulder, arms folded. He was looking at the professor with new eyes. "Just where is the McMurdo house?" he asked abruptly.

In a voice that trembled with exasperation, John gave him the address. He explained Tess's sudden suspicion that there might be something hidden there. "Which, as a matter of fact, there was." He told them about the false wall and the collection of Victorian pornography. "I didn't take time to really assess it, but it's probably quite valuable," he concluded.

"Is it?" Nightingale asked. His eyes were hooded as he looked at Soame. "Of course, you'd know more about that than I would—that period is your specialty, isn't it?"

"Yes, but that's not the point," Soame argued. "The point is, this mad Australian followed her there and tried to get her out of the way—either by killing her or putting her in hospital."

"To what end?"

"To get at the boy, obviously."

"Why would he want the boy?"

"To force her to hand over what he thought was his."

"Which she had just found and offered to him, anyway? That hardly makes sense, Mr. Soame. You can't have it both ways—either he wanted what was hidden in the house, or he wanted the boy."

"Well, then, *you* tell me what's happening here!" John practically shouted as he moved toward Nightingale. "Give me *your* theories. Give me *your* explanations!"

"Take it easy, take it easy," Abbott said, taking hold of his arm. Soame glared at him, struggled for a moment, then stepped back.

Nightingale was being patient, but it was difficult. Considering all he had learned in Cambridge about

Soame, from both Bardy Philpott and the friendly local sergeant, it wasn't surprising the man's nerves were so shot. On the other hand, he was reacting rather strongly to someone else's troubles. If they *were* someone's else's troubles. He got out his notebook and opened it. "Let's go over it a step at a time and see what we've got, all right?"

"We just *did* that. You're wasting time, dammit!"

"I don't think so, Mr. Soame. What we have here is agreement on the facts and disagreement on their interpretation."

"No," Soame said. "What we have here is people being pigheaded, obstinate, and dangerously lax in doing their duty!"

"That's a matter of opinion too," Abbott said sharply.

"Then why aren't you looking for Archie McMurdo?"

"We are," Nightingale said.

"We're checking with the biggest hotels," Abbott explained patiently, knowing without having to ask that that was what Nightingale had put in operation during his whispered colloquy with the constable in the hall. It was the obvious step to take. "Then we'll move down to the smaller—"

"Fine, yes, fine," Soame said, barely controlling himself. "Good."

"Right. Now, Mrs. Leland went to the McMurdo house this morning, leaving you in charge of the boy."

"No. Her decision to go was unexpected, and I had made other arrangements for this morning, so she called Mrs. Grimble and asked *her* to come over and stay with the boy. Which she did."

"Very obliging of her. So you left here at what time?"

Soame frowned. "About ten-thirty, I suppose. My appointment was for eleven."

"And that was with?"

"Clarissa Montague—she's a specialist at the V and A."

"A specialist in what?"

"Oh, for—" Soame gritted his teeth. "Does it matter?"

"It might."

"Well, in Victorian architecture, then."

Abbott raised an eyebrow. "Really? And what did you discuss?" He paused. "I *can* check with Ms. Montague, you know."

Soame's shoulders sagged. "We discussed the McMurdo house."

"Oh, really?"

"I thought I might be of some help to Mrs. Leland. And it pertains to the research I'm doing as well."

"I see. Interesting." Nightingale wrote it down and seemed to dismiss it. "And Mrs. Leland left the house—when?"

"Shortly after I did, I suppose. I know she was just getting her coat out of the closet when I closed the front door behind me."

"Fine. And she went straight to the McMurdo house."

"I expect so."

"How long would that take her?" Abbott inquired.

"I have no idea. You'll have to ask her." Soame was restless. He picked up a picture and looked at the wall above where it lay, searching for the hook that had held it. He hung the picture back up, but as he did so, the last piece of its broken glass fell out and shattered at his feet. "Damn."

"What time did you leave the V and A?"

"I don't know. About twelve-thirty or so."

"And you arrived back home at what time?"

"Again, I can't be certain. About three, I suppose. I stopped for a quick lunch at a café somewhere in Knightsbridge, and browsed around Harrods for a bit. Walked part of the way home."

"I see." Abbott stared at Soame and Nightingale made another note. "But when you arrived back here, Mrs. Leland hadn't returned?"

"No. Mrs. Grimble was worried, she had expected her back for lunch. We waited and waited, and then I decided I'd better go to the house and see if anything had happened to her."

Nightingale finished writing and waited for Abbott's next question. "What time did you arrive at the McMurdo house?"

"What?"

Abbott repeated the question, and Soame frowned. "Somewhere around five, I suppose."

"And how long did it take you to find her in the wine cellar?"

"I have no idea. About twenty minutes."

"But the nine-nine-nine call for an ambulance was logged at five fifty-five," Abbott said in a flat voice. "We checked it before we left the Yard."

Nightingale felt a jolt go through him. He saw it now. The way Abbott had set it out made it clear that it could have been Soame himself who caused the accident at the McMurdo house, because he had only a vague alibi for the relevant time. Equally, it could have been Soame who vandalized this house after pretending to leave it—thus arriving at the McMurdo house later than he'd said. Now *that* was a new and interesting kettle of fish.

Had Soame built up—on the basis of a few crank telephone calls—an entire edifice of threats and dangers surrounding Mrs. Leland, all because of his own paranoia? Was this another manifestation of his mental breakdown, seeing monsters in other people's lives as well as his own? And was this Archie McMurdo just a convenient scapegoat—or a real villain?

Soame didn't seem to see the dangerous course Abbott's questions were taking. He stared at him blankly, then shrugged. "Perhaps I arrived later than I thought. Or the search took longer than I thought. Christ, what does it *matter?* I found her, and she was *alive.*"

"Yes. That was fortunate, wasn't it? The way the racks fell just so. They are extremely heavy, but luckily—very luckily—Mrs. Leland was only trapped under them. Not even hurt."

"Would you rather she had been crushed to death?"

"Obviously not."

Soame scowled. "Do you think she *arranged* for the racks to fall on her like that?"

"I think somebody could have."

"But not Tess . . . Mrs. Leland. Why should she?"

"Indeed, why should she? You see, Mr. Soame, I *can* make a case for Mrs. Leland creating this situation—either consciously or unconsciously—to call attention to herself."

"That's ridiculous!"

"It's been known."

"She's not that kind of woman!"

"How well do you know her? You, on the other hand, insist that the phone calls, the intruder, the attack on Mrs. Leland, and now on this house are part of a pattern. Well, I could make a case for *you* creating that pattern—consciously or unconsciously—yourself."

Soame's chin came up. "Why would I do that?"

"You've done it before." Abbott's voice was perfectly calm.

Soame's face went paper-white. "You . . ."

"Yes. Sergeant Nightingale went to Cambridge and asked some questions about you. He got some very interesting answers."

"Soame looked at Nightingale, shocked and angry. "But why?"

"It was *necessary,*" Abbott said. "He was proceeding unofficially, but sensibly. It was sound investigation. There can be no exceptions in a case as vague yet complex as this—a good officer who senses wrongdoing must suspect everyone."

Soame turned away and stood rigid, facing the windows. Although he did not seem to move, both Nightingale and Abbott could sense the struggle he was having with himself. When he turned back, they were both tensed, prepared to cope with any reaction—except the one he showed.

"Quite right," he said quietly. "That's also good scholarship, Nightingale. One really can't draw a sound conclusion any other way."

26

Tim!"

Sherry stood in the open door, running one hand through her disheveled auburn hair, and using the other to hold her pale-pink terry-cloth robe closed. Now she reached behind her for the trailing belt and managed to cover herself properly—but not before Tim had seen she was naked underneath.

"I'm sorry it's so late," he said. "Maybe I should have rung first. But you always said—"

"Well . . . yes, of course," she said, and stepped back. "I thought you were going to Cambridge this weekend."

"Went and came back," he said, proceeding down the hall and into the large sitting room. "Fare was courtesy of the Yard, but everything else I had to pay for myself, and there wasn't much more I could do. Just as well I came back, too, because there's been a development. Any chance of a coffee?"

She had followed him through and now glanced at the ebony-and-brass clock on the wall as she closed the sitting-room door behind her. After eleven—she had barely dozed off when the doorbell had roused her again.

"Yes . . . yes, sure." She went into the kitchen and reached for two mugs. Dirty dishes were stacked in the sink and on the counters—plates, cups, bowls, cutlery—hurriedly rinsed but not yet inserted into the dishwasher. "You'll have to have it black, though—I ran out of milk about three hours ago and was too lazy to go out and get any. I thought I'd pick it up with the Sunday papers."

He sat down on the sofa and stretched out his legs. "I can do that," he said, yawning. "You can have a lie-in. Least I can do after waking you up, right?"

She stood in the kitchen, holding the jar of instant coffee high in the air between cupboard and counter, pausing for a moment before completing its transfer. "Mmmmm," she said after a moment, and began to unscrew the top.

"You remember that case I was worried about—the widow and her little boy?" he said over his shoulder, as he loosened his tie.

"Mrs. Leland?"

"That memory of yours never ceases to amaze," he said. "Mrs. Leland it is. She nearly got herself squashed under about five hundredweight of assorted lumber this afternoon. It all fell on top of her—but she escaped with only scratches, bruises, and a possible concussion."

"Lucky woman." The kettle gave its little characteristic internal moan as the water began to simmer within. Sherry added sugar to Tim's mug and ducked her head to glance in the small hand mirror set on edge in front of the spice jars on the rack. She made a face at her messy hair and chapped chin, remembered that she had an old lipstick in one of the drawers and began to root among the spoons for it.

"Maybe." He was silent for a moment, listening to the comfortable clatter from behind him. "But while she was lying unconscious, somebody tried to lure away her little boy—and when that didn't work, he vandalized her house."

"How awful!" she called. "Was the boy hurt?"

"No. And neither was his kitten, which was found safely shut into the bathroom."

"What has a kitten to do with it?"

"I'm not sure. But it bothers me. Why would someone who vandalized a house stop short of hurting a kitten?"

"Even killers are kind to their mothers," Sherry observed. "Maybe the vandal is a cat lover."

"Maybe. Or maybe he isn't a vandal at all." He told her some of what he had learned in Cambridge, and some of what he thought about Soame, and about Tess Leland. Not all, just some. He also threw in what he knew about Archie McMurdo—whom they had so far been unsuccessful in locating at any hotel. But hotel searches take time, and he was patient. There were so many possibilities to consider. He sensed her coming up behind him, and recalled another, more distant, aspect of the case. "By the way, did you manage to dig up any of the information I asked you to get for me? On Roger Leland's business?"

She put the coffee mug down on the table in front of the sofa, then perched herself opposite in the easy chair. He raised an eyebrow. "That's not very friendly—am I in the doghouse for coming around so late?"

"Of course not," she said. "But I feel a bit . . . you know . . . messy and unprepared. Caught with my pants down." She heard her own words and raised a hand. "No gratuitous remarks—I'm too sleepy to keep up."

"Fair enough." He picked up his coffee and sipped at it, burning his tongue. "Ouch."

"No milk, remember?" she said.

He put the mug back onto the table and leaned his head against the back of the sofa, grateful for a little support at last. It had been a long day. "Well, did you?"

She'd been watching him with an odd expression that mingled affection, concern, and something else. "Did I what?"

He lifted his head and looked at her directly. "Get any information on Roger Leland's business?"

"Oh, yes. Quite a bit." She untangled her long legs and got up to go over to her desk unit, which obliquely filled one corner of the large apartment. Beyond the desk huge windows overlooked the Thames, giving a view rather like that from the high bridge of a ship. The building in which Sherry lived had been a sugar warehouse which some clever architect had converted to apartments. When she'd invested in it, Tim had protested. He hadn't much liked the idea of her living down here, where the streets were dark and lonely. But the architect (who still lived on the top floor of the converted warehouse) had had visions of the area developing one day into some kind of premier riverside village complex. In the event, Tim had been wrong, and the architect had been right. Sherry's original brave investment would net her a hefty profit when she decided to sell. If she decided to sell.

She often teased him about missing his chance at a similar place and now being stuck renting a tiny flat in Putney. He absorbed these shafts with equanimity because he could, he pointed out, have been right. The odds had been even, and predicting fashion trends—whether in couture or property—was a risky business. Almost as risky as becoming a copper.

Now she returned from her desk bearing a large folder. "Here you go," she said, handing it to him.

"My God," he said, hefting it. "This will take me all tomorrow to get through."

"It's Sunday," she told him. She glanced at the clock again. "Or it will be, in twenty minutes or so."

"Can't you give me a précis?" he pleaded, putting the folder down beside him and trying the coffee again.

"Better still, can't we go to bed and you can tell it all to me as a bedtime story?"

"Too many details," she said. "You have to look at the figures to get the idea."

"And what is the idea?"

"Well, *my* idea is that it was a very peculiar public-relations company," Sherry said, resettling herself in the easy chair, but not looking much at ease in it. "On paper it was doing really well. A lot of money was going back and forth between here and the Continent, for example, but there weren't that many clients."

"You got that far into it?"

"Oh, it wasn't difficult. I know a lot of people in the City," she said.

"So I remember," Tim said.

She avoided his eyes. "Yes. Well . . . you have to admit, it's useful. Apparently Roger Leland was a real charmer, shot out creative ideas in all directions, really produced for his clients. There's no question—in his hands the company was a real goer. You get the feeling from the figures that they would have been in a terrific position when the Common Market opened up. But there was some talk just before he died—nothing you could put your finger on . . ."

"Saying what?"

She shrugged. "Odd stuff. That maybe he was losing his edge, or he was ill, or something."

Tim scowled. There had been no evidence of serious physical illness revealed by the post mortem. "You mean mentally ill?"

"Maybe. It was more like terminally pissed off."

"With his partner?"

"I don't think so. More like with the world. You know—ratty, irritable, slamming phones down, storming out of meetings, that kind of thing. For no apparent reason. I think that was what worried the people over at Philadelphia Mutual."

Tim made a dismissive sound. "Typical insurance

company, balking at paying out a measly few thousands to a widow."

"More like half a million. But it wasn't to the widow—it was to Richard Hendricks. Partnership insurance."

"Half a million?" Tim said incredulously.

"It was based on Leland's 'unique creative ability,' apparently. They paid, in the end—but not without a fight. They raised the question of suicide, based on Leland's apparent depression."

"Oh?"

"Yes. But it was pointed out to them that suicide was pretty unlikely, because Leland's son had been in the car with him, and it was decided a devoted father like Leland would never have risked injuring or killing the boy."

"I see."

"Anyway, once Hendricks got the money out of Philadelphia Mutual, he closed down the old business, which was really built around Leland's talent, and used the insurance as seed money for his new company, which, by the way, is called Salescan. It specializes in profiling prospective international markets. It's doing all right, but it doesn't have anything like the potential his partnership with Roger Leland had. Hendricks is respected but not particularly well liked. A good numbers man, but *not* a genius."

"Yes." Tim was still absorbing the fact that Richard Hendricks had gotten paid off handsomely for Roger Leland's death, but his widow had been nearly impoverished. Of course, Hendricks was under no obligation to give her any of the partnership-insurance money—that had been a normal business arrangement. But it wouldn't hurt him to drop her a few thousand, would it? On the other hand, maybe he had, and she was hiding it—say from someone in Leland's family? Or from his past? A former wife, perhaps? He knew so little about the dead man, but he did know that in any victim's personality or life-style or history there were always the clues to why someone wanted him dead. The trouble was, they were often buried deeper than the victim himself.

"Well, that insurance payoff gives us a motive for Hendricks."

Sherry shook her head. "Not really—Roger Leland alive was a lot more valuable to Hendricks than he was dead. In the long run, anyway."

"Maybe Hendricks needed money fast, for some other reason."

Again she shook her head. "The man is fairly solid in his own right. He could have managed to finance the new company out of his own pocket—it just made good business sense to use the insurance payout. That's what it's *for*, Tim."

"I know, I know." He scowled. "And then there's Soame."

"The nutty professor?"

"Yes." He scowled.

"You like him."

"Yes, I like him, but . . ." He paused. "I like Tess Leland, too," he murmured, half to himself, as he idly turned the first few pages in the folder. "Good Lord."

"What?" Sherry leaned forward slightly.

"It says here that Leland and Hendricks part-owned Brevitt Interiors."

"I told you, Hendricks is a good numbers man. He knew the value of outside assets, especially for a firm that was so dependent on the talents of one man."

"What would have happened to that interest when Hendricks closed down the company?"

"He could have transferred the asset to the new company, or sold the interest to someone else—any number of things. It may be in there, somewhere."

"Could he have brought any kind of pressure on the people in Brevitt Interiors?"

"Pressure to do what? And why? Leland and Hendricks's interest wasn't the major one, from the look of it. Maybe it was sentimental. It wasn't a big asset, and certainly not their only asset. It wouldn't be worth the bother, I shouldn't have thought."

"Unless there was something else there. Say maybe that Brevitt Interiors had hidden assets of its own. Do you know anything about them?"

Sherry laughed. "Good God, Tim—you must think I'm omniscient or something. I only know what's listed there—their name, their value, and the amount of Leland and Hendricks's investment. You said to look into Leland and Hendricks—not investigate everyone else in the City or out of it. It would take weeks to check them all out. I do know Adrian Brevitt is considered sound, rather than flashy. His boyfriend was the flashy one—but they've split up, of course."

"Oh? When was that?"

"A few months ago, I think."

"About the time Roger Leland died?"

She stared at him, and shook her head. "That's pretty farfetched, Tim. What possible connection could there be between that and Mrs. Leland? You sound like a man grasping at straws."

"Got it in one," Tim said. "But Mrs. Leland now works for Brevitt Interiors. She worked for them before she was married, too. Brevitt took her back eagerly—I gather she's pretty good on restorations."

"And all this kerfuffle, all this 'case' you're trying to shape, revolves around her, doesn't it?"

"Yes."

"And now somebody tried to squash her—she says."

"It was a pretty lucky escape."

"Luck—or careful planning?"

"I don't know. I really don't know. I can't see any advantage to anyone for persecuting her in the way she claims, yet I do believe someone is."

"And why do you believe that?" she asked, playing at devil's advocate.

"Because *she* believes it, I suppose."

"What's she like?"

He thought back. "Scared. Tired. Defiant. Stubborn. A little naive." He paused. "And innocent, dammit. If I ignore her, or dismiss it all as Soame's paranoia, and I'm *wrong*, I'll never be able to forgive myself."

Sherry shook her head. "I told you when you left Lloyd's, and I'll say it again—you've got too much damn conscience to be a cop."

"And you're a cynic."

She sighed, and glanced again at the clock. "Never denied it, love." There was a shade of something in her voice that was almost bitterness, and it surprised him. "Most of us vote the straight bitch ticket, these days," she said. "That's the price for getting what you want."

"What's that supposed to mean?" Tim asked in some confusion. What was it about her? She was looking nervy and seemed restless. Somehow exasperated with him. Somehow . . . uneasy? "Look, maybe I should have left this until morning," he said, getting slowly to his feet. "I didn't mean to wake you up."

She stood up, too. "Oh, you didn't wake me. I was just lying there, thinking," she said. Now he got what the sound in her voice was—some brand of sadness he hadn't encountered there before. She glanced toward the closed sitting-room door. When she spoke again her voice was soft, but very clear. "You didn't wake either of us, Tim."

He looked at her for a long time, and she let him look, meeting his eyes levelly, waiting. After a while he edged out between the sofa and the low table, went down the hall to the bedroom door and opened it, very quietly. He looked in, then closed the door again. Very quietly. He came back to the sitting room and, without looking at her, picked up his jacket, put it on, then leaned over and collected the folder containing the information she'd gathered about Roger Leland's business life.

Only then did he look at her.

Her face was pale, and there were tears in her eyes, but her chin was high. "I'm really sorry," she said. "But I think I'm going to marry him, Tim."

He just managed a smile. "Then there's nothing to be sorry for, is there? We made no promises."

"I know, but . . ."

"We made no promises," he repeated. "Forget it."

She followed him to the door. "Shall I send you an invitation?" she asked, trying to keep it light and failing.

"No," he said. He raised the folder. "Just send me the bill for your expenses on this."

She looked as if he'd slapped her. "That was unfair," she said reproachfully.

"Yes," he agreed. "Unfair." The word bounced back and forth between them, and she couldn't meet his eyes.

He opened the door into the chilly concrete corridor that betrayed nothing of the income received or spent by the twenty tenants of this vast and peculiar edifice. At the end of the hall a tall narrow window gave a slightly more angled view of the black river that divided one diamond-spangled bank from the other. The reflections on the water made it look oily, slow, and full of menace.

"I feel like I'm a long way from home," he said softly.

"Putney isn't so far."

He glanced at her. "That isn't the home I meant," he said.

And left.

27

Tess never did remember much about Sunday morning.

The clink of a cup in a saucer woke her from her exhausted sleep, and she opened her eyes. Mrs. Grimble stood beside her bed, holding a large tray.

"What time is it?" She struggled up against the pillows and looked at the clock on the bedside table, but avoided looking at Roger's face in the photograph beside it. She didn't want to have to explain to him what had happened to his house, his wife, his son, their life. Twisted, torn, all of it. Gone.

"Near noon, as you can see."

"Where is everybody?"

"The professor's upstairs. That blond bit of his is here again. Or still, maybe I should say. She arrived yesterday while the coppers were grilling him." Her tone of disapproval only just covered a deep and salacious satisfaction at sin uncovered and proved. "Disgusting, I call it. Her only a slip of a thing, probably no better than she should be, and him old enough to be her father, if you ask me."

From the attic flat overhead there came a sudden burst of music, quickly muffled. Then silence.

"Perhaps she helps him with his research," Tess said weakly. Oh, Tess—grow up, she told herself.

"Research, is it?" Mrs. Grimble sniffed. "That's a new name for it."

"How's Max?" Tess asked.

"Max is proper wore out, that's what he is. White as a sheet and too weary to complain, poor mite, what with the police and all making him so excited he was up half the night. He's gone back to sleep."

"What did the police do?"

"Which police? you might ask."

"Which police?" Tess responded dutifully.

"The police from around here, they did this and that, poked about a bit, took photos, threw some kind of powder all over everything, just more for me to clean up, *they* don't care. Them from Scotland Yard, all they did was ask questions. Put Mr. Soame through it proper. Asking him when did he come, when did he go, why did he this and why did he that. All sorts."

"But why should they do that?"

Mrs. Grimble shrugged. "Why do they do anything? To make themselves look good, that's all. They talked to Max. Wanted to talk to you, but I said you was asleep, and that was that. I said you'd had enough, and showed them the door. They're coming back this afternoon, so eat your breakfast. You'll need your strength."

Mrs. Grimble thumped the tray down onto Tess's knees. "Come on, get it down, while I run you a bath."

She went into the bathroom and there was a sudden rush of water thundering into the old lion-clawed bathtub Roger had brought home in a taxi one evening, rescued from a skip near King's Cross. A scent of peach and primrose filtered out in a cloud of steam that hung around the bathroom door and dampened the edge of Tess's dressing table. Condensation formed on the glass top and one side of the mirror.

"Not too hot, I don't want to faint in there," Tess called. She ate a little, just to be able to say she had, and spread what was left around the plate. "About the mess downstairs—"

Mrs. Grimble reappeared in the doorway. "Oh," she said archly, arms folded across her scrawny bosom. "Don't you worry about that." She pointed upward at the ceiling, presumably in reference to John Soame rather than the Almighty. "*He's* going to arrange for some special firm to come and deal with it tomorrow, he tells me. Bunch of hippie students, like as not, probably steal you blind. That's why I'm staying on. I made up the guest room for me. *Somebody* has to keep an Eye on Things."

"That's very kind of you." Tess was beyond protest and very grateful. Mrs. Grimble had "stayed on" when Tess was ill on various occasions over the years, most notably after Max was born. It was bliss for Tess, but Roger would usually lose his temper after being told for the fifteenth time to eat up his greens, and would send her home in a taxi. "But—what about Walter?"

Mrs. Grimble looked uneasy at the mention of her brother. "He's gone to stay with his son and snooty daughter-in-law in 'ampstead." The old woman's glance slid away, then returned. "Well . . . they'll be after him again, won't they?" she said defiantly. "It wasn't him did this. You know that, and I know it."

No, Tess thought, I don't know that, but I hope it's true.

"Anyway, he's old now. He can't take all that questioning and knocking about," Mrs. Grimble went on, as if to excuse the warning she had very obviously passed on to her brother.

"They wouldn't knock him about, would they?" Tess asked.

"Well, they've done it before. Like to keep their hand in, that lot do. The trouble is, Walter won't stand up for himself anymore. In fact, he's been real quiet lately.

Wonder if he's sickening for something nasty?" She frowned, thinking back, then continued briskly. "Be a bit more grateful for all I do for him when he comes back, though, you can be sure of that. He'll be locked in his room out there, like as not, and fed scraps under the door, if *she* has anything to say about it. Stuck-up cow. *Her* family isn't exactly royalty, neither, come to that, seeing as how her old man made his pile scrapping cars that weren't always his. Bet her la-di-da friends would be interested to hear about *that*." Mrs. Grimble smiled grimly. "Anyway, here I am and here I stay until you're better, and I don't want a word said about it, so just finish your breakfast."

Tess looked down at the scrambled egg, which was coagulating on the soggy toast, and the greasy strips of bacon which bracketed the pale-yellow curds. There was an aroma rising from it all that was faintly reminiscent of school dinners. That, combined with the sweet steam from the bathroom, was too much for her. Her head was pounding and her stomach was clenching in protest.

Thrusting the tray aside, she threw back the covers and made a dash for the loo. As she closed the door behind her, she heard Mrs. Grimble gathering up the tray and muttering to herself something about "keeping it warm."

It was in the nature of a threat.

After her bath she slept again, mercifully spared the reappearance of her breakfast or any other offerings. When she awoke she was aware of bustle and conversation downstairs, interspersed by the tinkle of glass and the occasional thump. She slept and woke again, several times. In between the blanks, she caught glimpses of Max peering around her open door, looking worried. She saw John Soame standing over her, she saw her doctor standing over her, she saw Sergeant Nightingale standing over her, and once, just for a minute, she thought she saw Roger standing over her, looking sad. She smiled and spoke to them all, but never knew exactly what she said. Or they said. She would have liked to know what Roger said.

At four she awoke completely.

Simon Carter was sitting beside her bed, watching her. He smiled brightly and closed the book he was reading—from the cover, a fairly lurid thriller. "Hello," he said.

"Hello." Alarm shot through her. "Is anything wrong?"

"No, no, no," he said quickly, and patted her hand reassuringly. "Everything is just fine. Mr. Soame is talking to the police downstairs, and Mrs. Grimble has gone home to feed her canary and fetch some fresh clothes. Max and I had a nice chess game, and now he's asleep again."

"Is he all right? He hasn't got a fever or anything?"

The young curate shook his head. "No, Mrs. Grimble keeps checking, but it's just exhaustion, poor lad. I'm afraid all this has really upset him. He's found out about the other things that have been happening—he's rather cross at being left out of that. Mostly, I think, he's worried about you."

"That's precisely why I *didn't* tell him about all the other things," Tess said bleakly. "Losing his father was bad enough—I didn't want him to think the other props of his life were being rocked as well. Was that wrong?"

"Well . . . in my limited experience I've found that children generally prefer the truth, however difficult it may be. That was certainly the case in the hospital," Carter said. "And it seems to matter a great deal to Max. He is troubled, you know."

"I know," Tess said, feeling exhaustion sweep over her. "The nightmares and everything. I just don't know how to help him."

"Perhaps he'll just have to help himself." He smiled. "With God's support, of course. Max is stronger than you think, Mrs. Leland. He's bright, and he's clever. And he loves you very much."

"I'm very grateful to you for giving him so much of your time."

Simon Carter flushed a becoming pink. "One reaches out, you know. Stuck with the impulse, can't stop it, really. Too squeamish to be a doctor, too lazy to be a lawyer, too impatient to be a social worker—Church the only thing left. Embarrassing, sometimes—not much for incense and all that."

"A worker priest?"

"Mmmmm—but don't tell the Bishop." Carter grinned. "Speaking of work, I thought someone should be with you in case you needed anything when you woke up. Do you?"

She needed badly to go to the loo, but she could hardly tell him that. He looked so eager to please, so hopeful of some kindly assignment, that she requested a cup of tea. As soon as he bounded off, she slipped to the bathroom. When she came out again, it was not the young curate who awaited her return, but Detective Chief Inspector Abbott. He seemed entirely undismayed by the sight of a woman in a rumpled nightgown, with toothpaste on her chin and the beginnings of a black eye.

"Good afternoon, Mrs. Leland. Do you feel up to answering a few questions?"

"Yes—I think so."

But there were more than a few.

Sometime that night, Max came and got into bed with her. Waking in the semidarkness she discovered him beside her, curled tightly against her ribs. She murmured to him sleepily and wrapped her arms around him.

"Mummy, can I ask you something?"

"Yes, lovey, of course you can."

It was a long time coming, and when it did it was a

past-midnight question, perhaps not quite what he meant to say. "They can't put children in jail, can they?"

Simple reassurance rather than a semantic discussion seemed called for. "No, of course not."

"But they can take them away from their mothers if they're bad, can't they?" His voice was very small in the dark.

"They *can*—but they try very hard not to. It depends on how bad the children have been, and how often."

"If they've been very bad?"

Tess started to wake up. "Have you something you want to tell me, Max?"

"That's what *he* said." He took a deep breath, and it caught somewhere in his throat.

"Who?"

"The really tall one with green eyes."

So Abbott had been questioning Max, too. She wondered if he'd used the same tactics as he had with her—going over and over the same ground, asking for the same things again and again: the times, the words spoken, a hundred small details, things she'd forgotten, things she hadn't known she knew—and always, always, with that oh-so-patient air of faint disbelief that kept you babbling, rushing to testify, fretful of mistakes.

"He's only trying to help us."

Tess felt the shivering begin, and held him more tightly. She waited, giving him a chance to continue, but he was silent, and the silence stretched. Tess sighed, blowing his hair gently away from her mouth, like feathers lifting and falling. "Go to sleep, darling. We can talk about it all in the morning. Mummy's head hurts now, and we're both pretty tired, aren't we?"

He twisted around and kissed her on the chin, which was all he could reach. "Don't worry," he said. "Don't cry anymore. They won't take me away, I promise. I won't let them." He hugged her and snuggled down again, his arms around her as protectively as hers were around him. His breathing steadied, slowed, and became softly even.

She was puzzled and worried by his questions. What could be bothering him? She frowned, and found that her face was stiff with dried tears. Realization swept over her—she must have been crying in her sleep. Ill and exhausted as he was, Max had heard and come to her—not only seeking comfort, but offering it as well.

For a long while, until she herself was overcome by sleep, she lay in the dark, holding the solid little shape, silently apologizing.

On Monday morning, when she awoke, Tess gritted her teeth and stretched all over, until she knew the worst. It was not so bad. Except for her head, of course, which was no longer muzzy, but still ached dully.

There was a pale, diffuse light in the room. She rolled over and looked at the clock—nearly ten-thirty, yet it was dark enough to be much earlier.

She could hear Max's voice down the hall, talking to Albert in a scolding tone. Apparently the kitten had committed some small, furry crime, and was being chastised. Feathers and pillow seemed to come into it, but there didn't seem to be much anger in Max's voice.

Tess stretched again, remembered, and groaned.

Mrs. Grimble, who was either psychic or lurking in the hall, immediately appeared in the doorway. "They've started," she announced ominously, and disappeared. After a moment she stuck her head back around the door. "Breakfast in ten minutes. Brush your teeth."

Tess stared at the empty doorway, and then, hearing noises and men's voices from below, realized the firm that John Soame had engaged must have arrived to put the house to rights.

Tess hauled herself to the bathroom, groaned again at the sight of two no longer faint black eyes, and decided to do more than brush her teeth. She was back in bed, toweling her hair carefully, by the time Mrs. Grimble returned with a breakfast tray.

"They're thorough, I'll say that," she announced with grudging approval. "But they won't find any cobwebs in *my* corners."

Tess crunched a piece of toast and found it good. "What are they doing?" she asked in a muffled voice as she cut her bacon.

"Well, two are picking up pieces and putting them together, so to speak. There's one sewing up upholstery, and another one is sweeping and chucking out. Don't worry, I gave him a box and everything he *thinks* to chuck out I tell him to chuck in, instead. Up to you, I said, what goes out. Even a piece of something might be important to you, sentimental the way you are."

"Am I?"

"Course you are. Why not? Them little things might seem like junk to other people, but they have memories attached, don't they? Worth more than the price," she said. After a moment, she added, "Have to be."

"Where's John?" Tess asked.

"If you mean Mr. Soame, *he's* gone to Scotland Yard to play with the detectives." The scorn in her voice could have been usefully employed removing tarnish from the copper pans hanging on the kitchen wall. "Full of investigating, he is, all mouth and magnifying glass." She paused, then plunged ahead. "His lady friend was here again. Left last night about eleven, made a big noise of it so's I'd hear." She sniffed. "Wouldn't be surprised if she crept back after, though. Butter wouldn't melt her."

"I'm sure she's very nice," Tess said, keeping her voice carefully neutral.

"Hmmmm. Well, I don't care if he is some sort of professor—sometimes I think he's not quite right in the head. This morning he announces they're going wrong down at Scotland Yard, and off he goes to put them right. Honestly. Maybe *I* should go down there and tell them about what I found him doing this morning. Maybe they'd be interested in *that!*"

Tess pushed the tray away, and was surprised to see that someone had eaten everything on it. "What was he doing?" she asked.

Mrs. Grimble leaned forward as if to grasp the tray, but merely glared at short distance into Tess's eyes. "He was *measuring*."

Tess felt inclined to laugh at the menace with which this announcement was imbued, but managed to control herself. "Measuring what?"

"The *walls*," Mrs. Grimble said, and snatched up the tray. "He was measuring the walls, as bold as brass." With this announcement, and the tray, she departed.

Tess slid back down in the bed and decided she was not going to think about anything ever again. Everybody else could take over her life—like the men downstairs, other people would have to put it all back together. She felt heavy with fatigue, and her headache was tightening again. The nausea she had felt yesterday was gone, but she still felt empty—hollow in arms and legs, dreamy in mind, and sad throughout.

She allowed herself to be cocooned by weakness, and stayed that way for another hour or so, listening to the mutter of the radio beside her. She tried to concentrate on a short story about an elderly cat burglar making a comeback and a program on the virtues and value of double-glazing in saving energy. Supine and defenseless, she received a stern talking-to from a man with a squeaky voice about the waning butterfly population, and a warning of bad visibility from several coastal stations. But when asked to consider the dangers of allowing the present government to continue on its wayward course unchallenged, she lost her nerve and switched off.

No solace there.

None anywhere.

Except from Max.

She sat up, suddenly.

Max, who had asked her about children going to jail. Despite her efforts to remain unconnected to the real world, the memory of those small troubled questions had snaked past her defenses and was now hissing in her ear. Sending children to jail?

"Max?" she called out. "Can you come here a minute, lovey?"

There was no reply, although his room was only down the hall. Perhaps he'd gone downstairs to watch the men working. He was allowed up for brief periods now. That must be it. Throwing the covers back, she got up, put on her dressing gown, and went along to his room.

Empty. Not even Albert in sight.

A little wobbly, she went slowly downstairs. The men in the sitting room looked up at her approach and smiled encouragingly. "Coming along, ma'am," one said. "Be back to normal in no time."

"Thank you," she smiled, and went on down the hall to the kitchen, where she discovered Mrs. Grimble rolling out pastry for a pie. "Is Max with you?" Tess asked, looking around the big kitchen. Mrs. Grimble put her rolling pin aside and headed for the cooker.

"No. He's in the garden with the kitten." She came back with a coffeepot and a mug with red and blue frogs on it. "Now, don't you fuss. He's dressed up warm, and I told him it was only for ten minutes. Can't come to harm in his own garden, can he? And a few breaths of fresh air will do him the world of good. Here, sit down and have some coffee."

But Tess was heading toward the side door.

"Now, stop that. Don't go out in your dressing gown, it's damp and chilly!" She slapped the mug down on the table for emphasis, but her orders were ignored.

Tess stepped out onto the damp flagstones of the patio. The garden was garlanded with drifting wisps of mist that had broken away from the thick fog that hung over the roofs and shrouded the treetops of the park beyond the next street. There was a still, dank heaviness in the air—fog was flowing in to weigh down the afternoon. The birds were silent, and the fat brown rose hips glistened with moisture.

There was a soft touch at her ankle. She looked down to see Albert, his fuzzy kitten-coat glittering with mist, weaving small, intricate patterns around her slippers. She picked him up and nestled him under her chin. He began to purr.

"Max? Time to come in, love. It's cold."

Her voice seemed to hang in the air, the words pegged out like washing drooping limp from the line. "Max?"

She stepped farther along the patio, emerging from the shelter of the vine-covered trellis. The garden stretched away to the rear, hedged in by tall laurels on one side and the weathered brown board fencing Roger had put up on the other. At the far end, the garden gate stood open.

Wide open.

And Max was gone.

28

The fog had flowed up the river from the sea, flooding across the Essex marshes and creeping over the city stealthily, silently, under hedges and over rooftops, curling around chimneys and eddying at street corners as the cars moved cautiously through it, their engines strangely hushed, their drivers shadowed and mysterious within. Pedestrians moved, isolated, within the circles of their own limited vision. Sounds were distorted, seemed to come from nowhere, anywhere—a drift of conversation, a ping, a thud, a footstep, a whistle, a whisper—all were enfolded by the moist and suffocating shroud. Untouchable, uncatchable, unescapable. The fog was everywhere.

And Max was lost within it.

Was he alone?

"How long has he been gone?" It was John Soame, coming through the front door at a run, followed by Abbott, Nightingale, three other detectives, and several uniformed police officers from the local station. Tess's call to Scotland Yard had been both rushed and hysterical, but had produced immediate results.

Mrs. Grimble, wringing her flour-covered hands, told him about forty-five minutes. "I shouldn't have let him go out," she wailed. "But he kept pestering me, and I thought . . ."

Already the men from the cleaning firm were out, calling Max's name, moving away from the house and down the misty streets, but the cotton wool of the fog deadened their voices, twisted their words into useless echoes that summoned no one save the occasional curious cat or dog.

Beyond the next street stretched the park, its great trees hanging still and shadowy in the mist. They were the only things visible within the perimeter of the fence—everything else was hidden, and secret.

Everything.

Everyone.

Quickly, Abbott produced a street map, and they divided the neighborhood up into sections. "He may just have gone for a walk, to get sweets or a comic," he said. But there was no real conviction in his voice. There was, instead, the bitter awareness of failure, and the memory of all those threats and "coincidences" Nightingale had produced and he'd dismissed. Until now.

Tess Leland stood in the middle of the hall, as if standing watch over entrances front and back, a slight figure huddled into a faded blue chenille dressing gown, her arms crossed over her chest. Nightingale watched her throat convulse as a sob struggled with a scream, and felt his own chest tighten—not because of her pain, but because of her courage in trying to overcome it. He had seen a lot of pain over the past few years, had learned to face it without flinching, but bravery always undid him.

Stable doors, he thought. Regrets, apologies, but the boy is gone and I am here too late, with too little. I can say nothing that will provide either comfort or hope, nothing that she will believe, because I don't believe it myself. And with all the possibilities we have, all the things we know or suspect, there is the additional ever-present danger of a purely chance encounter with a pervert. Every family it touches once lived in complete certainty that it would never happen to one of their own—until it did. Until its foul darkness fell forever on them. That chance was as real here as with any other child. All the other dangers that hung over his small tousled head did not provide any immunity for Max Leland from the lying smile, the quick grab, the fumbling hand, the knife, the rope, the shattering blow.

How long does it take for that twisted hunger to overcome self-loathing and caution, for the fog to offer its rare and cloaking opportunity, to take a child, to rape a child, to mutilate, stab or strangle a small body, to thrust it under a bush, to run and run and run, haunted, breathless, sated for now. But only for now.

He knew, as every policeman knows, that it takes only a few minutes. Only minutes.

And they were passing so quickly.

Abbott was ordering Max's description to be circulated immediately to all car and foot patrols in the area, with underlined urgency. Out of the corner of his eye he saw Tim Nightingale, as unobtrusively as possible, slip a photograph from a frame that still held shards of glass broken the day before, and pass it to one of the patrolmen to take back to the station for duplication. Their eyes met, and Tim's mouth tightened in a face already pale with anger. He, too, was blaming himself.

And it was worse for him, Abbott realized. Because there would always be one terrible thought within him. Did I cause this by asking too many questions? If I'd left this whole thing alone, would the boy be here now, and safe? This was the bad part, he wanted to tell Nightingale. This is the hard part, where you watch the pain and wonder what you should have done, could have done, to prevent it. You did your best, you scented danger, cried out on discovery, and were not believed. That is my fault, and I'm sorry I let you down.

Whether here temporarily or permanently, I am your superior officer because I am supposed to know my job. Most of all, I am supposed to listen. But in the busy day, so many dangers walk past us, wearing disguises, whistling casually, looking like promises or excitements or security. There isn't time to follow them all, stop them all, put them through the tests. We try, of course. And in this pursuit we may even, quite innocently, catch the eye of Death and cause Him to turn our way. He doesn't notice everyone—but He has a special soft spot for coppers. You might as well learn that now as later. We have a stink He likes.

He went over to Nightingale, and though he wanted to say that, all he could manage was, "I should have listened to you sooner." For a moment it seemed to ease the pain in Nightingale's eyes. But only for a moment.

"Perhaps if I'd . . ." he began.

The phone suddenly rang, louder and more insistent than any phone ever rang, and they all froze where they stood. Tess was closest, and, stiff as an automaton, picked it up.

It was Richard Hendricks. His voice was casual, relaxed.

"Tess, I've just got home from the airport. I've been going through my post. I know you won't like this, but I wasn't satisfied with what my banker friend found out, so while I was away I've had a private investigator looking into Soame's background, because I never quite—"

"Is Max with you?" Tess interrupted. Her voice came out in a croak, emerging from a throat that felt as if it were closing forever.

Richard was silent for a moment. "With *me?*" he finally asked. "Why on earth would Max be with me? He doesn't even know where I live."

"No special reason. Look, Richard, I can't talk about this now. Maybe if—"

It was his turn to interrupt. "Is Max missing?" he demanded. "I *am* his guardian, too, Tess. I have a right to know what's going on. Is he missing?"

"Yes." There was no point in denying it, and Richard might be able to help. He'd always been so good before. So strong, so very strong. Why hadn't she listened to him? Why hadn't she realized he cared so deeply? "He disappeared from the back garden about forty-five minutes ago."

"Oh, I see." There was relief and indulgence in his voice. "Well, I would hardly call that *missing*, Tess. For goodness' sake, he's almost ten, he's quite capable of going to the shops on his own—"

"Not without telling me," Tess said flatly. "It's a house rule he's never broken. We always say where we're going, we *always* know—" Her voice broke, and Abbott gently took the phone from her. He talked quietly to Richard while Mrs. Grimble took Tess over to the sofa and sat down beside her, patting her hands as she wept.

John Soame, watching her with concern, spoke quietly and firmly. "You ought to go back to bed now, Tess. You're still wobbly from that blow on the head—"

"No!" She rose up, braced herself, and her eyes blazed in her wet face. "He's *my* child, *my* baby, and if you won't do anything, I will. I'm going to look for him myself."

Abbott had replaced the phone and came over to her. "I wouldn't do that, Mrs. Leland. When we find him we'll only have to come looking for you. It's best if you stay here—Max may well come home on his own, you know. He'll expect to find you waiting for him."

"Let them do their job," Soame urged, reaching out to take her arm. "They know what to do and how to do it—"

"Oh, yes, they know what to do," Tess said bitterly,

shaking him off, backing away from his touch. "They know that everything is coincidental, that you have to wait until you have *proof*, that hysterical women don't make sense, that there are rules and regulations. . . ." She knew it was untrue and unfair, but their oh-so-reasonable tones infuriated her. She didn't care, she couldn't care now, not with Max gone. She drew in a quick, sharp breath. "What if somebody took him?"

Soame looked uneasy. "If you mean Kobalski, I don't think kidnapping is quite his style."

She stared at him. "Who?"

Abbott explained. "That's why Mr. Soame's been with us down at Scotland Yard, Mrs. Leland. When I spoke to you yesterday—"

"Did you?" Tess's voice was vague. "I don't remember."

"You didn't make much sense, I agree. But you did say one or two things that needed looking into. Particularly about this Archie McMurdo. He was a puzzle piece that didn't fit."

"It looks like Archie isn't a McMurdo, after all," Soame said. "I thought his accent slipped a little the other night—you said he was Australian, but he sounded more like Brooklyn to me—so Sergeant Nightingale arranged for me to look at some pictures. We aren't sure, but we think the man who *claims* to be Archie McMurdo is actually an American named Kobalski. He's . . ."

"A twisty son of a bitch," one of the other detectives muttered, then stifled a grunt as Nightingale kicked him in the ankle.

Tess had heard his comment, though. She looked at the circle of men around her. "You mean he's some kind of criminal?"

There was a brief silence, which Abbott finally broke. She might as well have the truth, she would go on demanding it, more and more loudly, anyway. "It's remotely possible, Mrs. Leland. And now that we know about Kobalski, there could be some kind of pattern showing up here. Possibly something to do with the drug trade." He looked at her, and there was compassion in his eyes. "Were you ever aware of your husband having any connection with drugs?"

She was astonished. "Drugs? You mean . . . real drugs?"

"Yes."

On this she could be completely clear. "Absolutely not. You see, Roger's younger brother was a registered addict and . . . well, he died. Roger loathed drugs and everything to do with them. Why would you think he had any connection with drugs?"

"Because of Kobalski," Nightingale said. "If this man who calls himself Archie McMurdo really is Kobalski, then there *has* to be some drug connection. He is a bright and ruthless operator, and he works for one of the main American drug syndicates. They use him over here because he speaks several languages, and can mimic dozens of accents."

Tess took a long breath. "Such as Melbourne and Sydney?"

"That would be easy for him," Nightingale said. His tone was almost apologetic.

"I see." But she didn't. She didn't *want* to see.

"We think Kobalski was sent to pose as Archie McMurdo by a third party. Perhaps with the help—unwitting or otherwise—of someone who knows all about your work and your life and the boy and all the rest of it. Someone who would know where you were at all times, and possibly had access to your house keys."

Irresistibly, Tess found herself looking at Mrs. Grimble, who had gone white as a sheet and was sinking down onto the telephone bench, horror in her eyes. And Tess knew she was thinking of Walter.

Nightingale hadn't noticed—or if he had, he gave no indication of it. "It may be someone who is involved in drugs in some way—either using or distributing. Perhaps someone who has gotten into financial trouble and is looking to you to get them out of it. Someone who is desperate. Someone in need of money. Someone you trust."

The doorbell rang, and Mrs. Grimble—her steps unsteady and her face stricken—went to answer it. They all turned and went to the archway that led to the hall, waited as the door swung back.

Adrian Brevitt stood on the top step, dapper in his fur-collared overcoat, his pale-pink-and-white-striped shirt gleaming behind his rose silk necktie, his white hair silvered by the mist. In his hand he carried a colorfully wrapped parcel, banded and bowed in blue ribbon.

"I have come to visit my godson," he announced.

The stunned silence by which this was greeted puzzled him. He frowned, then caught sight of the faces behind Mrs. Grimble. He brightened. "Are we having a party?" he asked.

"I tell you, it's impossible!"

Tess was precariously seated on the edge of her recently reassembled mulberry chair, and she was outraged at the suggestion that Adrian Brevitt might be the mysterious person behind all her persecutions, leading up to and possibly even including Max's kidnapping. "Why, you might as well accuse Simon Carter!"

"It's interesting you should mention him, Mrs. Leland. We're looking into the very helpful Mr. Carter, and the recently solvent Mr. Walter Briggs," Abbott said smoothly. "In fact, we're looking into the background, whereabouts, and habits of everybody who has been in this house or had anything to do with you or your family over the past six months, as a matter of fact. We have a great many people to do this—but it still takes time. At the moment we are interested in Mr. Adrian Brevitt."

John Soame, although obviously angered by the sudden and rather rough reception that had been visited on his ex-brother-in-law, was nonetheless listening to Abbott's explanation. Tess seemed to have stopped just short of clapping her hands over her ears.

"He knows you well, and his company is in financial difficulties," Abbott pointed out.

"Companies like Brevitt Interiors are *always* in financial difficulties, until they make the big breakthrough or until they find a backer who will cushion them," Tess snapped, briefly distracted by this attack on another pillar of her existence. "We work on long-term arrangements, and all too frequently our creditors do the same. Adrian has come up the hard way, with just his talent to work with. No private fortune, no titles in the family, no millionaires willing to sponsor him. At least, not anymore—there was one, but Jason took her with him when he went solo. I suppose Adrian has been struggling a bit since then, but I'm certain that if there's a problem it's only temporary and can be straightened out. He *works* for his keep. He's a genius, not a businessman. And he's one of my oldest and dearest friends."

"But are his friends your friends?" Abbott asked in a reasonable voice.

She hung her head. "That's what Richard said," she mumbled. And maybe, she thought, Richard had been right. About everything.

Abbott glanced toward the kitchen, where Tim had taken Adrian for questioning. "What else did Mr. Hendricks have to say about Mr. Brevitt?"

"I don't remember." Tess would have stamped her foot if she had been wearing shoes instead of slippers. "And I don't care! I just want my son back safe and sound." Tears of fear and frustration again overflowed, but she paid no attention to them—her entire concentration was on Abbott, willing him to make Max reappear.

John Soame put his arm around her reassuringly. "The search is going on right now, believe me. The police are doing everything they can in that direction—leaving us free to look in other directions. There have been these threats and the break-ins, Max has been upset and having nightmares—there may be some connection there that will give us a lead. He may know something without realizing it—and so might you. Chief Inspector Abbott is only trying to find it."

"Well, he's looking in the wrong direction if he thinks Adrian is behind it," Tess said, standing up and shrugging Soame's arm away from her shoulders. She had no time for sympathy now—she didn't deserve it. Why hadn't she paid more attention to Max? Why hadn't she *seen* the danger?

Abbott was looking out of the bay window at the front. At the curb stood two police cars, the men inside acting as coordinators for the various search parties. Neighbors, at first limiting themselves to peering around the edges of curtains, were now standing around openly staring, talking to one another, pointing, nodding or shaking their heads. The streetlights had come on, adding a false yellow glow to the scene. Condensation dripped from the trees in the gardens on the opposite side of the road, and the fog seemed even thicker than before, blurring the house, obliterating the ends of the crescent.

"There's been some question concerning Mr. Brevitt's circle of friends," Abbott said slowly, turning back to face Tess. "He attends parties where cocaine is available—"

Tess sighed. "So do half the people in London, it seems to me," she said. "People who can afford interior decorators can also afford cocaine. Naturally they come in contact, but that doesn't mean that Adrian—"

"See here, am I under arrest?" came Adrian's voice. He stood in the archway, hands on hips, glaring at Abbott. Nightingale stood behind him, looking exasperated. "If so, I demand to see my solicitor *immediately*. If not, I refuse to sit in that kitchen any longer to be glowered at by your sergeant here and that gorgon in the chintz apron. Tess, my dear, my poor dear . . ." He swept across the room and took her hands. "Have they found our wandering boy yet?"

"Not yet, Adrian," Tess said thinly.

John looked at him in some exasperation. "By the way, where have *you* been? I've been looking for you everywhere."

Adrian took a deep, dramatic breath. "I have not *been* everywhere. I have been somewhere, which is quite a different thing. And Max is somewhere, too." He whirled on Nightingale. "Get out of here, young man. Climb onto your white steed and comb the byways for that innocent child. Whatever interest you have in me can wait. *I* shall wait, as a matter of fact, until Max is found and restored to his mother's arms."

Adrian went over to the rocking chair and sat himself elegantly down, crossing one knife-creased trouser leg over the other and placing both hands on the top of his silver-headed cane. After a moment he raised one hand in a fluttering, scattering motion. "Get on with it, get on with it," he directed grandly.

"Adrian . . ." John began.

Adrian fixed his ex-brother-in-law with a skeptical eye. "I should have thought you had sufficient experience in dealing with students to keep track of one rather small one, John."

"He was at Scotland Yard," Tess said.

"Oh?" Adrian looked at his ex-brother-in-law with interest. "And what were you doing there?"

"I was looking into the activities of an imported crook called Kobalski," Soame told him.

"Also known as Archie McMurdo," Nightingale volunteered.

Adrian glanced from one to the other. He looked suddenly crestfallen, and much, much older. "Oh," he said in a small voice. "So you *know* about him."

29

Tess had retreated to the kitchen to drink coffee, away from the questioning, and, more importantly, away from the temptation of the stairs that led upward to her bed and oblivion. She had only been there a few minutes, it seemed, when the door crashed back and Richard Hendricks strode in.

Tess flew into his arms and clung to him, all ambitions to be independent lost in the terror of what might be happening to her child. "Oh, Richard . . . Max is gone. . . ."

He held her close. "It will be all right, Tess. I promise, it will be all right. I'll make sure they find Max, I'll look after you both from now on. . . . Don't fret, love. Don't fret."

"Hmph!" snorted Mrs. Grimble. She began banging pots and pans about, but she kept glancing over her shoulder at him. She didn't seem able to decide whether to smile or sneer.

Tess stood quietly while he whispered reassuring phrases into her hair and patted her over and over again. She was grateful to be encircled with care and love, if only for a minute or two. She was still there, her face blank and her eyes closed, when the kitchen door swung back again, and John Soame came in. He glanced at the pair of them, but his face remained as blank as Tess's.

"Hendricks, the police would like to talk to you," he said after a moment.

"Oh, really?" Richard relinquished his hold on Tess. "Running errands for them now, are you? If they knew about you what I know, they might not be so trusting."

"They know all they need to know about me," Soame said.

"Oh, really? I wonder." Richard's tone was threatening.

Soame's mouth tightened, but he said nothing, just stood holding the door open, waiting. Richard turned to Tess.

"I won't be far away, my love. Don't be afraid. I'm certain we'll find him soon." He gave John a malignant glance and then walked out.

"Going out looking himself, is he?" Mrs. Grimble asked the cooker. "Get his expensive shoes dirty? Not likely."

Soame cleared his throat and spoke to Tess, who was standing where Richard had left her, as if she had no more will of her own, not even enough to sit down again at the kitchen table and finish her half-drunk mug of coffee.

"Why don't you take just ten minutes, Tess?" he said in a quiet voice. "Even ten minutes rest will do you some good."

"He's right, for once," Mrs. Grimble agreed grudgingly. While she was desperately worried about Max, she was also a practical woman and accepted that others could search better than she. Her concern here and now was Tess. "I'll come up and get you the minute we hear anything, I promise you that. Anything at all.

You can trust me." She put a hand on Tess's arm. "Go on, lovey. Do as he says."

When Tess spoke it was in a dead, empty voice. "What is Adrian saying now?" she asked tonelessly, her eyes looking between them at the blue-and-white porcelain jelly molds arranged on the wall beside the door.

"Still nothing. He just sits there, glaring at them. He says he's waiting for his godson and his solicitor, in that order."

"Oh." She reached up and rubbed her temples with vague irritation, as if something within annoyed her. "Why won't he speak?"

"I really don't know," John said helplessly. "I've never seen him like this before."

"It is an unusual situation," Tess said in an oddly formal tone, like a newsreader giving the latest headlines, or a teacher instructing recalcitrant students. "None of us has been like this before." She walked past him, down the hall, and up the stairs. She did not even glance into the sitting room, where Abbott was talking to Richard and Nightingale was looming over Adrian, apparently trying to intimidate him by telepathy.

Soame and Mrs. Grimble watched Tess ascending the stairs, as stiff and erect as a model in a fashion show, her face blank, her throat taut above the turned-in collar of the old chenille robe. When she had disappeared, they looked at one another. "She's going to crack soon," Mrs. Grimble said.

"I know," Soame said. "I know."

"Why haven't you put Soame in a cell?" Richard Hendricks demanded.

"Because we have no evidence of his committing any crime," Abbot said. "No reason to bring a charge."

"I can give you evidence," Richard snapped, reaching into his inside coat pocket and producing a thick envelope. "He's a psycho. It's all in here." He handed it to Abbot, who gave a quick glance at the name in the corner and put it into his pocket.

"Aren't you going to read it?" Richard asked, annoyed that his offering was being ignored.

"At the moment, my main concern is for the boy," Abbot said. "Have you any idea where he might be?"

Richard flushed. "Why should I? Despite my best efforts, I don't know him well. I don't know his friends or his habits or—"

"I thought you were planning to be his stepfather," Abbott interrupted.

"I have asked Tess to marry me, yes," Richard said.

"Dear God in Heaven, what a prospect," Adrian muttered.

Hendricks glared at him. "It has damn-all to do with you, you old poof."

Adrian took this calmly. "He *is* my godson," he said.

"Do you know a man who calls himself Archie McMurdo?" Nightingale asked Hendricks. "Or Kobalski?"

"Never heard of them," Hendricks said over his shoulder, still concentrating on Adrian Brevitt. "If he is your godson, and I do marry Tess, I shall have you exorcised, or whatever it is they do to sever an unsuitable godparent."

Adrian managed a smile. "The Bishop will hear of this, do you mean? I am *terrified*, absolutely *beside myself*."

"Mr. Hendricks," Abbott said loudly, before further fighting broke out. "I want to know more about Roger Leland."

Hendricks turned back slowly. "What about him?"

"Why was he upset just before he died?"

"Was he? I didn't notice anything."

"Philadelphia Mutual did. Or perhaps you've forgotten the fight you put up for your half-million-pound payout? A payout, I might add, that Mrs. Leland apparently knew nothing about and did not benefit from in any way."

Hendricks went white, then bright pink, then white again. "That was a straightforward business arrangement, it had only to do with the partnership. I did nothing wrong, it was all—"

"Half a million?" Adrian Brevitt said, standing up so suddenly that Nightingale nearly fell over. "Do you mean to say you were paid half a million pounds in insurance when Roger died? And you let Tess suffer, let the boy suffer . . ."

Hendricks turned on him. "It had nothing to do with them," he said, biting off the words. "It was a perfectly standard business arrangement. As to letting them 'suffer'—I have repeatedly offered to marry Tess. I've also begged her to let me look after her and the boy, but she has always refused my help *and* my money, by the way, which was also offered freely and frequently. For some reason, she was determined to survive on her own—she's a very stubborn girl. And she was encouraged to do it, no matter what the consequences." He glared at Adrian and Soame, then turned back to Abbott. "I'm not ashamed of taking that insurance settlement. I paid heavily enough in premiums over the years, and so did Roger. If *I* had died in a car crash instead of him, he would have done with the money exactly what I did—used it for business purposes."

"And you're a very good businessman," Abbott said.

Hendricks drew himself up. "Yes, I am, dammit. I don't see why I should be pilloried for it. Tess had insurance—"

"A pathetic five thousand pounds," Soame said abruptly. "And bills to pay out of it."

Richard's glance went to him, and his lip curled. "Well, you know all about having bills to pay, don't you? You know all about being in debt, don't you, *Professor* Soame?"

"I am not a full professor," Soame said evenly. "I do not claim to be."

"And you never will be, with your history—"

"This is not relevant," Abbott said loudly.

But Hendricks was in full, self-defensive flow. Allowed back into the situation by Tess's apparent capitulation and gratitude, he spoke with authority. "As for Tess suffering, I could hardly call living in this house suf——" He stopped and seemed to glance around for the first time. "What on *earth* has happened here?" he demanded in some dismay. "Is Tess redecorating?"

"What's the matter, Hendricks?" Adrian said. "Not to your taste?"

Tess sat down on the bed, but she did not lie down. Instead she folded her hands in her lap and gazed at them. They looked old, like her mother's hands. When she flexed her fingers the skin on the back of them became marked with hundreds of tiny lines—a phenomenon she hadn't noticed before. After a moment her glance traveled down to her slippered feet. She saw that a thread had begun to come loose around the appliquéd flower that adorned each scuffed toe. There was a star-shaped mark just above her ankle bone where a capillary had burst during her pregnancy. Her feet and ankles looked white, like those of a person in hospital. She felt white all over, drained and parched and almost weightless. Moving her body—in the interest of purely scientific inquiry—she found her joints were slippy and moved unpredictably. It was disconcerting. She felt she was held together by taut and tangled wires—she would not have been surprised to have her head drop into her lap and turn to grin up at her, or to see her kneecaps slide slowly down her legs and roll like empty teacups onto the floor.

She waited quite patiently for everything in her to

unsnap, unbuckle, fly apart into every corner of the room like an overwound watch flinging itself into spare parts.

When nothing of the sort happened, she stood up and got dressed.

30

The street stretched before her, long and diminishing to a no-point between the gray curtains of the fog. On her right, in the vast and silent expanse of the park, the sentinel trees loomed dark and motionless, their outlines blurred by the twisting skeins of the fog. The fog, the fog . . .

Damp against her face, betrayer of light and sound, clammy fingers sliding down her throat, encircling her legs and hands, muffling the scream she could not, would not utter.

She had waited at the top of the stairs, listening to them all talking, arguing, wrangling downstairs. They all sounded so angry. Doors crashed open and slammed shut, voices rose and fell—and what good was it doing? What point did it have? All that mattered was Max.

When the moment had come, it had come quickly, without warning, and she had lost a precious second or two in realizing that Mrs. Grimble had gone into the sitting room with coffee, and had thoughtfully closed the sliding doors behind her. Down the stairs, through the hall and kitchen, out the back door and through the garden gate . . .

The way Max had gone.

Just to be away, to be moving, to be doing something was better than lying on her bed, wide-eyed, pretending to rest when there was no rest to be had, pretending to be passive and good when she was filled with rage. No. Her head throbbed with each step, but she just dug her hands deeper into the pockets of her coat and went on.

Such a long street. How strangely empty it seemed. And then the next street, and the next. Empty? Or were there footsteps following? She turned once, twice, three times—but there was never anyone there. Perhaps it was her own footsteps she heard, held high in the fog and then dropped, gritty, furtive, faster and faster, like scuttling rats gathering behind her.

But no shadows moved there, high or low.

Only one car, at the far end of the street, a moment of motion, a glitter, a hum, and then only the blank, dank, unembroidered hanging of the fog. She shivered and went on.

All around there seemed to be a low thrumming, the sounds of the city wound together into one steady purr, a perfectly level harmonic pierced now and again by the stab of a car horn, the rumble of a tube train emerging momentarily into the open, the snap of a twig, or the disconsolate chirp of some stranded bird clinging to a branch or chimney, caught high over invisible ground.

She turned corners, moving instinctively, imagining herself a ten-year-old boy and going—where? Now the street was a narrower one, the next narrower still. Away from the park the buildings diminished, becoming more and more mean, frowning closer and closer to the pavement, crowding in on her.

How dead the houses seemed. As if no one lived within, had ever lived or moved in those rooms, looked out of those windows, tended those small squares of garden. The fog hung them all with cobwebs, like Miss Havisham's room, caught and suspended in time. This strange little street was as silent as the rest she had passed along—as if everyone in London was elsewhere, attending some celebration or party to which she hadn't been invited.

Now she realized where she was heading. At the far end of this street there was a cul-de-sac containing a line of derelict buildings that had always fascinated Max. She'd mentioned them to the police and they'd added them to their list of special haunts. Perhaps the police had already been there, found nothing, and gone on. Perhaps it was pointless to hope—but she was determined to find out for herself. Max had been told never to go into the houses, but he'd been so odd lately, so moody and strange. Maybe he'd just been sick of being cooped up. Maybe it was just defiance. Maybe she would find him exploring the empty rooms, full of his own mischief.

She prayed for a naughty child.

A live, laughing, naughty child.

She looked at her watch. Nearly five o'clock, and the day was darkening. It would probably be pitch-dark in those houses. The street lamps were only creating useless pools of sickly light, deepening the shadows in between, so that her progress was stroboscopic. She visualized herself flickering on, off, on, off. She slowed, hearing again that odd echo of footsteps, and whirled around. Nobody, nothing. Just the empty street hung with misty curtains, and, far away, the hum of the rush hour.

A car passed down the street, and then another, seeking a shortcut around stalled or slow-moving traffic, the drivers intent only on their journeys home, hunched over their steering wheels, androgynous silhouettes, as unknown to her as she to them, and as uncaring. They could not help her find her child.

Maybe they'd taken Max away in a car.

Who?

Don't think about that, she told herself. Think about finding a naughty little boy in a bright-red anorak and school scarf. Expect to see him any minute, around this corner, around the next, here, there, anywhere, everywhere.

Now.

Yes!

As she turned the final corner she thought she saw a flash of red in the distance, going into one of the derelict houses.

"Max! *Max!*"

She began to run.

The house was the last in the row, at the end of the cul-de-sac. A high brick wall ran the width of the street between it and the house opposite, closing off the road from the open drop to the rails of the Metropolitan Line which surfaced here, briefly, before plunging once more into subterranean darkness.

These houses had been condemned two years before, unfit even for restoration. But a preservation order was holding up their demolition, and they continued to be slowly shaken to pieces by the vibration from the passing trains. Another went by now, the sound of its passage transformed into the rumbling of electric animals kept behind beyond the brick wall: dangerous, powerful, large.

The pavement vibrated beneath Tess's feet as she stood staring at the door of the condemned house. Boarded up, like all the rest, it had a boy-sized hole at the bottom where two bits of wood had been pulled away—so tempting.

"Max! I saw you go in there, young man! Come out here this instant!"

But there was only the sound of the train, fading fast as it entered the tunnel, and then only silence and the steady drip of condensation from a broken gutter.

"Max! Max Leland! Come out here this instant!"

A rattle of grit, the creak of a board—something *was* beyond that boarded door. Something or someone.

Was it her son?

The prospect of entering that filthy, crumbling house was terrifying to her, but she had to do it. She had to *know*.

She took her hands from her pockets and went up the uneven path to the gap in the boards, bent down, and peered through. Faint streaks of light from the street lamps illuminated the hall beyond and showed the shattered lower half of the stairway which led upward, to darkness.

Taking hold of one of the boards, she pulled hard and nearly lost her footing. It hadn't been nailed shut at all, merely balanced there to provide the illusion of closure.

For someone, for some reason, the house was still alive.

She put down the board and crouched slightly to step through the opening. The house smelled odd, as if work were going on here. What was it, that sour, penetrating odor?

The light from outside was very faint now, and she had neither torch nor matches to show the way. Twice she skidded on what felt like plastic bags, once she put a foot through a hole in the floor, cutting her shin and nearly losing a shoe.

There was a brief flicker of light from the door at the end of the hall. "Max? Don't be afraid, love. It's Mummy—and I'm not angry. Please come out."

"Ooohh, Max . . . it's only Mummy . . . and she's not angry. . . . Nooooooooo. . . ."

Tess froze in the doorway as she found herself facing a ring of pale faces, watery-eyed, grinning, wavering and rocking, the floor in front of them littered with plastic bags and rolled-up tubes of glue and cigarette butts and empty cider bottles and spoons and squares of foil and four or five disposable syringes.

None older than twelve, she thought in that first shocked moment. Boys or girls, it was impossible to tell. And any one of them could have been Max.

But wasn't.

They giggled as she stared, and then the grins became feral, defensive, vicious. "Piss off," one of them snarled. "Piss off or we'll cut you." When she didn't move, one of them, the largest and oldest, began to gather himself up.

"PISS OFF!" he shouted, balancing himself precariously and then stumbling toward her as his foot rolled on a bottle. Instinctively she caught him by the shoulders before he fell. His breath, fetid with decay and the acrid tang of solvents, whooshed into her face. She waited a moment, pushed him away, and spoke in a cold, hard voice.

"Have you see a little boy in a red anorak? A little boy named Max?"

The boy looked at her blearily, caught unexpectedly by a question rather than the expected accusation. "Go away," he said thickly.

She looked past him. "Have any of you seen a little boy in a red anorak?"

They stared back at her, uncomprehending, uncaring, lost in their haze of glue and drink and whatever else they had been sold. Their clothes were cheap and worn, their faces thin and surrounded by matted tendrils of unwashed hair, and she did not blame them or dislike them or pity them or excuse them.

She just wanted her child.

"The police are searching the neighborhood for my little boy," she said quietly. "They will be here soon, I expect. They weren't far behind me."

"Shit," the oldest boy said.

There was a whining scramble as they all struggled

to their feet and pushed past her, running down the hall, out the door and into the street beyond.

Tess, knocked to the floor by their frantic passage, tried to get up and cried out at the sudden pain in her ankle. This room had obviously been the kitchen, and her foot had caught in a corner of the torn linoleum as she went down. The house suddenly shook with the passage of another train behind and below it. There was a brief faint flashing from the rear window, and in its light she saw a figure standing in the hall doorway.

Before she could get up, the figure moved forward and lifted a foot to press her down into the filth of the broken floor. The foot was between her shoulder blades, squeezing the breath out of her, forcing her face down into the plastic bags still reeking of glue. Just inches from her eye, the exposed needle of one of the used syringes glittered in the faint, treacherous light. High above her, a voice spoke.

"Time this was finished, Tess. Time for the game to end."

31

It was Archie—or Kobalski, they'd said his real name was. The fake Australian accent and slang were gone—as were the lovely manners he'd displayed at the Ritz.

He was big and strong and terrible—strong enough to hold her down with one foot while he lit a cigarette and enjoyed the spectacle of her squirming there.

She looked up over her shoulder and saw his face momentarily illuminated by the flickering flame of his lighter. The handsome features, once so warm and lively, were cold, and there was cruelty in his beautiful eyes.

"Now we can do this easy, babe, or we can do this tough."

He lifted his foot from her back, and for a moment she thought she might get up and run, but it was only so he could kneel beside her. And there was no running away from those hands.

"Where's my son?" she demanded. "What have you done with Max?"

"I haven't done anything with your damn kid. Maybe

we'll deal with him later, after we've finished with you. After *I've* finished with you." Suddenly his hands were in her hair, twisting it around his fingers, pulling her head back. She cried out with the sudden pain of it, her eyes filling with tears.

"Where's the money, babe? Where's the money your husband stole off us, hey? Got it stashed away good, have you? Keeping it a secret, biding your time waiting for that rainy day? That stupid old man didn't take it from the car, like I thought at first. And I couldn't find it at your place, so I figured you'd got really smart and maybe stashed it at that old house you were working on. I tried being nice, but you don't fall for nice, do you? And I'm fed up with waiting around. So where is it, hey? In some safety-deposit box somewheres? Yeah, that's it, isn't it? Not a bank account—the tax man might be nearly as interested as I am, right? No, a box. Or maybe you buried it in the garden, how about that?" He jerked her head back even further, and she heard the sudden, horrifying click of a flick-knife opening. "Did you bury it in the garden, sweetheart?"

Because he'd pulled her head so far back, her throat was tight, and the words could barely crawl out. "There's no money. Roger wouldn't steal money from anyone."

"That's what you think. He stole it from my main man, and my main man doesn't like getting stolen from, on principle. Leaves a nasty taste, makes him look a little foolish. Makes him mad. And when he gets mad, he gets even. Capisce?"

"I don't have any money. I don't know what you're talking about," she gasped in a strangled voice. The cold edge of the knife was under her ear, but after a moment of staring down at her he took it away and laid it down on the floor. Then he rolled her over onto her back, half across his knees.

Tess screamed at the half-seen expression on his face—greed and anger and lust combined to twist his handsome features into a demonic mask—and then her scream was cut off by the pressure of his cold, wet mouth over hers. He tasted of garlic and stale whiskey and cigarettes, and she twisted her head away to scream again.

It was a mistake,

His snaking hand left her body and returned with the knife.

He drew the razor-edge blade down the side of her neck—she could feel the sting of air on the thin wound—and then dug the tip of it into the cleft between her breasts.

"Like I said, it can be easy or difficult, sweetheart. If I don't get the money back, my main man is going to think I can't do my job right. But I can do it—when I'm not interfered with. 'No violence,' he said." He mimicked a voice she thought she recognized. "'Don't hurt her,' he said. Pigwash. I handle assignments the way *I* want to, and not anyone else. What I start, I finish, you understand? I have a reputation to maintain. I lay off one, maybe they think I'm going to lay off the next one, or the next. Or that I can be bought off, maybe. That's no good for business. No good for me. I have an investment in myself, you might say." Though he kept the knife pointed toward her throat, held lightly in his fingertips, he rubbed the palm of his hand over her breasts, lingering over the nipples, pressing down, and all the while breathing into her face. Another underground train rumbled past, the faint flickering light from its windows showing the white of his teeth, the strong lines of his nose and jaw. Oh, the betraying perfection of those handsome features behind which lurked a cruel and greedy man. "Mmmm," he said. "Nice little knockers, sweetheart. What else have you got to offer a hungry man?" He laid his knife between her breasts and his hand slid down her body until it reached the hem of her skirt, and began to slide upward again, beneath it.

"You obviously don't have a very good memory."

A voice, hard and harsh, came from the hall.

At the sound Kobalski jerked around, caught by surprise. The knife slid onto the floor, and his hand loosened in her hair. "I remember what I want to remember," he snarled. "And I remember we have some unfinished business."

"Then let's get it sorted out, shall we? You can deal with her later."

Kobalski pushed Tess off his knee and got slowly to his feet, squinting into the darkness of the hall. He bent down and snatched up the knife, held it blade-out toward the shadow in the doorway. "Right," he said.

As he moved forward, the man in the hall stepped back into the darker shadows. "I think we should talk about the money first."

"Oh, yeah? You have it?"

"I know where it is. I found the hiding place you were too stupid to find. I can put my hands on it anytime I like."

They moved down the hall, the newcomer backing away, Kobalski coming after, drawn inexorably by the lure of the money. Drawn away from Tess. She lay there, unbelieving, her mind refusing to accept what it heard. It wasn't true. It couldn't be true. But she knew the voice so well, had heard it in the dark before, had heard it in the light, had heard it and been grateful.

Fool.

The man in the hall was John Soame.

She got up as quietly as she could and looked around her. The door from the kitchen to the rear of the house was no more than a black gap in the wall, covered by a couple of loose boards. She edged over to it and quickly ducked under the lower one, stumbling down a stone step into the pitch-black yard beyond. Her ankle stabbed pain up into her leg, and she gasped with the shock of it. It was weak and wobbly, but it did not give way. She nearly did, the pain was so great. But she must not give way, she must *get* away.

There was still Max.

He wasn't here, so Kobalski had taken him somewhere else. She *knew* she could find him—if she could just get away.

She couldn't see the fog, but she could feel it against her face, cool and clammy. Overhead the lights of the city diffused into it a pale-gray glow, tinged with orange from one side of the sky to the other. A glow that gave no light, but only absorbed it, so that here, on the ground, she was blind. In the darkness her stumbling feet encountered a bottle which skittered away and smashed against something metallic.

"Hey!" came a shout from the house behind her. "She's out!" And she could hear Kobalski cursing as he kicked away the boards over the door.

She ran down the littered, overgrown yard, stumbling and lurching as she prayed for escape. But there was no escape—and she realized why the glue-sniffing children had chosen to risk running straight into the arms of the police rather than escape from the house this way.

The yard was enclosed on all three sides by a brick wall, its surface slimy and cold under her scrabbling fingers. It was very high on either side, but against the sky she could see that the rear wall had tumbled down in one place. It would have to be there—she had no other alternative. She could hear Kobalski coming down the yard toward her, closer and closer.

Desperately she climbed up the wall, sticking her fingers and toes into the chinks left by fallen or broken bricks, trying to reach the top, planning to go over into the next yard and get away. As she reached the top and swung a leg over, another tube train rumbled past, shaking the ground, the wall, and—seemingly—the whole world. The *was* no other yard on the far side of the wall.

Just a straight drop to the Metropolitan Line.

And its electrified rails.

As she hesitated, she felt Kobalski's hand clutching at her legs, and realized that she, like the wall itself, was outlined clearly against the oddly pale fog-lit night sky. There was no real choice, no other way.

She kicked out at him, felt her toe connect with what she hoped was his head, heard him yell, and then swung herself over the wall. For a moment she hung there, a moment that was as close to eternity as she had ever known. Then she let go.

And dropped to the tracks below.

32

Tess lay perfectly still where she had fallen.

She'd been stunned for a moment, but now her mind was clear—terribly clear. She sensed, but could not see, the electrified underground rails beside her. She could smell the acrid presence of high voltage, rubber buffers, oil. Lifting her eyes, she saw a long narrow strip of sky high above her—the diffuse luminous orangy glow of the city under the fog. Beneath her, dirt and grit pushed a thousand points into her skin, penetrating even the heavy wool of her skirt.

She was afraid to move for fear of touching the live rail. That was certain death.

Gently she flexed her arms and legs and neck, testing to see if pain shouted the news of broken bones, torn muscles. No—she was bruised, but aside from the throb of her previously twisted ankle, she seemed whole enough. Despair had made her go limp as she fell through what had seemed like miles of space—as if the ground, seeing her descent, had pulled away to avoid the impact.

Overhead, where the wall to which she had clung

edged the sky, she could see the outline of a head—Kobalski had reached the top and was peering down into the cutting. She could hear shouting, but the words were not clear because of the noise from the approaching train.

The approaching train!

Her stomach lurched and her heart seemed to go into suspended animation. A train was coming and she was lying within inches of the rail.

The rumbling grew louder, filling the long narrow declivity, growing, swelling. There was a screech of metal on metal as the wheels scraped the rails. The ground beneath her shook and trembled as if it were as terrified by the approaching monster as she. Suddenly light came, the light of a train bursting from the tunnel, emerging one-eyed from its lair, bearing down on her.

She screamed but could not hear herself at all, curled back against the filthy wall, a small terrified animal transfixed by the light. Beneath the dumbfounding roar of the train, echoed and amplified by the enclosing walls, she could hear the crackle from the thousands of volts of electricity that propelled it, felt the wind of its passage sucking grit and paper and discarded rubbish into a whirlwind that rose and surrounded her. She screamed again as the train thundered past. She knew she screamed only because her mouth stretched and her breath was expelled and there was a tearing in her throat—but she heard only the deafening clack and clatter and thunder of the train itself.

And then it was gone.

Disbelievingly, she lay there, her breath coming painfully from her constricted chest, her hearing numbed by the explosion of sound that was even now diminishing as the train disappeared into the far tunnel, the last of the lights from the coaches flickering against the sooty walls.

Darkness came again.

Tess began to sob, great racking sobs of relief. But that relief was tempered by the realization that this was not the end, that more trains would come, and that she could be—would be—battered again and again by the maelstrom of noise and wind. She had survived one onslaught—the thought of others inevitably coming was almost impossible to bear.

The tube trains stopped during the night, didn't they? Maintenance crews came along then, so the electricity in the rails would be switched off eventually.

She clung to the thought, even as the ground again began to shake beneath her and once more the distant rumbling began. From behind her, this time. The last train had gone by on the far side—this one would probably come close, for it was traveling the other way.

"Oh, God, please help me," she sobbed, and again curled against the wall as the light burst forth from the tunnel and noise became a pounding ram of force that would surely crush her or tear her apart.

But it didn't.

This train also passed by on the far side.

Breathless, grateful, she lay there and tried to sort out her impressions. She had closed her eyes each time the trains had burst out of their respective tunnels. There were tracks next to her, she had glimpsed them momentarily before she blindly cringed away. Why weren't the trains using them?

Someone was shouting from above. She paid no attention. Kobalski, John Soame—they had nothing to do with her now. Whatever danger they represented paled in comparison to the danger only inches from her.

After a few minutes the ground began to vibrate once more, and again there came the distant mutter and rhythmic pulse of an approaching train. She was ready, she could bear it, she would keep her eyes open this time.

At the last minute she lost her nerve, and her eyes

closed involuntarily against the wind and the spinning grit and rubbish. But she had seen enough. The tracks next to her were overgrown and barricaded at the tunnel's mouth. They were not being used. She could move.

Maybe.

Just because they weren't being used was no guarantee that electricity still didn't pulse through them when the trains passed on the far side, did it? Wasn't there something in electricity about completing a circuit? Isn't that why lightning didn't hurt you if you were earthed?—whatever being earthed entailed. Not for the first time, she cursed her ignorance of the way things worked. She knew nothing about the underground system or how it functioned—she only knew how to get from one station to another. To touch the wrong rail—the center rail?—was certain death, she knew. On the other hand, she knew that she had read of people falling beneath the trains and surviving—or was that simply in the stations, where there was a deep channel beneath the rails?

At any rate, it was simply a matter of staying where she was until the trains stopped, and then perhaps a maintenance crew would come along and—

Something touched her face. She screamed and flailed out wildly with her hands. Was it an insect? A bat?

After a moment she saw it against the sky and realized it was a rope. A rope! Lowered down to her—was this salvation? She struggled to her knees and looked up.

"Come on, sweetheart, grab on and we'll pull you up," came Kobalski's voice, sweet again with lies. "You don't want to get electrocuted down there, do you? We won't hurt you—I promise. I only want the money, honey." He chuckled, he actually chuckled, and the sound whispered back and forth in the small canyon of the cutting, reverberating between the walls in a mockery of the thunder that had gone before.

She waited for John Soame to add his treacherous voice to this less than tempting lure. But he was silent, perhaps realizing she would not trust him any more than she would trust Kobalski, who was apparently under the impression that she was stupid enough to climb back up to him.

She sat back down, ignoring the rope that dangled before her. Then it began to jerk about wildly—did he think that would increase the temptation? She looked up, preparing to tell him what he could do with his damned rope, and saw he was already doing something with it.

He was climbing down to her.

Perhaps to make certain she fell in front of the next train.

"Oh, God—" That was twice she had invoked the Deity. She was sure there was one, but He seemed to be looking elsewhere at the moment. She struggled to her feet, gasped at the pain from her ankle, which she had momentarily forgotten, and began to edge away down the wall.

"No! No!" she yelled. She saw the figure on the rope turn toward her, spinning awkwardly against the sky, searching the dark shadows for her and stiffening angrily when he realized she had moved away.

To what?

She didn't know, she didn't care. Sheer terror robbed her of reason, gave strength to her legs, and drove her before it. Mindless and blind, she ran along the wall, squeezed past the barrier, and went into the black mouth of the tunnel, where even the faint luminosity of the night sky could not reach.

In the distance, she heard the fresh thunder of an approaching train.

33

The noise in the brick-walled cutting had been bad enough, but the crescendo of the passing train within the tunnel was like a fist to her head and a hammer to her body. Tess turned and pressed her face against the grimy wall and felt her skirt whip around her legs as the train went by.

Out of the corner of her eye she saw the passengers in the coaches, peacefully reading their evening papers or staring blankly at the advertisements that ran in a line above the windows, oblivious to her existence or her terror. Some were even chatting, hanging from the straps and exchanging polite but weary evening smiles.

It was the crackle of the electricity that was the worst—and the strange metallic smell it left in the air. The space within the tunnel was even more restricted than it had been in the cutting, although this was still a double tunnel. There was no shoulder of ground here. Just a ledge, barely walkable. The curved walls seemed to press her over as her feet edged along.

For a while there was silence, blessed moments of relief. She didn't know how long it would last, but she wanted to make the most of it. She could hear her own breath, panting, and a low moaning whimper that seemed to originate in her throat—a throat already sore from screaming.

And someone else was in the tunnel, too. Scraping sounds overlapped her own, more than echoes. So Kobalski had followed her in. He was intent on her destruction, one way or another.

She tried to remember the distance between stations. Surely she'd come this way a hundred times over the past years. But which station to which station it was she didn't know, because as she'd wandered the streets looking for Max she hadn't kept track of distance or direction. She could have gone in a circle for all she knew—where were those derelict houses?

It couldn't be far, she thought. This is still London, not the suburbs. Not more than two minutes between stations here, surely. Unless she was under the park. The wall curved under her outstretched hands, seemed to go on and on and on.

Now she could see signal lights ahead. Didn't that mean a station was near? Or was it a junction? She moved along, then paused beneath them to catch her breath.

Beside the signal lights there was a small niche in the wall. On the floor lay some tools, discarded or left deliberately for the next man or the next job. She bent down and ran her fingers over them. She grasped what felt like a pipe or a wrench. It was heavy, about a foot long. At least she had something to defend herself with now. She could wait until he came along and—

But he can see me here, because of the lights, she thought, and moved on.

About twenty feet past the lights and around a last sharp bend, she came to a place where the rails divided. A faint light came from a grimy light bulb set high in the tunnel roof, showing her two ways to go. Obviously the left-hand tracks would eventually lead to a station. It was a narrow tunnel, holding only one track—a live track—with no more than inches between the wall and the sides of the racing trains.

There hadn't been a train for some time. Odd, considering this was the rush hour. Looking back she could see that the signals were still red. If she chose the narrow tunnel she might make it to the next station before a train came. Or she might try to go too fast, and fall onto the live rail. Or a train might come and smear her along the wall, crushing her like an insect.

The right-hand tunnel only offered blackness, but safety from the terrible voltage of the live rail, and perhaps from Kobalski, too. What else it might offer she would not think about.

She went right.

This tunnel was wider, with a margin of cinder track beside the rails. And there was no smell of electricity here, either. Perhaps only because the circuit was not complete. One touch and she could become the last arc. She kept on, blindly, holding her hands out in front of her, keeping her shoulder against the wall so as not to stray onto the rails. The ground seemed to slope upward slightly. After what seemed like an eternity of slow, groping progress, she sensed an open space ahead. Perhaps through some change in the quality of her own breathing and the sound of her shuffling footsteps? A draft of fresh air? Was it yet another junction? She knew there was an absolute maze of tunnels and junctions beneath the London streets of which ordinary people like herself knew little. Like the sewers and the conduits for electricity and phone cables, it was a secret and hidden world.

She began to move along more quickly, hoping for another niche in the wall in which she could rest or hide. Instead, her groping hand encountered what felt like the edge of the wall. She could thrust her arm all the way back and still she did not encounter anything but space.

It was a platform!

With some difficulty, she climbed up and felt her way onto the flat space. She moved forward until she ran smack into another wall. Splaying out her hands, she felt the cold shininess of tiles, some missing, and then stepped to the side and barked her shins against a rough bench, onto which she sank. It was a station!

But there were no bright lights, no gaudy advertisements, no crowds of people impatiently waiting. Nothing. It was deserted, abandoned. She sat there, panting, gathering herself together. She ran a hand down her leg and encountered a large swelling—the ankle had bandaged itself. She could hardly flex it, but the pain had diminished a bit.

Her breath was coming in hiccups and sobs now. Had she been seen under the faint light at the junction? Had Kobalski followed her into the blackness or not? There was no way of knowing, but she had come to expect the worst. God still seemed to be looking the other way.

She couldn't risk it, couldn't stay where she was. She had to hide—or better still, find a way out of here and into the open air.

She forced herself to her feet and, arms outstretched as before, began to work her way along the old platform. She could still see nothing, and the air was dead and still. Claustrophobia, which sheer terror had kept at bay while in the tunnel, now began to press in on her.

Her groping hands suddenly went forward into space, and she nearly fell to her knees again.

She moved forward, feeling ahead of her with her good foot, and almost immediately banged into another wall. Right or left? She tried both and realized she was in a pedestrian tunnel that turned after leaving the platform and led—where?

To some stairs, she discovered, after falling painfully up the first three. Pressing her back against the handrail that was fastened to the wall, she started to edge up the stairs one at a time. They were wood, and creaked alarmingly under her weight. For all she knew, the staircase was incomplete. For all she knew, she could fall through on the next step. Or the next. Or the next.

She continued to climb, she had to climb, there was no other option. From below her she saw, reflected in the dusty tiles, a brief flicker of light. Kobalski and his damned cigarette lighter. The light disappeared. He wasn't wasting it—just giving himself brief illumination now and again.

And he was still coming after her.

Tess continued to climb, a step at a time, until she reached the top. She sensed a great space ahead of her, and began to move through it, arms outstretched, testing each step before she transferred her weight to it.

By the time Kobalski reached the top of the staircase behind her, she was in the middle of what—in the flare of his lighter—seemed to be the booking hall. She froze where she stood, arms out as if she were preparing to fly, her tear-filled eyes starred by the reflection.

"Well, hello there," he said. He sounded quite cheerful.

"Stay away from me," Tess croaked, raising the metal bar she'd found in the tunnel. "Just stay away."

"My goodness, you scare me half to death," Kobalski said, and smiled. He came toward her, holding his lighter at shoulder level. The light reached out faint fingers all around, and Tess could see that the ticket booths were shrouded in cobwebs and dust, and the walls contained shreds of old advertisements, half torn away and faded. One said "Careless Talk Costs Lives"—telling her when the station was closed.

And possibly why.

She started to back away, glancing over her shoulder, prepared to see a yawning gap of bomb damage or some fallen timbers. But the way was clear—only a rusting folding gate drawn across a solid wall of wood. Station closed. What lay beyond the gate and the boarding she could only guess at. She didn't remember seeing a deserted station anywhere in the streets of the area. Perhaps it had been bombed. Perhaps there was an entire building beyond the boards.

Her tomb was going to be an impressive one.

When, one day, they reentered this place, what would they think when they found her body lying here—or even, by then, her skeleton? Would they think she was an ancient war casualty? Would she haunt the hall, wandering forever down the tunnels, searching for a way out, for a way to her son?

"Where's Max?" she demanded hoarsely.

"How the hell would I know?" he asked.

"Didn't you kidnap him?"

"Hell, no. But it would have been a good idea, come to think of it. You'd have handed over the money then, wouldn't you?"

"If she had it—which she doesn't," said John Soame, emerging at the top of the stairs behind Kobalski. "I told you that before. She never had it."

Kobalski whirled so quickly at the sound of John's voice that the lighter went out, and he had to flick it into life again. As he did, she saw him reach into his pocket.

"He's got a knife!" she shouted. But then, John knew that, didn't he? Why on earth had she bothered to warn him?

"Yes, I know he has. And I have a gun." He moved a hand inside his jacket pocket, extending it as if there were a pistol inside. Kobalski sneered at such a pathetic subterfuge.

"Oh, wow," he drawled. "A two-finger thirty-eight. Why, shucks, you can't hardly get them no more." His tone was bored—he'd seen it all before. "I thought you'd run for it," he said. "Thought you'd turned tail. Persistent bastard, aren't you? Well, you can't pretend you have anything to offer me anymore, because I know you haven't." Flicking his knife open in one movement, he thrust the naked blade toward Soame. It was a mistake.

The sudden movement caused him to slide on the gritty surface, and he dropped the lighter. It cracked onto the marble floor and lay there, its fluid flooding out and burning brightly for a moment before flickering out.

Darkness again.

There was a sharp intake of breath, a scuttle of steps, a grunt, a moan, and then the noise of struggle. Tess backed away, afraid to strike out in the dark, although she still held the metal pipe. She kept backing until she hit the wall, and then just stood there helplessly.

The sounds, the terrible animal sounds, seemed to recede from her, and then there was a sudden shout and a crash of splintering, rotten boards. They had broken through the stairway and fallen, locked together, to the platform below.

Tess covered her face with her hands.

And then there came a new sound.

A high, thin whistle.

Suddenly there was light. Faint and pale yellow, two of the three globes in an overhead fixture came to life, throwing barely adequate illumination onto the vast, dusty hall. They brightened for a moment, and then one flickered and popped out, leaving only one to shed its light, creating more shadows than sense in the big space.

At the same time there was a loud noise and more light poured in—this time from a slowly widening gap in the boarding beyond the metal gap. Men stood there, silhouetted in a bright light that scalded Tess's eyes. She could see them moving, peering through. Then she heard Abbott's voice. He sounded almost bored—certainly annoyed.

"All right, that's enough. I am a police officer and I am armed." He stood to one side while a man in a London Transport uniform unlocked the gate. With a protesting shriek of rusty metal they pushed the gate aside. Policemen poured in and stood staring around them.

"They're down there," Tess shouted, pointing.

A torch beam swung around and revealed her pressed against the frame of a torn advertisement for Cadbury's Chocolate. "Good God," said Tim Nightingale.

She was never to know how she looked standing there—face filthy with soot and grime, clothes torn, legs bleeding through ripped tights, white streaks of tears dividing her face like river channels, hair strung with cobwebs, eyes wild.

"Are you all right?" Nightingale asked gruffly, coming over to her, while other men went over to the stairway and peered down. She leapt forward. "Make him tell you where he's got Max!" she screamed. "Get him, make him tell—" She was hammering on his chest desperately. What if Kobalski was unconscious? Hurt? Dead? He'd never speak then. "I'll do it. Let me do it. Let me hurt him, let me kill him, make him tell me, make him—"

"Mrs. Leland!" He grabbed her arms, shook her. "It's all right. We've got the boy—he's quite safe."

She cried out with the sudden relief and felt the floor giving way—was she, too, to fall into darkness? But Nightingale was there, holding her up with one strong arm, helping her over to a bench, saying encouraging, peaceful things until the vast dust-fogged hall ceased spinning and humming around her. Some of the men by the broken stairway had edged forward, clinging to the handrail and one another, tentatively descending via the surviving edges of the stairs.

"Is Max all right?" Her throat was so raw from screaming that when she tried normal tones they were no more than a croak.

"He's fine."

"Where—" she began to ask, but then the men who

had gone down the stairway reappeared, hauling Kobalski and John Soame with them. As she watched she saw John hold out a bleeding arm while one of the officers tied a handkerchief around it. He looked across the man's shoulder at Tess.

And she looked at him.

There was a sudden burst of voices from the direction of the rusty gate, and Tess turned to see Adrian Brevitt being led through the gap in the boarding. He stood there staring at her. From beyond him there came the sound of traffic—just ordinary street traffic. So there was a street out there, after all, and she hadn't climbed from the tunnels merely to find herself entombed beneath a pile of concrete.

Then Richard pushed past Adrian and the man in the London Transport uniform. He came straight over to Tess, put his arm around her and tipped her face up. "Are you all right? Did he hurt you?"

"I'm fine, Richard."

"Christ, you're bleeding," he said, and produced a handkerchief which he used to wipe the long, thin cut that was still oozing blood into her collar. She had forgotten that—it seemed to have happened many years before. "And your legs—" he bent to wipe those, too, and saw her swollen ankle. "Oh, Tess," he said. "My dear."

Adrian came across too, and gazed down at them. "All this is not very nice, is it?" he said in a strange and sorrowful voice. "So . . . unnecessary."

There was a snort of derision, and they all turned to see that Detective Constable Murray had moved to the center of the hall and was holding Kobalski's arm in an iron grip.

"All she had to do was tell me where the money was," Kobalski said to him in a perfectly reasonable tone.

Abbott went over and stood next to the handsome American, whose good looks were not lessened by the dirt on his face nor the fact that his hair was tumbled over his forehead. If anything, he looked more attractive then ever, Tess thought. Only the anger in his eyes spoiled things. That, and the cruel twist of his mouth.

It did not seem at all strange to her that she could think that he was attractive, even now. All the men around her seemed frozen in a tableau so that she could examine them one by one, as if she were suspended in a bubble of time. All the men in her life. Richard, so solicitous, so protective, his good square face earnestly gazing down at her; Adrian, elegant and impeccable, but still with that odd and distant expression in his eyes; John Soame, dirty and disheveled, watching her intently, his narrow face scratched and bruised, his expression strained.

Detective Chief Inspector Abbott, tall and self-contained; Detective Sergeant Nightingale, who had believed her when no one else had; Detective Constable Murray and the other detectives who had been at the house. Even the London Transport man looked familiar standing there in his uniform, twisting the keys in his hands, gazing around the empty booking hall making a mesmerized inventory.

And Roger, who was not there, but whom she could see clearly now in her mind's eye, the way he'd looked when he'd left that last, terrible morning. His dear, familiar face had been haunted, his natural ebullience dulled—as if he'd been invisibly bruised and was hurting inside. "Don't worry, Tess," he'd said. "It's a bit of a mess, but at least I've decided what to do about it. I'll sort it all out."

But he'd never said what it was.

And he hadn't lived to sort it all out, either.

She'd been left to pay the bills.

All the bills.

Abbott spoke to Kobalski. "Perhaps you'd like to make things easier for yourself now," he suggested. "Perhaps you'd like to bring someone with you for company when we take you to the Yard. Your local contact, for instance?"

"Yeah, sure, why not?" Kobalski agreed. "Misery always loves company—not that I intend to be miserable for very long." He walked forward, Nightingale coming with him on one side, Murray on the other. As he moved, Kobalski spoke with a kind of resigned disgust. "My main man warned me about you and your damned English caution. Always interfering. Always making me slow down, back off. You should have let me do the job right from the beginning," he sneered. "We could have finished it long ago, if you'd let me do it right."

And Nightingale's hand closed on Richard Hendricks's arm.

34

Adrian Brevitt sat down beside Tess and rested his chin on his silver-headed cane. "One should have known," he murmured. "He had absolutely no taste. And as for his clothes . . ." He shuddered delicately.

"I can't believe it," Tess whispered, shivering.

"I can," Abbott said quietly. "Richard Hendricks is the kind of man who is always right, in his own eyes. When that kind of man is crossed, he is very dangerous indeed, because every argument is a threat to his ego and his self-image. We spent most of this morning with the Fraud Squad, going over and verifying information Tim had gotten from—somewhere." He glanced over at Nightingale, who flushed and managed to look both proud and sad.

Abbott went on. "We were pretty certain Hendricks was behind the trouble, but we didn't know how he fitted in, and how far back it had begun. At first we assumed it was just the accident—that perhaps he'd been driving the car that old Ivor Peters thought was chasing your husband—and that Max could identify him—"

"Where *is* Max?" Tess demanded. "You said he was all right, but where is he? I want to see him!"

"You might better ask where *was* he," Adrian said. "All the while we were searching for the little devil, he was sitting in Hendricks's outer office, waiting to see him. That young curate drove him over, apparently under the impression that you knew all about it. Hendricks's secretary finally rang through because she wanted to go home and didn't want to leave Max sitting there alone. Sergeant Nightingale went for him in a police car—I expect riding in that made his day."

"He went to see Richard? But why?"

"To return the money, in a manner of speaking," Nightingale told her. "You see, he had it all along. His father had given it to him."

"Three hundred thousand pounds," Adrian murmured.

Tess stared at them, aghast. "Where did Roger get three hundred thousand pounds, for goodness' sake?" Her head was spinning again, and it had nothing to do with the concussion, or the terrible flight through the darkness of the tunnels below. "Are you telling me that Roger *did* steal some money? That he *was* involved in drugs?"

Abbott shook his head. "Not in the way you're thinking. I'm sorry if this upsets you—"

"I think I'm beyond being upset," Tess said weakly.

"Yes, I suppose you are. Well, I had a word with the pathologist—and it's quite likely that your husband didn't die instantly in that crash. He and the boy were trapped there, together, for perhaps ten minutes or so before the ambulance came. He must have realized he was dying. He managed to tell Max something about what he had done—although it was probably pretty incoherent—but before he could tell him why—he died."

"Oh, Lord." Tess felt as if she had been stabbed, the

pain in her chest was so great. "My poor Max. No wonder he had nightmares," she said. "But why didn't he say something? Why didn't he ask *me* about it?"

"Your husband may have told him not to tell you. We didn't question the boy closely—there wasn't time—so you may learn more eventually. But it's obvious that he was upset and confused about it all. It was quite a dilemma for a youngster. And then he became ill. That meant he had a perfect excuse to delay doing anything—but the delay also made the burden of guilt heavier. The time went on—and so did those nightmares. Max knew that by rights the money was Hendricks's, but he didn't *like* Hendricks. He may even have blamed him for his father's death. So he didn't *want* to give it back. And, of course, he didn't know anything about what you were going through, did he?"

"No—I didn't want to frighten or worry him," Tess said slowly. Then the enormity of it hit her. "But how could Max have had all that money? I mean, that much would be very bulky, wouldn't it? I've cleaned his room dozens of times since Roger died, and there was no money there. And Kobalski didn't find it, either." She remembered something and turned to John Soame. "You told Kobalski *you* knew where it was."

He didn't look at her. "I was bluffing," he said dully. "Trying to buy time."

An ambulance siren sounded in the distance, muffled by the fog, coming closer. Some blood was still trickling down John's arm and splashing onto the marble floor by his feet, combining with the dust to make small, muddy crimson puddles. She could feel the warmth of him beside her, and was ashamed. She had been so wrong, so quick to assume he was associated with Kobalski when all along he had been trying to protect her. The blood he was shedding, the struggles he'd had, the time he'd lost from his work, all of it was because of her, and when the final moment had come, she had not trusted him.

"Oh, Max has told me where it was," Nightingale said. "I talked to him in the car on the way back to the house. I have a couple of younger brothers of my own." He grinned. "You might not have seen it, but it was in his room all the time."

"But where?"

"In his stamp album." Nightingale smiled at their astonishment, enjoyed the moment. Then his face saddened, because he knew he had to tell her the rest, and it wasn't easy. It was never easy to tell someone that they had been deceived by a person they trusted, in whatever way, and for whatever reason.

He took a deep breath. "You see, for quite a while your husband and his partner were involved in a little more than public relations, I'm afraid. Under cover of servicing their actual clients they'd been running a nice little sideline in smuggling stolen or proscribed works of art or even occasionally transferring money for some very questionable clients on their 'private' list. I think your husband did it for fun—but Hendricks was always interested in profits. There came a day—perhaps inevitably, considering the kind of people they were dealing with—when Hendricks was shown there would be even *more* profit in drugs. Hendricks was willing—but there your husband drew the line. Little tricks to cheat the tax man or customs were one thing—sort of glamorous, I suppose—but drugs were something else again."

"Roger would *never* have touched drugs," Tess said.

"Your husband went to France just before he died, didn't he?"

"Yes, that's right. Marseilles."

"It would be. Hendricks probably gave him money to make a 'purchase,'" Abbott said. "The contact had been prearranged, but when your husband realized it was to be drugs he was to carry, and not negotiable bonds or some work of art, he couldn't bring himself to do it. He never made the meeting. There he was in Marseilles with all this money. He was furious with Hendricks, and worried about being implicated in some way because of it, so he bought something else instead. Something that would look quite innocuous if he was stopped at customs at either end."

"What?"

"A set of stamps. Not so much to look at—just very, very rare. When he got back, he slipped them into Max's stamp album. And when Max saw them, he loved them. That *also* made it difficult for him to turn them over to Hendricks. But in the end, seeing the house torn apart and, most importantly, seeing you hurt, was more terrible to him than losing any stamps, however rare and wonderful. So he decided to give them back to Hendricks—as his father had wanted. He thought the trouble would stop then."

"Did Richard . . . kill Roger?" She was almost afraid to ask.

"We don't think so," Detective Murray said. He had returned from handing the prisoners over. "Anyway, it would be hard to prove, with Ivor Peters dead."

Abbott became reflective. "It *might* have been a genuine accident—Peters could have been totally wrong about the intentions of the following driver. Just one of those terrible things that happen to the very people who least expect it. And it came at the worst possible time, because it left you facing a great deal of unfinished business."

"When Roger kissed me good-bye he said he was going to clear up 'the mess,'" Tess said sadly. "I didn't know what he meant, but I saw he had come to some kind of decision about something that had been worrying him."

"Well, for what it's worth, I tend to trust Ivor Peters's instinct," Nightingale said. "I always did. I think it *was* Kobalski driving the chase car, and Kobalski who frightened Peters sufficiently to precipitate a heart attack."

Tess remembered something. "He said something about thinking the old man had taken the money."

Nightingale allowed himself a glance of satisfaction at Abbott, who raised an eyebrow but said nothing. "Perhaps the car-rental clerk will recognize him," Nightingale said.

Abbott shook his head. "It won't make any difference," he said. "Kobalski will simply say he never intended to kill your husband, just frighten him into handing over the money. And it could be true, because it was early in the game, after all. We could never prove otherwise."

"And Richard hired him?"

"Not exactly," Abbott said.

"But Kobalski—"

"Kobalski was wished on Hendricks by the American dealers—he didn't have much choice about it."

"He said something about 'a main man.'"

"Yes. You see, Hendricks never suspected your husband had done anything with the money except what he had been *told* to do—he assumed he'd made the buy and passed on the goods—until the Marseilles dealer got in touch with him a few days after Roger's death and asked him if he was still interested in the shipment. That was the moment Hendricks realized your husband had stolen the money. By then, the client knew it, too. At first they assumed Roger had either given the money to you or hidden it at home—hence the break-in during the funeral. When nothing was found, Hendricks was told to get close to you."

"And that's why he was so attentive," Adrian put in. "Not that you're not worth pursuing, my dear—but he had ulterior motives beyond the obvious, I'm afraid." He patted her hand in a fatherly fashion.

As he spoke, the ambulance drew up outside—and then the ambulance men came through the gate.

"Here," Abbott called, gesturing them over and indicating John Soame's bleeding arm. One of them ripped the sleeve open and got to work.

"Did Hendricks ever hear about your son's nightmares?" Abbott asked Tess.

She nodded. "He actually witnessed one, in the hospital, when Max was delirious."

"Mmmmm. I'm afraid that may be what first made him think that *Max* knew something about the money, rather than you, and that there was still a chance he could get it back. But he couldn't get at Max in the hospital, and once Max came home he was never alone. You and Mr. Soame and that housekeeper of yours saw to that."

Nightingale spoke. "Kobalski had tried the phone calls and the break-ins to frighten you. They didn't work, and now Mr. Soame was in the way, too. Hendricks tried to turn you against him, but that didn't work, either. So, Archie McMurdo was invented."

"But why?"

"At first, to charm you. But you weren't having any. So he tried kicking up a fuss, to make you lose your job and perhaps either start spending the money or turn to Hendricks. I think Hendricks was genuinely fond of you, Mrs. Leland, and insisted that Kobalski go gently."

"I suppose I should be grateful for that," Tess said.

"Yes. But there was increasing pressure on Kobalski from the 'client' to get the job done."

"I don't know why Hendricks just didn't pay the client back out of the insurance money," John Soame put in. "Or from his own funds, if he's so well off."

Abbott shook his head. "I don't know if you know much about organized crime, but there was a lot more than just money involved here. It wasn't the money, it was the *getting back* of the money that was so important. The big men don't like to be seen as soft, and they don't like to be made fools of. What they do like is revenge, and making their position clear. That's why, whenever Hendricks was out of town, Kobalski got a little rougher. He was under pressure, too—and eventually he stopped listening to Hendricks."

Tess turned to Adrian. "You seemed to know Archie was a phony."

"Oh, I did," Adrian agreed. "But *only* after I'd flown to Italy and tracked down Dolly McMurdo herself. When I saw what you had done at the mansion I knew there was nothing wrong with your work or your ideas, so there had to be something wrong with *him*. When I finally found her in her little 'hideaway'—my God, Tess, you should have seen the frescoes in that place—she told me flatly that she had no nephew named Archie or anything else. I came back all full of my news, only to find it was old news." He sighed. "I felt quite miffed when you all turned on me."

"And promptly went into a sulk," John said, wincing as the ambulance man bound his wound.

"I am a sensitive creature," Adrian said, but his eyes were twinkling as he spoke.

Abbott wanted to finish this now. "Time was passing. Kobalski was waiting for Hendricks when he came back this morning. When Hendricks learned Max had gone missing, Kobalski leaned on him. Hendricks was frightened—he had begun to realize the kind of people he'd so lightly taken on as 'clients,' and that they had no compunction about killing even useful people if they wanted to make a point. Fear for his own safety finally overcame his better judgment, as well as any finer feelings he might have had about you and the boy. When he came over, he knew Kobalski was on watch outside, waiting for a chance to get you out of the way."

"And I gave it to him," Tess said contritely. "By leaving the house and going out to look for Max myself."

"Come on, in you get," the ambulance man said, taking hold of John Soame's good arm. Soame staggered slightly as he got up, and they supported him out of the hall and through the gate to the waiting ambulance.

Adrian looked at Tess, who was staring at the floor. "He followed you," he said softly. "He knew you wanted to look for Max, but he didn't want you to be alone."

Nightingale cleared his throat. "Soame saw Kobalski go into the house after you, and managed to ring us from a box on the corner. We told him to just watch and wait but—he went in. When you went over the wall Kobalski knocked him out and went after you. As soon as he came to, he went after Kobalski, even though he knew the man was a killer. He was over the wall by the time we arrived—he wouldn't wait—so all we could do was contact London Transport and get them to turn off the power. After that it was just a matter of covering all the stations to which you had access—including this one."

Tess looked at them, and then toward the gate.

"Go on, Tess. Mrs. Grimble and I will look after Max," Adrian said encouragingly. "And you *should* have that ankle strapped."

Tess stood up.

The ambulance doors banged shut and the ambulance swayed as the driver got in and started the engine. John Soame opened his eyes when Tess sat down beside him. "What about Max?" he asked.

"Mrs. Grimble will feed him bangers and mash and Adrian will tell him all about what he missed." She cleared her throat awkwardly. "Thanks for saving my life, by the way."

He shrugged, his old half-moon smile curling up in his pale face. "Thanks for saving mine," he said.

"I don't know what you mean."

"Oh . . . it's hard to explain. You see, last spring I had a nervous breakdown."

"Yes, I know."

"Oh?" He seemed surprised, but not embarrassed. "Well, it happens to a lot of people, I guess. They got me functioning again—I could walk and talk just like a real person." He smiled wryly. "But I simply felt dead inside. I couldn't seem to care about anything or anyone. I hoped coming to London, a change of work and scene, might help. At first it didn't make a bit of difference. And then Adrian suggested our 'arrangement.'" He managed another smile. "I won't say it's been *relaxing*, exactly—but it has stopped me thinking only about myself. And I don't think I've felt so alive for years. You did that. You and Max."

"And the beautiful Julia?" Tess asked before she could stop herself.

He looked at her in surprise. "What's my niece got to do with it?"

She stared back. "Julia's your *niece?*"

"Yes, of course. My ex-wife wasn't Adrian's only sister, you know, and they're all pretty overwhelming. Is it any wonder he turned out the way he has? Julia is not only my niece, she is a very intelligent girl who is doing medicine at Barts, and whose parents have several other children to support. I'm helping to finance her—hence my present extreme poverty—and in return she's helping me do my research. What did you *think* she . . ." He paused. "Oh, I see."

"Well, she *was* wearing your dressing gown."

He nodded. "Yes, she was. It was raining that night you saw her, if you recall. She had gotten her clothes soaked by a passing taxi and was drying them in front of my gas fire. You ran off before I could introduce you." He sighed. "She's just broken up with her boyfriend—I've been hearing all the gory details of a broken heart. Poor girl can't move into her new place until the end of the week. She'll have to stay with us until then." He started to put his good arm around her, then paused.

"You *did* call me 'darling' that night, didn't you?" he asked warily.

"Yes, I'm afraid I did."

He looked relieved. "That's all right then," he said.

He pulled her close, bent his head to kiss her, then slid slowly off the seat in a dead faint.

The ambulance man, who had been listening and watching with great interest, stared down at him and sighed. "I was expecting that," he said resignedly. "These intellectual types are all alike, aren't they?"

Tess smiled as she knelt to help him lift John onto the stretcher. "Not quite," she said. "Not quite."

35

Nightingale stood on the pavement watching the ambulance pull away. People were still pausing to stare, clotting on either side of the precipitately revealed tube station. A few ignored the broken boards and thick dust and were trying to buy tickets. Accustomed to stations that were vandalized, dilapidated, or in the throes of renovation, they assumed this was a functioning station, and did not like being told to move on. The man from London Transport looked on the verge of either strike action or a magnificent tantrum.

The fog was still with them—now visible only in lamplight and headlight beams—and he could feel the damp cold penetrating his jacket. "Move these people on, will you?" he asked one of the uniformed officers. "That poor sod from London Transport is going under for the third time. And get somebody to call LT—they'll need to send a crew to board up the place again."

"Yes, sir," the constable said, and moved off to do the usual six things at once.

Chief Inspector Abbott joined him, looking amused. "We located Carter. He *is* a curate at St. Winifred's. Or was. When we found him he was in bed with the vicar's wife, the vicar being out at his regular Monday karate class. So much for the worry that Carter was some kind of pedophile. I tell you, Tim, the Church is not what it was."

"No," Tim agreed.

"And we could have discounted Walter Briggs from three o'clock yesterday afternoon. He's been in the Hampstead lockup since then, taken there after some kind of domestic punch-up with his son concerning a bottle of ten-year-old brandy that had been reserved for some important guests."

"Thus we spread our largesse throughout the population," Tim said. "Bringing joy into every life we touch."

Abbott ignored the sarcastic tone. "Well, clearing this Leland thing up ought to look good on your record," he said.

"I wonder," Tim said wryly. "They aren't going to like the expense sheet—getting London Transport to turn off the juice on the underground line, then having to send in extra men to handle the traffic jams as people poured out looking for buses, ripping open this place, mounting a search for the boy—they'll go raving mad." He sighed. "And all because one old cop was curious about one man who died too soon."

Abbott looked at him. "Everybody dies too soon," he said gently.

"Yes. But if Roger Leland had lived even a day longer, it would all have been different. I like to think he'd decided to come to us."

"He might have come up with some other scheme," Abbott said. "Something not quite so noble."

"I prefer my version. We do know that, at the last minute, he did his best. I hope the boy eventually realizes that." He shook his head. "Funny—the way Max hung on to those stamps. He showed them to me when we got back to the house. Very boring—not even attractive pictures on them. And worth all that money. Disgusting, really."

"You mean, when you think of all the starving children in India?" Abbott asked, trying to raise a smile.

"Something like that."

Abbott looked at him, recognizing the tone of voice, the slump of the shoulders, the emptiness. It always happened, every time, to everyone, at the end of the long, long run. There was nothing anybody could do, except ride it out. "Go home," he said quietly, wishing it didn't sound so banal. "Put your feet up, have a drink, let it all go. Just let it run out the ends of your fingers, Tim. It's the only way."

But Nightingale didn't answer, and Abbott knew there was nothing he could do for him now.

Maybe later.

Maybe tomorrow.

But not now.

Tim stood looking at the grimy street and the passing people. There weren't that many now—it was well past the rush hour—but they looked whey-faced and weary. Their feet made a sullen, shuffling sound on the pavement. Their eyes were down, their expressions blank.

He felt the weight of the crowd, and it crushed him.

You don't see me, he thought. You don't want to see me. I only come bringing trouble, after all. I walk through people's lives and out the other side, trailing disaster. I picked up a thread of Ivor Peters's life because I thought it would be exciting, because I thought I was doing the right thing. How many people are destroyed each day by someone like me, trying to do the right thing? And what difference did I make, in the end? Five years from now, none of them will remember my name.

Abbott will go home to his hills.

Detective Chief Inspector Spry will come back and growl at everyone for a few years, then retire, glad to be out of it.

Murray will make sergeant.

Hendricks will soon be running whatever jail he lands up in.

Kobalski will get a smart lawyer and probably be deported.

Sherry will marry her stockbroker.

Tess Leland will marry Professor Soame.

Maybe Max will even grow up to be Prime Minister.

After a brief interlude, they will all continue as before.

I won't have changed them.

But they will have changed me, because I can't turn them out. They'll stay within me, because I can't forget. And gradually I will be so full of them that there will be no room for me.

He looked at Abbott, now deploying the uniformed men to various tasks, clearing up the mess, tidying up the details, probably already planning the report he'd write tomorrow. He looked so calm, so controlled, so damned *able*. How do you get through it? he wondered. You're standing there, scratching your ear, looking up the street, listening to Murray telling a joke and you're smiling. How did you learn to pretend it doesn't matter? Where do I sign up for the course?

Because there will be other cases, other victims, other villains. The City breeds them, and it is breeding them into me, too. Any one of these people walking by me now could be part of my next case. What will I be like when I've absorbed all the pain and the anger and the sorrow and the evil this City can create? Do I really want to be that man?

He glanced at his reflection in the darkened window of a nearby chemist. His shadowy self looked attenuated, hollow, and misshapen.

He turned away.